MARY, Behold Thy Son

A *Mother's Story*

A Novel By

ROXCY JEPPSON

Table of Contents

Preface

May I share with you my testimony of the divinity of our Savior and the awesome calling of his dear mother.

I began researching and studying for this book more than fifteen years ago. I have found little to cause a change of ideas and feelings. Rather, my testimony is stronger than ever.

If you search the scriptures to see which parts of my work are true, and renew your acquaintance with Mary and her son, this work will have achieved its purpose.

I took the facts as given in the Bible and Book of Mormon and read about the customs and history of the time. From there I wove a possible storyline about the life of Mary. For example, I found nothing about Mary's early life or of her parents, and, taking note of Jesus' concern and teachings about the widows and fatherless I was led to believe He may have experienced the feelings caused by such a condition. From this perspective, I wove the present storyline.

This is only a story, but I pray it will lead you to study more about the family of our Savior.

Roxcy Jeppson

Chapter One

WHO AM I?

Joseph! Joseph! Will you understand? Will your love be strong enough? If only I could tell you about the angel.

The angel had appeared as Mary finished her nightly personal prayers. The message—not the messenger—had surprised her. It seemed only natural for him to come. Hadn't she asked for direction and guidance, and wasn't it promised to those worthy? Mary had always tried very hard to be an obedient daughter. Having such loving parents made it easier. They had chosen Joseph to be her husband.

Joseph. Would he believe that she spoke the truth? When should she tell him? He was so busy preparing their new home. Perhaps the angel would tell him, also.

Mother, my dear sweet mother. It should have been you, not me, to have this great honor. You were the Queen of Jewry. You were the special woman.

Mary sat by the window, watching the moon as it rolled by. Her thoughts fled from the visit. Instead, they took her back to her very first memories. They were of her sweet mother's wrinkled face as she sang the winnowing song. Mary, too, had a small woven tray and threw the grain into the air to let the wind blow the chaff away. The winnowing song was still one of her favorites.

At her mother's knee, Mary had learned to card the wool, spin the yarn, and weave the cloth. Jacob, her father, had carved a beautiful doll's head and asked her mother to make the body. The doll was finished just in time for Mary to make its clothes from the scrap bag and cloth she'd woven. Who cared that the cloth was coarse and uneven. Rachel, her doll, surely didn't. She smiled even if the dress itched and didn't fit too well.

Mary still clearly remembered her father's tears as he attempted to eat her first bread, trying not to laugh at its awful taste. When she tasted it, Mary spat it out. Then and only then did Jacob, her father, brother of Heli, allow his laughter to roll forth. Together they went to find the swine herd. Even the swine refused to eat the bread.

Her favorite memories were of scripture reading. First Father, then Mother, would read and lead the discussion. Their favorite scroll seemed to be Isaiah. As Mary learned to understand the meaning, she recognized many passages telling of the coming of the Messiah. Surely the chosen virgin who would be His mother would be blessed above all women.

Patiently Jacob had taught of the blessedness of the Chosen People. Moses was a special friend who had the power of God to perform many miracles. As the lessons grew deeper and more detailed, Mary began to understand the need for a Redeemer. Judah was not free. Due to wickedness and evil leaders, Israel had been scattered, gathered, and scattered again. Now, only the tribe of Judah remained together in any great size and force.

The harshness of Roman rule was stamped forever in her memory the day the legion rode upon the sleepy town. Abusing all, taking what they wanted, paying a token in return, and destroying at will, the Romans rode in and out in less than an hour. The lesson of Roman rule lasted much longer. Old Shillem had been brutally struck when he demanded payment for his wife's figs and bread.

"What! Pay for such poor quality? Surely you jest. But no, I see you are in earnest. So here, I'll pay you." The whip had not cut through the tough Nazarene garments, so the officer used his club about the old man's head and face. His loyal wife had received the same when she tried to pull him away. Two days later they were laid side by side in the tomb. The Romans had taken their entire store of food and smashed the goatskins of water.

No, Judah was not free. She had great need of the Messiah—her promised Redeemer.

Mary had always been full of questions. Each answer brought more questions to her mind. Her favorite in childhood had been, "Mother, are you truly the queen of Judah? If so, then I'm a princess!"

2

Neighbor children, not Jacob and his wife, had given Mary this bit of information. She'd been playing with her doll and a group of rowdy, dirty boys had come around the corner, kicking a stone. Seeing Mary so clean and pretty, they immediately began to tease and torment her. She begged them not to get her doll dirty saying, "Rachel has just had her bath." This caused the boys to throw dirt at her. Determined not to cry, Mary stamped her foot and demanded they leave at once.

"Who do you think you are? The queen? Well, you're not. You're only the fair princess. So there!" Immediately the boys formed a circle around her. Chanting and dancing, they disclosed to the bewildered child her royal lineage, adding a taunt to overthrow the hated Roman rule. They suggested she hurry up and marry the Tetrarch and free her people as Queen Esther had done. Mary broke away from her tormentors and ran to her mother demanding an explanation.

As she grew in wisdom, the answer to the question became more rich and detailed. At first Mary had wanted to know why they lived in such a small house. Why did they dress and eat so poorly?

One day Mary had watched the Tetrarch and his family travel to Caesarea from Capernaum. Their rich trappings and their servants had been carefully recorded in the child's mind. It was some time before she understood why Mother had cried with shame and pain when Mary and her 'train of servants' trooped through the yard. Each child had added details from their meager store and the result was strikingly pagan. This was one memory which was pushed back as soon as it popped into Mary's mind.

Scripture study had been doubled for a while. "When pride cometh, then cometh shame," seemed to be Jacob's favorite. Whole sections of Proverbs were committed to memory. Mary had no idea so much of that book dealt with pride. It was no wonder Mary learned to read faster than the other children her age. Most girls were not even given the opportunity of learning to read. Parents felt it wasn't necessary for their roles as wives and mothers. Yet, serious study did not keep Mary from roaming the hills in search of wildflowers. Sometimes with Mother, sometimes with friends, Mary always found enough flowers to share with the older people in the village. Mary's smiling face framed with shining golden brown hair always left the dark, cool rooms brighter and happier. If she had no flowers, then she would sing a song to cheer their

. . . Behold Thy Son

hearts.

Yes, Mary was indeed the beloved child of the village. Everyone knew of her parents' longing for a child. No one was more deserving. Yet, like Sarah and Abraham, it was their elder years which were blessed by the extraordinary child. Right from the beginning, Mary had been the joy of the whole village. Even old, crotchety Aaron smiled at the pretty face. He would hobble far out of his way just "to see that vision of beauty."

As she learned the duties of a home, Mary became capable and proficient. And as Mother became increasingly feeble and stiff, Mary took over more and more of the responsibilities. Jacob could be forgiven his 'prideful' boast of having the cleanest home in Nazareth. Many people found their door at supper time in order to taste the delicious, though simple, food of this humble household. Many a traveler left Nazareth, grateful for the suggestion that they try Jacob's home for a place to stay.

Mary had been trained as every daughter of Judah should be. She was prepared to take her place in the home of a son of Judah. Gone were her early childhood dreams of castles and riches. No longer did she secretly plan how she would marry a prince or tetrarch and free her people. Dreams and longing for the Messiah now filled her hidden thoughts.

Mary's thoughts were troubled as she approached her thirteenth birthday. She knew it was time for Father and Mother to arrange a suitable husband for her.

Why, oh, why does it have to be so? Why can't I choose? It's not fair! It's just not fair!

If she could only be certain of being given to a choice man like her father, Jacob, then she knew she'd have a happy life as her mother did. She knew she could keep house and be a dutiful wife as well as the next girl. But if there could be love, sharing, and appreciation it would be so much easier. She didn't want to be like Sarah—always at the neighbors seeking the appreciation and love not found at her own home. Jeremiah was always drunk or "with that woman." However, Sarah wouldn't force the issue. She had three small children to care for. And then there was Miriam. She was the shrew to poor Zeke.

In contrast, Rachel never let a day pass without someone hearing how blessed she was because her parents insisted she be given to wonderful, manly Reuben.

4

Do you suppose that is why he treats her so much like a queen? She has nearly doubled in size since their marriage, yet he has never given one cause for sorrow or regret.

Yes, if Joseph proved to be as good as Reuben and Father, Mary would be happy. But how could she be happy? Joseph seldom laughed. He smiled only if very pleased and then only a faint smile.

Mary had heard the women talking. All the women were afraid of Joseph's eyes. "He seems to be able to pierce your very soul and see all the evil thoughts you have or ever did have," they would say.

"Besides, he is many years past marriage age, and he has refused all offers from any of the fathers."

"Yes, who does he think he is—a king or something?"

But Joseph is king. If the Jews were allowed their own government, Joseph is the rightful heir. He wants someone who could be queen if the opportunity comes. But it never will. Herod is too powerful, and Rome isn't about to give any freedom of government.

The men, too, spoke of Joseph with great respect. He seemed too wise for his age. They say it came from too much scripture study and long, lonely walks over the hills. Still, everyone had to admit he was the best carpenter in the village—no, the whole area. He could fix things faster and better than even old Zebulon who held top place for years and years. Yes, Joseph was honored and respected, yet feared, too. He seems to have more inner peace and strength than even the rabbi. Perhaps that is why he seldom smiles. His thoughts are above these worldly things.

Oh, why won't sleep come? Why must I worry so? Father loves me. He'll not do anything unwise. Yes, I still see the joy in his eyes as he told Mother the reason for Joseph's visit. I can hear the tears in his voice when he cried, 'Jehovah has heard our prayers.' Mother, too, looked extraordinarily joyful. They are good parents.

They waited so long for a family. Yet, they have never felt it a disgrace that I, a daughter (soon to become a woman), opened the womb, and no brother or even a sister was sent to relieve this old cursing upon Jewish women. No. They've loved, taught, and enjoyed me as if I were sent straight from Jehovah.

Mary tossed, turned, and tossed some more. If she didn't soon sleep the cock would crow and she would have to rise. Her red, puffy eyes would tell of her sleepless night. And then there was her snarly hair. Oh, why hadn't she braided it after washing it? Vanity

. . . Behold Thy Son

had convinced her it would be more full and fluffy if she didn't braid it. Now she'd have to spend two hours just getting the snarls out.

Serves me right. 'When pride cometh, then cometh shame.' I can just hear Mother quoting that proverb with a twinkle of 'I told you so' in her eyes. Oh, dear! There's the cock! How can I face Joseph with red, puffy eyes? If only he hadn't insisted on coming right after breakfast to talk to me. Oh, what am I going to do?

Mother had indeed quoted her favorite proverb, and with a twinkle of merriment had suggested Mary wear her red scarf to bring out the lovely color of her eyes. Mothers could be so exasperating at times. Mary made a silent vow to never quote that proverb to *her* daughters. Breakfast brought again the telling of her genealogy. Joseph's was the same. His father was Heli—brother of her father, Jacob. Joseph and Mary were first cousins. This knowledge had done little in the past to set her mind at rest, and it still didn't help.

True to his word, Joseph's knock came as they finished breakfast chores. Mary's heart nearly stopped beating. Then she wished it would. If it continued to beat so hard and loud, Joseph would hear and think her a foolish little girl—not a woman of nearly thirteen years.

Father had wisely decided she should have one extra year at home before accepting anyone's offer of marriage. Most girls were married at twelve and mothers by age thirteen.

Watching her father's joy and quick step to the door, Mary suddenly realized why they had waited a year. The answer had been given last night when he'd said, "Our prayers have been answered." Father and Mother had been praying that Joseph would come and seek her hand in marriage. Their trust and faith in Jehovah had been such that they were able to refuse the other offers given them, knowing that Joseph would someday come and offer his hand in marriage.

He must be a good man. I must trust in their love and wisdom. Oh! Then why won't my heart stop beating so loudly?

As Joseph came to her and took her hand, Mary looked timidly into his face. He was smiling. Yes, not a faint, smug smile, but a fearful, hesitant smile as if he, too, were frightened. Could he, Joseph—the strong, calm, and wise—be frightened of her? The thought made her laugh right out loud. She tried to stifle it, but couldn't. Joseph's face crinkled into a broad smile and he, too, laughed—nervously.

"Could it be that you can hear my heart beat, my beautiful Mary? It is so loud I can hardly hear anything else."

"No, Joseph. I see the fear in your eyes. Imagine, you—the most revered and learned man of all Nazareth afraid of me, the most humble of the daughters of Jehovah."

"Yes, humble is a good description. But we must add lovely, radiant, and kind. Mary, I came alone (that was true, Rabbi wasn't with him—Mary had not realized it until then) so that you might know my feelings and give your true answer. Your wishes are of utmost importance. If, after you hear me out, you wish to refuse, you may. I'll not press you. You, not your father, mother, or I, must make the decision."

Why have I been so afraid to meet this man? He is even more handsome up close. And he does smile—a lovely, wonderful smile.

Mary's thoughts were reflected upon her face as she looked over this giant of a man.

He is a giant of inner strength as well as size. His face is gentle and his hands are, also. I can feel the callouses of hard labor, yet he makes me feel like the purest glass. Joseph, you do look into the inner soul, but not for sins and errors. You are searching for love and understanding.

"Mary," the gentle voice began to tell of his love for her. At first he had been drawn to her as the other rightful heir to the Jewish throne. But as she had grown and matured, it became apparent she would teach their children true and correct principles by word and by example. No truer daughter was to be found in all Nazareth— nay, not in all of the province of Galilee. His thoughts had frightened him for he knew he was in no real position to seek her hand. He was poor—even by Nazarene standards. The early death of Heli, his father, had cut his formal schooling short. He had been forced to continue his studies on his own. Besides, Rabbi had a son whose eye was also on the fair Mary. His offer was sure to be accepted.

Could Mary begin to imagine his joy to learn of Jacob's reply to Nathan's offer just prior to Mary's twelfth year? Could his answer of wanting to give his wife one more year of Mary's help at home mean that Joseph might stand a chance? Praying fervently that this be the case, Joseph had worked extra hours to become a better carpenter and better able to support her as she had a right to expect. Long hours at night by the fire had given him greater insight into the scriptures. His feelings for her had grown deeper each day.

. . . Behold Thy Son

Jacob had labored fourteen years for Rachel. He'd do the same for Mary if need be. Only, please, Jehovah, he had prayed, let Jacob not accept any offers until he could come forth.

Nathan had brought a wooden chest to him yesterday to be repaired, Joseph continued, and stated it was to be used in his new home. Mary's thirteenth year was nearly here and Jacob could not afford to refuse a second offer. He even had a home built by the stream—a huge one with plenty of garden space. Joseph's thumb hadn't been hit by a hammer for many years. But as Mary looked at it, she smiled to think of Joseph's consternation and frustration.

Imagine his being so afraid when Father and Mother have been praying so hard for his courage.

"After Nathan left, Joram said he was reminded that he was now able to sell his father's old home," Joseph hesitated, then continued. "It is small, Mary, but it is in good repair, on a big lot, and I can add rooms as needed. Joram has set a fair price which I can meet. So, Mary . . . (again, that look of anxiety and fear) Mary, if you say so, I will make an offer to your father. But *you* must decide."

The silence that filled the humble home lengthened as Mary's parents prayed in gratitude adding, "Please, Jehovah, let her say yes." Joseph prayed, "Jehovah, God of Abraham, Isaac, and Jacob, surely I've not been amiss in my request. Please give me strength if she says . . . no. "

As she looked from Joseph's face to the faces of her aged and beloved parents, Mary knew they had never taught her amiss. They had only her welfare at heart. Why should she not trust them now? For this very purpose they had planned and prayed since she was born. Surely it was Jehovah's will. Another look into Joseph's eyes assured her of his deep love. No longer would she fear him. Already she could feel love growing in her heart. She knew what she must answer. "Yes, Joseph. I do wish to become your wife. Father has chosen wisely."

The sudden releasing of breath caused each to laugh in nervous embarrassment as their inner feelings were disclosed. Each avoided the other's eyes. "Hurry, Joseph, go get Rabbi. I, too, heard of Nathan's boast. I want to see his face when he hears I have accepted your offer. He's such a pompous . . . I know, dear, but he is! Imagine—him as our son-in-law. I shudder to think of it." Mother's face mirrored the joy of her husband's words as she hastily wiped away the tears, offering a fervent, silent prayer of thanks.

8

The bargaining and setting of a bridal price brought all of Nazareth to the humble courtyard of Jacob. All but Nathan agreed it was a perfect union. Mary and Joseph would bring the royal lineage to one household. Their children were indeed rightful heirs to the throne of David. By the end of the ceremony, even Nathan had to agree they were "made for each other." Joseph's reverent manner had added the grace and solemnity needed for such a sacred occasion. As usual, Mary's eyes and face betrayed her joy and excitement. She kept wanting to sing when she should be silent.

"My, what handsome children they will bring forth."

"Yes, but can you imagine how Joseph will change under her happy influence? He'll not stay sober and quiet for long!"

"Can't you see, Rachel. He is changing already. Twice, he has nearly smiled."

"I am glad. He is too serious," whispered Sarah. "I say if a man can't smile or laugh, you'd better watch out for him."

"Sarah! Shame on you! You forget the hard life he has had to face—supporting his family with his mother's long illness since Heli died. Joseph also feels deeply his position as heir to the throne. He takes nothing lightly."

"See, Rachel, what did I tell you! He *is* smiling. Joseph is actually smiling! My, he is a handsome fellow."

Mother's death had dampened the joy of Mary's marriage preparations. Home wasn't so cheerful now. Further lessons were learned by hard experience. Jacob tried to be cheerful, but he missed his beloved wife more each day. His thoughts seemed more with her than in the preparations for the wedding. Absently answering Mary's questions, Jacob would sit in "her" spot by the hearth and dream of the long ago days.

Sometimes these thoughts were shared in full—not the usual sigh, word, or sob. Thus Mary began to understand why the light had gone from his life. Mother had been a fine woman and Mary must strive to be the same.

"Mary, if Jehovah chooses to leave you childless or withhold this blessing for a while, know that you are not wicked. But you must prove as faithful and patient as did your mother. She was truly choice and clean. Be not ashamed of such a trial and burden. Listen not to the chattering women. But be as your mother—faithful and true to the end. Make Joseph as happy as I have been. Then

. . . Behold Thy Son

you will know Jehovah smiles upon you."

His eyes closed in restful sleep. Mary's tiptoed preparations for supper did not disturb him. A gentle kiss failed to awaken him, nor did the sobs of a mourning daughter. Jacob would no longer be lonesome—he had joined his beloved wife.

Who but Joseph could Mary turn to now? Joseph had made all the arrangements and had made certain Mary had a place to live the last five months of their betrothal. Mary mourned deeply, yet rejoiced at the blessings she received.

Surely, Jehovah was mindful of her—His humble handmaiden.

Chapter Two

GABRIEL

The moon rose majestically on a very hot summer night. Not even a breeze stirred. Yet, a lamp still burned at one home. Mary seemed more lonesome than usual tonight. She had not been mistreated. No. She'd received great love and favor from her friends and neighbors. All had opened their homes and hearts to her, and Joseph had made the decision to accept Rachel and Reuben's offer. Since they had only sons, this chance for a daughter—even if only for five months—was not to be passed up.

Mary had now seen firsthand that other children in a family meant adjusting and sharing. She could see she had missed out by being an only child. The boys had been shy at first, but now they treated her as one of them. She'd learned to duck when the play began or be hit with whatever came flying. Yes, boys could be fun as well as exasperating.

Could it really be one month? It had gone so quickly, yet so slowly. Rachel had given much instruction. She wasn't as old-fashioned as Mother, so new foods were added to Mary's list. Rachel's knowledge of healing herbs seemed absolutely necessary with a family of rowdy, rough boys. Mary's head fairly spun with all the added information she had been given.

Mother and Father seemed so close tonight. They almost seemed to be right there in her room. Her weeping finally under control, Mary took up the scriptures. Her eyes fell again on Isaiah. But thoughts of Joseph and their coming marriage pushed to the front. Surely, Father had been wise to choose Joseph as her husband. He was so like her father—capable, sure, and manly. Being his wife would never bring shame to her. And she would never bring shame to him. *Never!*

"Therefore the Lord, Himself, shall give you a sign; Behold, a virgin shall conceive, and bear a son, and shall call his name Immanuel."

The Virgin. The chosen daughter of Judah. Will this daughter know she is chosen? I wonder what her preparations will be. She will have to learn to cook, weave, and tend the garden. But, no. She will be a queen by then and have servants and maids. Will she be afraid to raise such a Son? I would be. How could you teach Him? Will He be so holy and pure that He will be unable to be as a child? He will probably be taught by the angels and his mother will just have to watch. Will the Virgin have a husband to help her? "Too many questions" *is what Mother would have said.* "Too many questions about the mysteries of God. Keep your mind on now and today. Then you will be ready to meet the Messiah when He comes." *Mothers are so practical. It seems they never dream!*

Her parents seemed even closer as Mary blew out the lamp and said her prayers. Perhaps that is why she prayed so fervently for help and guidance that she might be truly prepared to teach her children as she has been taught. Prayer helped ease the heaviness in her heart as she told God of her fears, her troubles, and her dreams. "Please help me not to blush when the boys tease me. I had no idea boys teased so much. They seem to delight in keeping my face a deep red. . . But, oh, Dear Lord, thank you for such a loving home to finish my final preparations. Rachel is as loving as Mother. Thank you, thank you! Amen."

Oh, dear. I forgot to blow out the lamp. How careless of me! It is bad enough to use it so late.

As Mary rose to blow it out, she realized the light came from the foot of her bed. There was a man standing there in the light. He—not the lamp—was lighting the room.

"Hail, thou that art highly favored, the Lord is with thee: blessed are thou among women.

"Fear not, Mary; for thou hast found favor with God. And, behold, thou shalt conceive in thy womb, and bring forth a son, and shalt call his name Jesus. He shall be great, and shall be called the Son of the Highest: and the Lord God shall give unto him the throne of his father David: and he shall reign over the house of Jacob for ever; and of his kingdom there shall be no end."

Jacob's worry was for naught. Mary was to bear children. A son would inherit the throne as rightful heir. But, wait! The message seemed immediate. She still had four months till she wed Joseph. "How can this be, seeing I know not a man?"

The message was too great—too awesome—to comprehend. She had never heard of nor even in her wildest dreams come up against such a thing. The angel answered and said unto her, "The Holy Ghost shall come upon thee, and the power of the Highest shall overshadow thee: therefore also that holy thing which shall be born of thee shall be called the Son of God."

She, Mary, daughter of Jacob, to be the Virgin bringing forth the Messiah? Yes, Mary was clean, obedient. She tried to be humble. She was rightful heir to the throne. Yet, how could it be? She was mortal, Eloheim the Supreme Being—a God—*the* God. How could it be?

As if in answer to her silent questions, Gabriel told of Elisabeth's coming event. Wonderful, old, barren cousin Elisabeth to have a child? The stories and rumors were true then! It was not just gossip. "For with God nothing shall be impossible."

Gabriel's words caused Mary's heart to leap with joy for her dear cousin. Mary was living proof that nothing was impossible. She herself was a child of old age—long past the years of child-bearing. Trembling with excitement rather than fear, yet subdued and humble, Mary fell to her knees and bowed. "Behold the hand-maid of the Lord; be it unto me according to thy word."

Opening her eyes, Mary found only the moonlight lighting the room. Gabriel was gone as he had come. Yet, he had left a very unsettled girl behind. Mary's thoughts were tumbling too fast to keep up with.

Why me? Why not my mother or my daughter? But why me? I've done nothing so special. I'm certainly not fair above all women. I'm not even a woman yet.

Mary wondered if Isaiah had seen her—Mary—when he saw the vision. The message had seemed urgent. Would it be next week? Tomorrow or yet, next month?

I'm not prepared! Marriage to Joseph is scary enough, but to Eloheim? Do I hurry up on my bridal clothes? Will I still be Joseph's wife? Where will I live? Oh, Mother, Father, please help me from where ever you are!

The Event came that very night. Thus, Mary had little time to fret and stew. Truly, such a wonderful experience should be shared with family and friends. But as Mary lay there the next morning,

. . . Behold Thy Son

she felt the memory fade farther and farther away. She realized it was too sacred to share even with Rachel.

Besides, no one would believe her. The Messiah was to be born in power and great wealth so He could free their people. He would be acknowledged King from the start. How many times had Jacob argued with the Rabbi as to the true meaning of those scriptures. Who ever heard of mortal woman becoming wife to God? Impossible! That only happened in Greek stories. She had been told to become Joseph's wife, but was forbidden to tell him of these things—yet. The time was not right.

Joseph! Joseph! Will you understand? Will your love be strong enough? If only I could tell you of the angel!

Mary's great and exquisite joy turned to anguish, sorrow, grief, and pain as she began to realize what she faced. How could she face it alone, with no mother or father to give her strength?

"Oh, God, please help me and guide me." The cock called the sunrise as Mary buried her head to muffle the sobs. Could Joseph bear the shame of her child?

Chapter Three

ELISABETH

Rachel observed the red eyes, shining first with joy and then grief. Arms placed lovingly around Mary confirmed the sobs still refusing to leave. Mary helped with breakfast. But the boys soon quit teasing. They couldn't understand that faraway look, followed so quickly by the tears and racking sobs.

"Sons, you've just never seen a woman in love before. She's just getting anxious to leave our company and join Joseph. Isn't that right, daughter?" Reuben's kindness brought only a fleeting smile, then again the sobs as the thoughts of facing Joseph chased it away.

"Now see what you've done. She's just very lonesome for her mother and father. They were so close. We are good to her but just not the same as her own family." Rachel shooed the men out and tried to get Mary to eat.

"No, thank you. I'm just not hungry this morning. I think I'll go get some cool water at the well." Taking the goatskin, Mary stepped out into the bright sun. Her tear-swollen eyes rebelled at the brightness and she stumbled slightly as she went. At the well she again heard the rumor of Elisabeth's impending motherhood.

"I don't believe it. It's all just gossip."

"Well, it's not! Simon was just over there and he saw Zacharias. And it is true! Zacharias can neither speak nor hear. Elisabeth was at home but the townspeople said she *is* with child."

Elisabeth! Gabriel had told Mary of her good fortune. Elisabeth would know and understand. Mary fairly flew home to Rachel. "Rachel! Rachel! I must go to Elisabeth. Simon has just returned and the rumors are true. I must go and visit with her. I'll not be able to go after my marriage. Oh, Rachel, say that I may! Please say that I may go!"

"Calm down, Mary. Of course you may. It is right that you should visit her. She'll feel sad to hear of your parents' passing. But I know you need family right now. Yes, Mary, I shall see to it immediately.

"Jason, run to your father's shop and inquire who is going to Juttah or close by. Mary can leave today if needed.

"Let's see, that's a hundred miles or less. Oh dear! It will take many days. We'll bake some quick hard bread and buy cheese and figs so you'll be prepared. And you'll need a new robe."

So, Mary made preparations to go to Elisabeth's. The excitement of the trip served to cover her mixed emotions. Her behavior seemed natural for the occasion.

At the end of a long and impatient journey, Mary approached the humble home of Elisabeth and Zacharias. Her thoughts became even more confused, nearly tearing her young heart out. Was she only dreaming? Did it really happen? Was the sickness real or imagined? It was very real. Mary rushed to the side of the road to find relief. It came more often each day. But then, it could be caused by the water. People often became ill when they traveled and drank strange water. Since the caravan leader had given her the herb tea to drink, Mary had felt relief—if she didn't eat anything till noon.

Rejoining the group, Mary's face was ashen and full of fear. It had been a few years since she had seen Elisabeth. At that time, Mary had been the "little grown-up daughter" of a dear cousin and lifetime friend. Now Mary was alone. Elisabeth was with child and would hardly be expected to rejoice at an uninvited guest with such unbelievable news.

Why? Oh why did I come? It was foolish and unthinking.

Mary's eyes betrayed her thoughts.

When the caravan passed on by, a lonely, sad, and frightened girl of nearly fourteen years was left standing alone. Picking up her bundle, stifling her sobs, trying to ignore the queasy feeling in her stomach, Mary slowly approached the gate. She saw Zacharias out behind the house with the goats. Thinking to attract his attention, Mary called to him. As he went on with his work, ignoring the call, Mary remembered he had lost the power of hearing and speech until his son was born.

Someone *did* hear her timid greeting. The door flew open and Elisabeth hurried down the path. "Mary, Mary, you *did* come! Oh, Mary, when I heard of Jacob's death I prayed earnestly you would come for a while. I am old and stiff and this being with child is hard at times, very hard." As Elisabeth held the girl in her arms, Mary's worries and fears melted into tears of relief. Her sobs caused Elisabeth to pat her on the back and talk soothingly to her, as if to a small child.

"Now, now, daughter, I'm sorry. How thoughtless of me to go rattling on when your heart is broken and you are so lonely. Now then, dry those eyes and we'll go into the house. It's hot out here, but our house is cool. Here, let me take that."

"No! No, Elisabeth. You must not lift, not in your condition. I will manage." Mary stooped to pick up her bundle. She had been so foolish to worry. Elisabeth was glad to see her; Zacharias would be, also.

Elisabeth gasped, loudly, then gave forth a cry. Mary dropped her bundle and steadied the shaken Elisabeth. "What is it?"

A light shone from the face of the pregnant woman. Her hand was on her stomach. She seemed unable to speak. Yet, joy and delight shone from her eyes and face as surely as if a light were within her.

Mary helped her to the garden wall under the fig tree. She had lost her look of fear and reflected the joy of the older woman. Impending motherhood had its moments of joy as well as pain.

"Mary, I felt him! I felt my son! He kicked me hard. I've wondered before, but I know for sure this time! My hand was here, on my stomach, and he kicked it. He kicked it so hard I felt it on my hand!" Tears mixed freely as they embraced.

"He is to be the forerunner of the Messiah. The angel said his name is to be John and he will prepare the way for the Messiah. Can you imagine that? Will I see and know the Messiah? I keep wondering and praying and rereading the scriptures. This is truly a humbling responsibility." Turning to look at her beloved husband, Elisabeth's voice trailed into silence. Suddenly, she sat upright, turned to Mary and cried, "Blessed art thou among women, and blessed is the fruit of thy womb. And whence is this to me, that the mother of my Lord should come to me?"

Mary could hardly believe her ears. Elisabeth knew her wonderful secret! She knew without a word from Mary. Furthermore, Elisabeth had sung praises and not cast condemnation upon her.

. . . Behold Thy Son

The angel must have told her, or else the Holy Ghost had.

"See! Mary, feel! My son, John, knows it, too. He is rejoicing at your presence!" Again the two women fell into each others' arms, tears mingling, sharing the sacred joy of the moment.

A stranger passing by would have stopped to marvel at the scene. Here were two women—no, an old woman and a young girl—crying with joy and happiness, all the while giving forth a strange light or glow. Yes, it was a glow. What could these two people have in common to cause such a visible happiness? A closer look would have revealed Elisabeth's condition. But surely that would not be the cause of such joy—even for an elderly Jewish woman—for the young girl, too, seemed to share the feeling. She was dressed as a betrothed, not a married woman. The stranger would marvel that one so exquisitely fair and beautiful would only now be betrothed. Surely, such beauty would have brought forth many offers as soon as she became of age.

No one but Mary and Elisabeth could know what secrets caused them such happiness. Mary seemed overwhelmed with joy. The fears and doubts had been swept away. Elisabeth had been told the secret through a heavenly power, so Mary again knew it was real, not imagined. She was with child—no doubt about the sickness now. And Mary knew her child was special—so extra special. In time his name would become Messiah. But until then, he would be her son, Jesus, to bear, rear, and love.

"My soul doth magnify the Lord, and my spirit hath rejoiced in God my Savior. For he had regarded the low estate of his handmaiden: for behold, from henceforth all generations shall call me blessed. For he that is mighty hath done to me great things; and holy is his name. And his mercy is on them that fear him from generation to generation. He hath shewed strength with his arm; he hath scattered the proud in the imagination of their hearts. He hath put down the mighty from their seats, and exalted them of low degree. He hath filled the hungry with good things; and the rich he hath sent empty away. He hath holpen his servant Israel, in remembrance of his mercy; as he spake to our fathers, to Abraham, and to his seed for ever."

Silence fell as they quietly enjoyed the outpouring of love—love for each other, their unborn sons, and for their Father in Heaven. But nature is never silent and to Mary's ears it seemed as if all nature were rejoicing with them. Never had the birds sung more sweetly, and never this late in the season. She seemed able to smell every single flower within a day's journey around. Looking about her, it seemed the colors of every flower, every bush, and tree were more vivid than ever before.

Her eyes fell upon Zacharias and the goats. What on earth was that man doing? Trying to doctor the foot of a kid, Zacharias had knelt down and then bent over. He appeared to be standing on his head. "Elisabeth, look at your husband." As they laughed together, sharing his 'foolishness,' the women realized something else was also aware of his position. The billy goat was eyeing that upturned end and getting ready to charge. Two horrified screams failed to arouse Zacharias' attention. As the goat connected and sent him sprawling, Elisabeth sprang up, waddled as fast as she could, muttering, "Oh dear, oh dear, I forgot. He can't hear a thing. He must be more watchful. Oh, I hope he isn't hurt. He should leave such stunts to the herder. He's too old to be doing these things."

It was the younger Mary who reached him first and helped the dazed and bewildered man to his feet. Seeing he was not hurt, the two women doubled up with laughter at the recollection of his mishap. Zacharias couldn't hear, but he could see and he, too, melted into laughter. Brushing him off, the women led him firmly to the house.

By nightfall, many secrets and plans had been shared. Mary was grateful for her ability to read and write. She had been able to share with Zacharias her feelings and questions. His smiles and pats had added strength to his written counsel and encouragement. Yes, Mary had been sent to these wonderful people. She had followed the right promptings. The world was bright once more.

Morning brought the sickness quicker than usual. Mary didn't quite make it. Embarrassed and crying, she was cleaning up when she became aware of Zacharias standing there laughing at her.

From his gestures and written words, Mary got the message—"Even the young ones get sick. So Elisabeth isn't so different." Then Mary realized Elisabeth had the same problem in her room. "Too many fig cakes and too much late talk. You'll learn to be more careful." As he left them to the cleanup, Zacharias laughed joyously to himself.

Mary accepted the warm drink. Elisabeth had to agree (begrudgingly, of course) with her husband. She'd not been sick for two weeks. Two blessed weeks of no morning sickness but her back had begun to hurt—dreadfully. As Mary rubbed Elisabeth's back, Elisabeth shared her secrets of 'getting along' while with child.

. . . Behold Thy Son

Mary was grateful to find there was help for the terrible feelings.

"Occasional tears and down feelings are a natural part of it all," Elisabeth confided. "But you can't give in to them. You should see the shirt I mended one day. Tears were so steady. I was so old, ugly, and sick. But Zacharias made me fix that hole. He knew best—or at least he thought he did. We keep the shirt as a reminder that if you try, you can. Bless his heart. He didn't laugh until I began, then we had a good laugh together. I'd sewn the front and back together in such neat, tight, little stitches I could never pick them out. It's my 'crying shirt.' Many a meal he's had to get for himself. But he's not complained. No one could have a sweeter, more loving companion than Zacharias.

"I remember your parents when you finally decided to come forth. It was so beautiful to see your father's love and concern, Mary." I'd cry just watching them and wonder how it would be for me." The older woman's hands framed the lovely face of her cousin as she made sure Mary got the full meaning of her words, "Mary, it is even more beautiful and wonderful when it is your own love being shared by a wonderful, loving husband. I pray you will be blessed to find such love with Joseph."

Joseph. Was he really to be her husband? Mary's face dropped to her hands and she sobbed as once again she thought of her future.

Joseph, Joseph, will you understand?

Elisabeth, not knowing how best to help, simply held the sobbing child in her arms. Now what have I said or done? Elisabeth thought. How could I be so thoughtless?

But finally Mary was able to share her thoughts with her cousin. Very wisely, Elisabeth listened without comment until the torrent of pain, anguish, and fear had ceased. Then, "Mary, do you really think a loving Father in Heaven would take a young daughter to wife, give her His seed, then leave her struggling to bear the burden alone?. . . No, I don't either. Here is a cool cloth. I am sure He will prepare Joseph to be at your side. Just have faith and courage. You aren't alone."

"Elisabeth, do you sometimes waver in your belief? It is so strange, wonderful, and awful that I wonder if I dreamed it all. But I did not. I *am* with child. He *did* tell me to go to Joseph—in time. At least, I think I remember Him telling me that last part. My memory of the time spent with Him is so vague, I can't be sure except that He . . . He told me not to tell Joseph, yet . . . Elisabeth, why can't I remember it all clearly? I can remember every word Gabriel said." Mary was frantic as she clutched Elisabeth's hands. "Why? Why? Why can't I remember my time spent with Eloheim and His words to me? I remember only how very loving and gentle He was with me. It was beautiful . . . Simply beautiful." Again, Mary's face reflected her thoughts.

"My child, some things are too sacred to be shared; so God puts a veil over our understanding that we may do nothing amiss. It is for your protection. Remember His gentle, loving ways, always! That is what He wants you to remember and to cherish."

In the silence, Mary again felt the close, warm presence of her loving mother. How thin the veil seemed at this moment. How like her mother was Elisabeth. No wonder God had sent her to this home. Here she could have help to sort her feelings. Elisabeth's warm understanding would enable her to prepare to face and tell Joseph—if the angel didn't.

Oh, please! Gabriel, go to Joseph and tell him. Please!

As the time for her wedding approached, Mary knew she could delay no longer. She must return to Joseph. If only she could wait until John was born. But the wise Elisabeth gently pushed her into the preparations. "You must be married on time, and before your condition becomes too apparent to prying eyes and wagging tongues. Joseph must be told. He is a man of God and will understand. Go to him. Seek his love and support and give him yours in return. You have a grave responsibility in bearing and raising the Son of God. Joseph is the man to help."

Zacharias supported his wife's position. They had so enjoyed her visit, yet they knew it must end. How grateful they were for her love and support. Elisabeth's time had been made so much easier.

As she packed, Mary gratefully accepted a gift of fine white silk for dainty underclothes and fine baby things. How could the world stay such a dreadful place with such fine people as Mary knew? Mary looked at the baby furniture standing ready for John. She'd learned much in helping Elisabeth in her preparations. No longer did it seem such a frightening thing to face. Besides, she had not experienced morning sickness for a week now. Her face was clear and lovely again, radiant with the excitement of the secret growing within her. Yes, Mary was ready to face Joseph and Nazareth— even the whole world if necessary.

. . . Behold Thy Son

Rachel was overjoyed at finding Mary at the door. "So, you finally decided to come home. We have only one month till the marriage date and so many things to do. Just listen to me! Come in out of the heat. It's just that I've never had a daughter to prepare for marriage, and I'm so grateful you are mine at this time.

"Tell me, how are Elisabeth and Zacharias? Is she doing fine? Your letters said she is well. But how is she, really? Does she have to stay in bed, or can she be up and around?"

Grateful for questions about someone besides herself, Mary answered as she laid her bundle on the bed and began to open it. As Rachel's eyes fell on the beautiful white silk, she gasped, picked it up and held it to her face. Temporarily speechless, Rachel met Mary's eyes and expressed the great love she felt for the lovely girl.

"Mary, what a beautiful piece. My, won't it make lovely underwear. It is so exquisite!" The words were as soft as the material. "Elisabeth and Zacharias love you very much. How blessed you are." Arms around each other, the two women sat upon the trunk and shared their experiences after a long separation. A noise at the door caused them to look that way.

"Aren't you going to fix supper?" Jason wasn't about to give voice to his joy at finding Mary back again. But his face could not hide his feelings. The women smiled, then stood up to go begin preparations. Mary caught him in a quick squeeze before he squirmed free. She'd not realized how she had missed the boys. As the other boys came home, Mary realized just how much she did love each one. Jason lost little time spreading the good news. Even Reuben was home early for supper. No one seemed to mind the delay in preparations. Mary could hardly keep up to the questions.

"What did you see? Was it hot?"

"Were you scared?"

"Did you walk or ride the camels?"

"Silly, there weren't any camels with her group."

"Well, maybe there were some that joined after. Or maybe better yet, elephants!" Jason's eyes widened as he thought of the possibilities.

"No," laughed Mary. "No, Jason. We didn't go where the camels and elephants go, only the donkeys and goats. They are very noisy. But it was good to be able to get fresh milk each day."

"Did you sleep in the open?"

"Yes, we did on the way here. It was too hot to use the tents."

Just as the supper chores were finished and the scriptures taken down for family study, a knock sounded at the door. Reuben went to answer. He was already on his feet and closest to the door, but Jason ran so fast he nearly beat him.

"Joseph, what a pleasant surprise! Do come in. Have you heard the good news? Mary is home." Joseph's nod assured him he had. "How thoughtless of us. We didn't think to come by the shop to tell you. Please forgive our selfishness. It seemed as if spring had come and I guess we just didn't think to share our good fortune."

As Joseph went to the hearth, his eyes searching the room for Mary, he assured his host he understood. He had heard the news just now from Simon who had brought his cart in to be repaired. Where was Mary?

"Rachel, what have you done with our daughter? Surely you have not sent her to bed so early." Reuben, too, looked in vain for sight of her.

"Oh, you men. Don't you know we like a bit of advance warning so we can fix our hair and wash our face and hands? Mary fled at the first sound of Joseph's name. She will be here presently. Remember, she's been away and is bashful by nature."

Philip snorted, "Mary bashful? Humph! She is just a tease. She likes to tease same as anyone."

"I do not!" Mary walked slowly to Joseph. Her hair shone from the brisk brushing it has just received. Never had she seemed more lovely. "Hello, Joseph. It is good to see you."

He took her outstretched hands. Forgetting everyone else in the room, solid, formal, "stuffy" Joseph put her hands to his lips and gently kissed them. "Mary, you are lovelier than ever." The family had to strain forward to hear his softly spoken words. "I thought you would never return."

"But I did."

CRASH! Jason fell off his bench. He had leaned too far forward trying not to miss what was said. The laughter and teasing didn't break the spell completely, though. The magic was still there, and stayed till Joseph was ready to leave. Rachel and Reuben shooed the boys off to their bedchambers. Then they, too, slipped away. Mary knew, though, that all were standing very close to their doors, anxious to hear every word.

From Joseph's greeting, Mary was sure the angel had told him. Why else would he be so happy? However, with the family listening so closely, she knew she must not bring it up. Joseph would

. . . Behold Thy Son

when it was proper. Oh, how glorious life was! How good God had been to her. Her fears had been in vain—again.

But as Joseph bid her goodnight, he pulled her gently into his arms to kiss her. As she felt his arms encircle her and her body draw close to his, she became aware of the development of her baby. Mary no longer had the shape of a young, unwed girl. Joseph, too, realized the change in her shape. How could he miss it?

He withdrew, puzzled, then instinctively pulled her close again. Looking into his eyes, Mary realized with mounting anxiety, the awful truth. The angel had not told him! Pain, bewilderment, and turmoil clouded his handsome face. "Mary!" He was just barely able to whisper. "Mary, you are with child!"

"Yes, Joseph, I am!" No more. She could not go on. Only, "Yes, Joseph, I am!"

The family heard his cry of anguish—saw his face as Joseph turned and fled out the door. They saw Mary sink to the floor, sobbing brokenheartedly. Try as they might, Rachel and Reuben could get no answer as to why. The cock crowed before Mary's sobs allowed her to sleep. Then and only then did they leave her bedside. What had happened? How could they help? What had they done—or not done?

Chapter Four

JOSEPH

Stumbling blindly through the streets, Joseph felt as though his heart would burst. How could this terrible, horrible, awful, wicked thing be? His pure, lovely, sweet Mary . . . with . . . child! It just could not be! Yet, Joseph had felt the change in her shape. And . . . Mary had admitted she was with child.

But she was happy, gay, and carefree, not full of guilt and condemnation as she should be.

She knows the Law. She has been well taught. How could she do this? God of Abraham, Isaac, and Jacob, what do I do? WHAT DO I DO? I cannot stone such a beautiful thing.

I can't live without her. These three months have been sheer torture. I thought they would never end. I never did understand why she left and had no idea when she would return.

Slumping onto the well, Joseph leaned against the post. A sudden thought caused him to sit upright, banging his forehead on the winch. Distraught and upset, Joseph failed to realize he had hit it until he was home and found the blood on his hands.

Was that why she left so suddenly? Was she raped? or what? Was it Reuben's boys? Or maybe one of the village men?

Unable to believe anyone he knew could do such a thing, Joseph slumped again. One thing was certain, it was not his child.

The Roman soldiers! They were in Nazareth the week before Mary left. Maybe they . . . but no, there had been no disturbance.

Rising to his feet once more, Joseph stumbled home. He felt lightheaded and dizzy as well as enormously confused. The

moon's rays revealed a man who appeared to be very drunk struggling home after a big night out. Only this man had never partaken
of spirits. He was very strict in his observance of the Law and it
forbade drunkenness. The Law also forbade adultery and that was
what it appeared Mary had committed.

*Another thing, Mary acted as if I should have known. She actually
thought I knew and . . . approved. How could she? How could I approve
such behavior?*

Maybe this explained her sudden departure for Juttah. It never
had seemed right to him, no matter how he tried to reason it out.
Rachel, herself, said Mary had been fine one day and extremely
upset the next, grasping at visiting Elisabeth as a drowning man
would a log. Could someone have broken in and . . . raped Mary?
There was a window in the room they gave her. But if his memory
served him, that room was right off the room Rachel and Reuben
slept in. There had been no door, only a robe across it when he had
helped bring Mary's things for her. They would have heard anything like that.

Not able to find peace in sleep, Joseph wandered from room to
room in the house he was making ready for his lovely wife-to-be.
His pain grew even greater and harder to bear. Each item had been
purchased, traded for, or made with Mary—pure, innocent Mary—
in mind. But now, what was he to do?

Work had to go on, so Joseph opened shop as usual in the
morning. But work was not as usual. He could not seem to find the
pegs and holes. Nothing fit after he cut it, and the lathe was no
place for a man in his state of mind. Why did everyone in Nazareth
have to come to tell him Mary was back and to see if he'd seen her
and to ask about his wedding plans? Why couldn't they just leave
him alone?

The townspeople left the shop, shaking their heads in puzzlement. Why was Joseph so upset? A wedding is a time of joy. Yet, he
seemed uninterested and refused to discuss it. He even snapped
whenever Mary's radiant happiness was mentioned.

Speaking of Mary, where was she today? Rachel and Reuben
seemed to be upset, too. What had happened to the wedding
plans? With only a few weeks to go, why the sudden halt? Rachel
had canceled a women's get-together until further notice. No
explanation—just Jason at the door saying his mother had something come up, so please forget the party.

Nazareth is a small, friendly village. Little happens that stays private. So the news spread quickly when the next day brought a locked door on the carpenter shop and the herders watched a tormented Joseph heading to the hills. He had forgotten to cover his head. *That* let the town know for sure—something was drastically wrong. Joseph—the strict observer of the Law—was too upset to observe and perform as he usually did. The whole village was humming with the news. This was the biggest event since last summer when locusts had descended on them like a plague.

No one had any answers. No one knew anything. Everyone guessed, but no one knew. Reuben and his boys only added to the mystery with their bewildered shrugs and silent shaking of heads. What was wrong? Surely, someone could explain the mystery.

Mary awoke at noon. The morning sickness returned, probably because of the upset. It seemed as if her body were trying to throw off the child who was causing Joseph such pain.

Hearing her heaving, Rachel hurried in to see what she could do. Mary was finally able to pull out the herbs Elisabeth had sent to help ease the awful sickness. Rachel took the herbs from her, sniffed them, and stiffened—rigid as a cedar post. A very white face revealed that she knew what these herbs were for. She now understood the heaving. But Rachel could not ask the question. She had no voice or will to speak.

"Yes, Rachel, I am with child. About three months." Mary's soft voice barely carried to Rachel's startled ears.

"B . . . b . . . but . . . why? . . . Who? . . ." Rachel choked on the questions. She still could not believe or understand.

At last! Someone in Nazareth knew. Someone could help as Elisabeth had helped. Surely she could tell Rachel all. But all Mary could say was, "It is not Joseph's. I am not an adulteress. I am clean." No more. Why? Why could Rachel not share her heavenly secret? But Mary was prevented from going further.

As the words sank into Rachel's heart, she felt a dagger turn and twist. Rushing from the room, she felt as if she, too, would be ill. What could she do? What had she not done? Where had she failed her dear friends, Jacob, and his faithful wife?

Just then Reuben stepped through the door for his noon meal. No need to ask if things had improved. His tired body slumped onto the bench and his head found a cradle on his arms. Rachel's hands rubbed his tired back and neck. Realizing Rachel was sobbing, Reuben looked up, then pulled her to the bench beside him.

. . . Behold Thy Son

"Have you found the trouble? Do you know why Joseph left so abruptly?"

Rachel nodded, unable to speak. No longer able to bear it alone, she fell into his arms, sobbing the same as Mary had last night . Reuben caught words in between her sobs, "Child . . . stone . . . Law . . . strict . . . fail . . . why?"

Allowing her to find relief through tears, Reuben waited patiently for his dear wife to talk. "There, there, Rachel, it can't be as bad as all that. You know our Mary is a pure, fine . . ." But he got no further for Rachel cried louder and harder at the words. Now what had he said? Women!

At last, Reuben learned of the scene in the bedchamber. He felt like crying, too, but sat tight-lipped and grimfaced. More able to reason things out, Reuben tried to see what he could make of it. Mary had been so radiant and happy on her return. A little shy, perhaps. But she had to get used to the boys' teasing again, so that was expected. And her greeting for Joseph was normal. Nothing went wrong till he kissed her goodnight. No, it had to have started before that.

"Reuben, do you think Joseph will stone her? Or divorce her? Go to him and convince him to give a divorce and let us keep her always. We must help her all we can. The poor child is all alone. We cannot send her back to Elisabeth and Zacharias. They are too old. . . . Do you think they know?"

"Yes, . . . they must know. She would have been ill while she was there."

"Remember that lovely white silk? So pure and white . . . If they, being priests and knowing the Law, could treat her so royally and not as a whore," Rachel stood up, shaking her finger to emphasize the point. "If they can accept it, then we must. We must protect her at all costs!"

"And we will, my dear, we will. If she says she is not an adulteress, I believe her. She has never lied in her life."

"Oh, thank you! Thank you, dear, sweet Reuben and Rachel. Surely, no one could have dearer friends than you are." A frightened girl had listened at the door, afraid they would turn her out . . . or worse, accuse her to the rabbi. A relieved young woman came to take the hands of her beloved friends.

As Reuben looked at Mary, he realized her face did show the signs of pregnancy. He just figured the mountain air and fresh goat's cheese had fattened her up a bit. "My daughter, tell us how we can help and we will."

"All we can do is wait . . . Wait for Joseph. I thought he knew. But he does not. Now we must just wait."

Jason burst into the room. "Joseph is surely upset. He can't do anything right . . . Oh . . . excuse me for interrupting." He backed to the door in embarrassment.

"Come, son. Come over here. Mary has a bit of a problem. We can help best by not talking of it to anyone outside the family. We will not answer questions except that Mary is home, well, and happy. Plans for the marriage are awaiting Joseph's approval." Reuben pulled his young son onto his lap. Hugging him gently, the father tried to help the boy understand. "Keep your ears open, but lips tight. It will all work out in time. But whatever you hear, I want you to remember one thing." Looking into his eyes, Reuben watched the fear begin to melt away. "Remember, son, Mary is now your sister. She is pure, innocent, and clean, no matter what you might hear. Do you understand?"

Jason nodded as he looked from his father to his mother to Mary. "Are you really my sister, Mary? Can I *really* claim you?"

"Yes, Jason. I need a little brother just like you." Hugs are allowed if a boy wants and needs them, and Jason needed to feel Mary's reassuring arms around him.

"Hooray! Hooray! Mary is my sister. Mary is really my sister!" His voice trailed off down the road as those left behind laughed in relief as one crisis passed.

Two awful, long, horrible days passed for the anguished Mary. Perhaps she was wrong. Perhaps Eloheim had not told her to go to Joseph. Maybe she just dreamed it. Surely if it were to be, he would know by now. The boys could not understand their parents' anxious looks and protective spirit toward their "adopted daughter."

Only Jason seemed to be unaffected by the mystery. Being the youngest, he had greater freedom to come and go. So it was Jason who kept them abreast with the news. "Joseph wasn't in his shop all day. No sign. Just a locked door. Mary, you must have upset him terribly. Daniel said he headed for the hills with his head uncovered. Sarah and Miriam are telling everyone. I listened to them, then I told them to be still 'cause you are clean and pure and a great big sister. They said they would thrash me for my impudence, but I can run faster than them so I did." His shrug showed his assurance of safety. Amused smiles cannot stay hidden behind hands when the eyes betray them. Jason knew he'd not be punished—

. . . Behold Thy Son

scolded, maybe, but not punished.

"Jason," Reuben knew he must say something. "You are not to be rude to your elders. However, you were right to defend Mary's honor. She *is* clean and pure as you said."

"Well, Joseph didn't come home by supper time. So I fed his goats. They needed water, too. You'll love them, Mary. They are very playful and friendly."

"Oh, dear! Joseph *is* upset if he forgot the animals." Mary's face was ashen. Rachel wondered if she would lose her supper and rose to get the pail. "No, thank you, Rachel. I am fine. The tea helps. I just have to wait, pray, and . . . and hope." Her voice trailed off into the stillness.

All the family were extra quiet as if listening for a footstep or voice. When a knock did sound at the door, all but Jason nearly jumped out of their clothes. Who was it? Joseph? Had he finally come? Jason went skipping to the door, whistling as he went.

But a stranger—not Joseph—was at the door. Would they feed him and allow him a place by the hearth for the night? He wondered at the crestfallen faces and Reuben's hesitant manner. He could not read Reuben's thoughts, "What if Joseph should come? He will not be able to talk to Mary with this stranger here."

But Mary was already getting the food for him. She sent Jason for the goat's milk. She seemed relieved to have something urgent to do.

The stranger's stories of faraway China gave them an excuse to stay up later than usual. Finally they had to say goodnight. Rachel and Reuben kissed Mary gently on the cheek. If only they could help. "Shall I go to him? I can, Mary."

"No, Reuben. He must come on his own. I must just wait."

"But why, daughter? *Why?*" Rachel's tears spilled to her ample bosom, making rivers on her cheeks.

"Because, Mother, that is the way it must be. I am prevented from telling him anything. He must come on his own."

"Then who will tell him? How will he learn the truth?"

"I do not know. I only know I must wai . . ." Mary could go no farther. Her tears mingled with Rachel's as they tried to comfort each other.

Reuben's arms went about them both. A man has a right to cry when his dear ones are hurting—and hurting they were. His silent prayers begged for strength and wisdom.

Please, God, send Joseph to this lovely daughter. Let him not stone her.

Let us shield her and protect her from the pointing fingers and wagging tongues.

"Are you sure you don't want to go to Salome and Zeebedee at Capernaum? They would let you stay till it is over and raise your child with theirs. James is nearly one. She loves you as a sister. You were so close as girls before her marriage."

"No, Rachel. I am to raise and teach my son. It is my calling. I must just wait."

"Your son! Your son! How can you be so sure it will be a son?" Reuben's teasing brought a smile to Rachel's face, at least.

"Reuben, don't you know we must have sons to open the womb. Besides, being here with all our sons, she would naturally beget a son first."

Mary smiled faintly at their teasing. Life can't stay so dark with such good, choice friends. She must have faith.

Why can't I tell them? They are so good, kind, and loving. Surely, they should know. But I can't. I am stopped. I told Elisabeth and it was easy . . . No . . . Elisabeth told me. I did not tell her . . . Perhaps they, too, will be visited.

Sleep refused to come. Mary tossed and turned then tossed and turned again. Finally in desperation, she sat at the window and prayed to her God. Something was stirring in the street. It must be a dog or stray animal. No, it was a man. A drunkard. See how he staggered.

The full moon revealed a bareheaded man staggering through the streets. He stopped at their gate and raised his face to look at the house. Mary shrank back into the shadows as she realized he was looking at her window. He must be a thief. Then she heard his mournful sobs.

"Mary! Why? Mary! Oh why? What do I do now? Oh, God . . . help . . . me. Please help me!" There was more but Mary was sobbing and Joseph had turned and returned down the hill.

Exhaustion overcame the young girl just before the cock crowed. No one awakened her. Even Jason sensed her need for sleep. Ezra, the eldest son, had heard Joseph at the gate. He related the incident and asked why Joseph was in such great torment.

"I don't know, Ezra. But this much I can say. We will stand behind Mary and protect her at all costs." Reuben's voice was extra firm, although soft.

A knock . . . no, a gentle tap . . . at the door caused all to jump. Perhaps the stranger had decided to eat breakfast after all. No one

. . . Behold Thy Son

seemed anxious to answer the door. The tap was repeated again before Jason answered the door in response to his father's nod.

"Joseph! *Joseph*! You've come! Father, Mother, it's Joseph! He's come! He's come! I knew he would! I just knew he would!" Jason slammed the door in his excitement and danced all around the room, shrieking like a peafowl.

"Jason, Jason, quiet down. You will awaken Mary." Reuben sprang to open the door again and to apologize. But Joseph's upraised hand and smile made it unnecessary.

"Reuben, may I come in and speak to Mary? I have something very important to discuss with her."

Ezra marveled at the change. Joseph was not the tormented man he had watched at the gate in the moonlight. He now appeared calm, collected, and joyously happy.

All the family marvelled at the change. Surely something was happening which was beyond understanding. Who would explain it? And when?

"Mary is still asleep? Poor girl. She must have been terribly distressed these past two days. How could I have been so cruel?"

Joseph's voice carried through the curtain into the room where the troubled Mary slept. She was dreaming that Joseph had come. He had come to stone her. She sat up in fright. It was so vivid, the dream would not go away. It had been so real, it was as if she had actually heard his voice. Mary realized a guest was with the family. Oh, yes. The traveler would eat breakfast. She must hurry and help. But as Joseph spoke again, Mary stopped dead still. She had not been dreaming! He *was* here, and he was angry.

But Joseph was angry at himself. "Reuben, I have been so blind. Mary is pure and innocent. How could I have doubted her? Rachel, please proceed with the plans. Only make it as soon as possible. We must protect her from wagging tongues."

Mary fairly exploded into the room. "Joseph! Joseph! You know! He came! Oh, thank the Lord, you know!" Joseph caught the sobbing girl in his arms. Tears of joy and relief are as wet as tears of sorrow and fear and his robe was soon damp. Joseph smoothed her shining hair and let her cry. Rachel shooed the men off without breakfast. She handed them fig cakes and dates as they tiptoed out the door. Jason shrugged his shoulders, picked up the water jug, and headed for the well. Boy, he could hardly wait to tell Sarah and Miriam the news. He would show those gossiping ladies.

Joseph thanked them with smiles and nods and patiently waited for Mary to calm down. After a while, the sobs slowed and became infrequent. Still, she did not lift her face or talk. Just being in Joseph's loving, strong arms was sufficient for now. At last her tear-swollen face looked into his. Radiant with joy, love, and relief, no face with swollen, red eyes had ever looked lovelier.

"Was it Gabriel? Did he come?"

"Yes, my darling. Gabriel came early this morning. I had finally made up my mind to a Bill of Divorcement and fell asleep. I think it was less than an hour before dawn. I dreamed a dream which caused me to awaken and sit upright. It was disturbing—yet wonderful at the same time. Unable to go back to sleep or to find peace of mind, I knelt in prayer to find the meaning of the dream. As I said amen, a light shone into my face. Lifting my head, I saw a man standing at the other side. His voice penetrated my very being, cleansing my soul of bitterness and confusion. 'Joseph, thou son of David, fear not to take unto thee Mary thy wife: for that which is conceived in her is of the Holy Ghost. And she shall bring forth a son, and thou shalt call his name JESUS: For he shall save his people from their sins.' He told me more, quoting scriptures and helping me to understand. You are to be my wife and I am to help raise your son . . . The Son of God."

Mary's relief was total. She felt an overwhelming love for Joseph and realized she was now free to share her sacred secret. She sat up, squared her shoulders, and confided in her sweetheart. Joseph's eyes grew wide as she told of Gabriel's visit and message. Then she told how the Holy Ghost had "overcome and prepared her" so she could enter the presence of Eloheim, the Eternal Father. Her eyes grew misty and her face softened as she told of her visit with Him. Her voice trailed off into silence as she gazed into space. Joseph waited patiently. He understood that some things are too sacred and wonderful to share—ever. He really did not want to know all of it. "Oh, He is so kind and gentle . . . and wonderful. Not at all like Rabbi speaks of Him. I have no words to describe the joy and peace I felt while with Him.

"As I was leaving, He put His arm around my shoulder—like this—and lifted my chin so I could look into His eyes. 'Love him, Mary. Love him and teach him. His is a most important mission. But you must not raise him alone. Joseph is kind, wise, and good. He will help you. Trust him . . . and me.' Then He led me to the door and kissed me good-by. There were tears in His eyes and great sadness mixed with joy. And He was right! You are good,

. . . Behold Thy Son

kind, and wise." A kiss planted firmly on his nose left no doubt as to her sincerity.

"But, Mary, I have been so unkind and . . . so unwise. When I left I felt I would rather die than face what I had discovered. First I felt anger at you for being with child. Then I was torn by the decision of stoning or divorce. The thoughts of living without you were torture. These past three months have been an eternity. I could *not* divorce you, nor could I have you stoned. Rather they stone me!

"Then I remembered your happiness at seeing me again and your apparent lack of guilt over your condition. Reuben and Rachel didn't seem upset. You gave no explanation—just 'Yes, I am with child.' No more."

"But you left before I could explain!" Mary stiffened in his arms.

Pulling her closer, Joseph kissed her forehead. "I know, darling, I know. But I am back and ready to become your husband and help you raise your son . . . Jesus . . . A common name for a very uncommon child."

"Yes, a very uncommon child. Oh, Joseph, thank you. Thank you! Thank you!" Could it be that after three days of continual crying Mary could still find tears to cry? She most certainly could and did. Only now her tears were not as the terrible thunder showers of summer, but as the gentle rain of spring.

Chapter Five

NEIGHBORS AND FRIENDS

"I still say Mary is with child. Look at her face. It is as plain to see as anything."

"If she were with child Joseph would never marry her! He is too strict in the observance of the Law. He would have her stoned or put away—privately. He would not have this quiet wedding. No, I think you are mistaken." Deborah moved away from Sarah and Miriam. She had been waiting too long for this day to let Sarah's feelings ruin a beautiful occasion. Joseph was too fine a man and Mary too pure and sweet to do such a thing.

Miriam, on the other hand, *knew* the suspicions were true. Hadn't she observed Joseph's strange behavior at Mary's return? She had taken a chair for him to mend, and he actually growled at her when she asked if he had seen Mary. He was so upset he cut the leg off too short and had to make another one. Yes, Joseph, was not the father. That sweet little innocent Mary was not so innocent after all.

"You would think Rachel and Reuben would have known better than to bring such a pretty, friendly, little thing into their house of boys. I'll just bet it is one of their sons who is the father."

"No, Sarah. I've been watching and they don't act a bit guilty. I can spot it right off. They are not the guilty ones. Rabbi can be thankful Nathan did not ask for her hand."

"Oh, but he did. Jacob refused him." It was a blessing Miriam could not read Sarah's thoughts. They were most unkind.

If you are so good at spotting the party, how come you are the only one who doesn't know Zeke's late hours are spent with women, not his work? You aren't as smart as you think you are, my dear.

Deborah found an open spot by Rachel. Rachel's radiance was nearly equal to Mary's. Anyone observing would think she really was mother of the bride. Reuben and the boys were equally proud. Could anyone doubt their love for the beautiful young girl? "Rachel, you finally did it. You are to be congratulated."

"Thank you, Deborah." Her eyes did not leave the faces of the couple under the canopy. Her tears made them appear even more ethereal and radiant. "Why do we always cry at a wedding? It is such a beautiful occasion and especially so today. Our king and queen are marrying. What a handsome pair!" Tears prevented further expression of joy.

"I was so afraid last week this would never come to pass. Why did Mary leave so fast? I understand she did not talk to Joseph—just left a note and . . . fled, so to speak."

Rachel turned abruptly and looked deep into her friend's eyes. Seeing no malice or mischief—only loving concern, her face relaxed and she explained, softly. "Mary became so terribly lonesome and frightened. We could not help. She needed family. When Simon returned bringing news of Elisabeth's coming event, Mary longed . . . No . . . It was a greater need than longing, much greater. She *had* to go and see for herself. We inquired and found a group headed to Juttah that very morning. We only had three hours to prepare. There just wasn't time. Elisabeth and Zacharias were so grateful to have her loving help they kept her as long as possible before sending her home, laden with gifts of gratitude and love."

"But why did Joseph react to her homecoming the way he did? I saw him and I *know* he was very upset."

"Hush, back there. We can't hear the Rabbi!" So Deborah did not get her answer, yet. But there was still time after the ceremony when she wouldn't offend those watching. The ceremony was nearly over, and she would soon be needed to help in the kitchen. Perhaps then.

As the men congratulated the happy groom, Reuben silently took his hand and looked into his eyes. Finding only love, trust, and understanding, Reuben embraced the man who had married his adopted daughter. "Love her, always, Joseph. I do not understand it at all, but you seem to. I only know she is as pure as the driven snow and not at fault in her condition."

"You are so right, Father. So right. She is pure, innocent, and clean."

36

No one else heard the whispers, yet they could see the happy smiles and tears. All knew Reuben approved of the actions of the day. Next to Rabbi, Reuben and Joseph were the most respected men in Nazareth. Some were sure Reuben was smarter than Rabbi.

But Sarah and Miriam were still discussing the "shamefulness of it all."

"Yes, Joseph was very upset and did not go near the home for two full days. He gave up trying to work and headed to the hills the second day. He didn't even leave a note—just locked up and left."

"Rachel told me the wedding wasn't for another month. Then all at once, I heard it was today. Joseph wanted it as soon as possible. That was a switch if I ever heard of one," said Sarah.

"I know. No matter how you look at it, we should have been throwing stones today—not rice and flowers."

"If anyone should be stoned, it is you two for gossiping!" Zeke and Jeremiah removed their wives from the spot with force matching Zeke's angry words.

"Yeah," flung Jeremiah over his shoulder as he pushed Sarah away towards home. "Let's see if Rabbi will allow stoning for gossiping and nagging. Surely would save a lot of misery if he would." As the two men laughed loudly at their joke, their wives rebuked them for their drunken rudeness.

Many of the women watching and listening had to agree with the men. Misery begets misery. It was a sure bet Joseph would never be driven to drink. Not with Mary as his wife.

Rabbi smiled as he looked on the royal couple. It was good to have the king married. An unmarried monarch, even though he has no throne, can be too tempting to the young women. Joseph had chosen wisely. Mary was radiant and capable. She had been well taught. A feeling of hurt still came when he remembered Jacob's refusal to Nathan. We would have welcomed Mary into our home, he thought. She would have been welcome and well cared for. However, I doubt Nathan would have loved her as deeply as Joseph does. It causes him to literally shine. I wonder about the torment and uncertainty he experienced at her return. It was certainly strange. But there is no torment and uncertainty now. He is very sure and very much in love.

Turning to go, Rabbi was called into the kitchen to give his benediction to the preparations of the feast. Weddings are such a joyous time. "We really should do this more often."

. . . Behold Thy Son

"Do what, Rabbi?"

"Oh. Was I thinking out loud? I didn't mean to."

Laughter added to the merriment as the Rabbi's face returned to its natural color.

Miriam and her friends were enjoying their few moments at the well. "I told you so. Only three weeks married and look at her!"

"I still say no adulteress could have such peace in her face. Mary is very much a queen."

"Joseph is more in love than ever. So tender and careful."

Water splashed into the pots which were lifted to their heads as they began their trip home. "Wish Zeke would be so loving," sighed Miriam.

"He would be if married to Mary. She appreciates and loves Joseph in return."

"Humph!"

A group of women were washing at the stream. Something had them buzzing like bees. The conversation was going faster than the washing. At this rate, the clothes would not get washed today. "I have it on good authority. Sarah says they sleep in separate rooms. She thought as much, so figured and figured . . ."

"Schemed and schemed you mean."

An angry scowl, then Miriam took up where she was when so rudely interrupted. "Last week when little Ben was sick, she ran over to their house. (Mary is so good to help.) Sarah barged right in with her lantern. There was Joseph's bed by the hearth. Mary came from the other room. They didn't even have the decency to look ashamed or to offer an explanation.

"And have you noticed? Joseph treats her as a precious doll, not as a wife or sweetheart. It's not his child, or he would be sleeping with her right now."

"Shame on you, Miriam! What right have you to pry? That is between them and God, not you. Besides, my Reuben often sleeps in by the hearth as I progress with my children. That way we both sleep better. After all, I can't sleep on my stomach and have to lie on my back. My snoring keeps poor Reuben awake. He works so hard and does need his sleep. My groaning adds to the problem. I fix him a bed by the hearth so he'll be warm."

"Not me! Zeke has to be right there. He got me in that condition. He can suffer, too. Why should *I* suffer alone? He has to rub my back and change the cool towel over my eyes. After all, it's his child, too, not just mine!" Such scrubbing and rubbing. Surely the clothes didn't deserve that punishment. But at least they were finally getting washed.

"You know, Esther, I feel like you do. Joseph isn't the father, but he knows who it is and why. His love for Mary is so great he has forgiven her. His waiting till she is 'cleansed' shows even more the love and respect he has for her. My, such love . . . Would my Dan love . . . me that much? . . . I pray so." The splashing, rubbing, and soaping seemed less vigorous, more tender and gentle.

Mary wasn't wearing her usual smile. Something was troubling her. Life seemed to be getting harder and harder. Now should be the happiest time of her life: she was newly married and expecting her first child. She knew it was going to be a boy. That is a great honor for a Jewish woman, but a must for a queen. So why the sad look? Neighbors and friends were becoming increasingly cruel in the little things said as she left their company. Why must she go to the well for water? Joseph would get it for her if he knew. Yet, he was too busy to take the time. Besides, she must do the marketing, and Miriam and Sarah always seemed to know just when she would be there.

Do you think they plan it? It surely seems so. I've not been to market or the well for two months now without finding one or both there. Nor do they ever fail to make me feel like a harlot—but not for long. For if I think back to Gabriel's visit, that glorious feeling comes over me anew. Me—Mary, wife of Joseph—mother of the Son of God.

The broom settled back to its place as if grateful to be done with the task.

Her smile returned as Elisabeth and her new baby John came to mind. Word had arrived in early morning. Too good to keep till night, the news was shared at lunch. Picnic lunches are fun—even if only in the carpenter shop. The wood shavings always smelled like the hills, and those white and yellow daisies by the door added the last touch. She was so glad she had planted them for him. Joseph had received many thanks for the bouquets he had sent home with his customers.

Joseph knew that something special had prompted the picnic. He had made his own lunch that morning. Mary had slept little because of her backache. It always got worse after wash day. Joseph slipped in and whispered that she must not stir. He had

. . . Behold Thy Son

awakened early to get the extra time to finish the crib for Dan's new baby who was due any day now. He had fixed a basket and said, "Please sleep in, my darling. You are much too tired."

Then the messager with that glorious message: Elisabeth had delivered, and it was as Gabriel had said—a boy!

Imagine, after all these years—a boy! I can see why the people would marvel at the name of John. We have had no one by that name for generations. I would loved to have been at the temple and seen their joy as their tiny eight-day-old son was circumcised. Yes, and I can imagine the priest really thought Elisabeth was terrible for not wanting her son named Zacharias. They would be upset enough at her 'going against tradition' but to go against her husband! Yes, I would like to have seen the faces when Zacharias supported Elisabeth and made known his wish for 'John.' The outpouring of words must have been marvelous as he praised God for His blessings.

Elisabeth! Gabriel is a true messenger. It all came to pass just as he said it would. It has for me, too. Oh, if only I can be strong. If only I can remember. I can ignore the remarks. I will not see the gestures and sneers. I will be happy and not let Joseph know how hurt I am!

Joseph! Yes, Joseph just had to know about John. It might help erase the worried lines that had come to be so much a part of his dear face. Dear, sweet Joseph. No one else would be so loving, understanding, and patient. Thank goodness Joseph realized that the tears which flowed so freely meant nothing except that she was with child and tears are a part of it.

Like yesterday. Everything had gone right—for a change. No Sarah, only Miriam, at the well, and Rachel was there with her. That always meant joy, for Rachel was like a special mother. She seemed to know what needed to be said or done without being told. Everyone loved her. Built like an elephant (at least that is what Rachel said) and strong as an ox, Rachel was so gentle and full of love that everyone was naturally kind and generous when she was around. And the baking had gone right. Supper was on time—Joseph, also. But as they ate, this awful, lonely feeling suddenly came over her. Before she knew what she was doing, tears had spilled over and made her milk salty. How could she explain to Joseph? It had taken almost an hour before a smile could be coaxed back into her eyes. Even his imitation of old David, the rabbi, didn't succeed this time. But he had been patient and seemed to realize it wasn't anything serious—just the usual feelings of a woman in her condition. It helped to be the oldest child of a large family. Joseph had watched his mother and knew what to expect.

But where is Joseph now! Zeb's cart was to be done by noon, and he didn't expect any more new work till next week. So where is he? The sun has been low for some time. He knows I hate to be alone. Is he hurt? Have robbers found him? Maybe he cut his hand on the lathe—or worse! Oh, I must sweep the floor to keep my mind busy . . . But I just did that . . . I know. The mending basket. But first, I'll put some water on to heat. Warm ginger tea will be good for supper.

The faint smile soon faded as the shadows deepened. Strange noises became more frequent as the time dragged by. Why does the imagination work so well at night when one is alone? A gentle knock caused the tense Mary to jump—dropping her mending with a clatter. "Who is it?"

"Joseph." Did he sound strange, tired, or maybe hurt? The latch always sticks if you are in a hurry.

"My darling, I'm so glad you're home. I've been so worried. Joseph! Your robe is torn, and your face! Joseph! What happened?"

"Nothing, dear, nothing. I just stumbled in the dark. I must have hit a wall or something." He slumped to the bench.

"A wall? Did it have a post sticking out? How could your robe get torn that much? Here, let me have it. Joseph, your hand is bleeding! What happened? Who was it!? Why . . . ?"

"Now, Mary, calm down. It was nothing. Really." He sat up.

"Nothing? Nothing? This is awful!"

"Really, dear. I am okay and it won't happen again. I promise!"

Angrily, Mary faced her battered husband. "How can you be so sure? Here, the water is hot. Let me wash that hand . . . that looks better." Tender once again, Mary very gently washed, doctored, and bandaged the cuts and bruises. "We must take care of that eye or you will not be able to see tomorrow. Maybe I better get Esther. She's so good at helping people."

"No, dear. See it's really only a few scratches. It isn't so bad."

"Then why do you wince every time I touch your hand? And . . . you can hardly open it without tears." Silence fell as the hand found comfort in the cool leaves and bandage. The lines were leaving Joseph's face, but growing deeper on Mary's. Softly and tenderly, Mary comforted, loved, nursed, and fussed. "It was because of me . . . wasn't it?" Tears and sobs began to gain control. Mary found herself in tender, gentle arms. There was no stopping the tears now. This time she had a reason to cry—a very good one!

. . . Behold Thy Son

At last her sobs nearly subsided. Joseph led her to the bench by the hearth. Smoothing her hair back and kissing the tears away, Joseph felt he could not love this precious girl more. How could he? He would simply burst if any more love tried to squeeze in. She was so patient and forgiving. Mary didn't fight back. Some of the neighbors and townspeople could be so cruel. Yet, Mary always managed to smile when she went out. Tears were saved for home.

"Joseph?" . . . barely a whisper.

"Yes?"

Oh, Mary, I love you.

"I am so sorry . . . Oh, Joseph! Why can't they understand? Why must some people be so cruel?"

A knock sounded on the door. Who could be calling this late? Rachel! Wonderful, good-hearted Rachel filled the room with her concern and warmth. "Reuben told me what happened. Shame on that Jeremiah! Who does he think he is anyway—a rabbi or judge?

"Here, Mary, I brought some roots. They will take that swelling out of his eye. Crush them, then pour boiling water over them. After a moment put them in a clean bandage. Make sure he holds it there for at least an hour.

"Otherwise the whole town will be talking, as if they aren't by now. Really! You men! Why must you get so physical about things? My Reuben has wanted to tear into Jeremiah for some time and I keep telling him it isn't his place."

How could such an immense woman move so quickly and softly? She was everywhere, calming, soothing, fussing. Things didn't seem so bad with Rachel in charge. And in charge she was. "Mary, you're getting too close to your time to carry the water jug. I'll have Jason bring your water. Once in the morning and again just before sundown. Joseph has no time to do it, but Jason needs something to do and this will be just the thing. And I wash the same day you do. We will drop by and help carry the clothes to the stream. You really shouldn't be doing all that heavy lifting. With most of my boys away working, I don't get to spend as much time visiting as I used to. I always run out of clothes too fast. So I will help you. No, there is no use to protest. Here, supper's all ready and you two sit up and eat. You must be famished. Keep that poultice on your eye, Joseph."

She paused long enough for prayers and began again. "Besides. Sarah and Miriam won't get to say a word with me there—they wouldn't dare. It's all their fault, you know. They are such gossips.

They make me angry with their hints and tales. After all, it is none of their business. No! They won't dare say a word. I'll see to that!"

An amused smile played on Joseph's face. *No*, he thought, as he looked at the dear woman, no one would dare say a word.

"Now, Joseph, don't you feel bad. Jeremiah needed to be taken down a peg or two. He is too cocky. Reuben has been wanting to for months, no—years, but didn't have enough reason. I guess you smelled his breath.

"Say, this *is* good bread, Mary. Joseph is right to be bragging about it. These figs are just right, too. Not too sweet and not too tart.

"Why does such a good man feel he needs extra courage? Drink doesn't give strength, but destroys it ... destroys good sense, too. Anyway, I don't believe anyone else will be so thoughtless. Your business is your own business. Anybody can see that you have made your peace with the Lord and know what is what.

"Now remember, Mary, I'll help on wash day and Jason will carry the water. And if you would be so kind as to stop by on your way to do the marketing, I will go with you. I do so enjoy your company. After all, I still claim you as my daughter." Then she was gone—just as she had come. As a cool evening wind dispels the hot, angry tears, this angel of mercy swept the gloom and darkness out the door ahead of her.

"How can we be grateful enough for her? Surely, she is a chosen vessel to help us in our times of need. God is mindful," cried Mary.

Peace reigned again in the happy home. God had heard their prayers.

Chapter Six

TAXATION

A lamp burning on the table enabled the happy young mother-to-be to put the finishing touches on a soft, white silk garment for the expected baby. As her fingers sewed the tiny, even stitches, she listened as her handsome husband read from the scriptures.

This was their favorite time of the whole day. Safe and snug in their tiny, clean home, they could forget the rudeness of some of their neighbors and ignore the not-so-subtle counting from their wedding day and the wagging of knowing heads as they watched Mary's growing size. Instead, they could remember the kindness of loved ones who did all they could to bring the light back into their eyes. Thank goodness most of the people were good, kind, and forgiving. Rachel and Reuben had done much to stem the wagging tongues.

Joseph felt that only a knife could still Sarah's and Miriam's tongues. He wasn't sure but what they would then each grow another tongue to again spread bitterness and hate. He paused to feast his eyes on his lovely wife. It is no wonder Zeke and Jeremiah drink. If only they could have part of the happiness he enjoyed. Why, he thought, he and Mary had never said an unkind word to each other. No, and they never would, either.

"Why did you stop? Are you tired? I will read for a while and let you rest your eyes." Mary blushed as she read the love in her husband's eyes. She wondered if she would ever get used to such love and devotion. What had she done to deserve it?

"No, darling Mary, I'm just feasting my eyes on your beautiful face. Motherhood is becoming to you. You grow lovelier and more radiant each day."

"You mean fatter and more awkward. I nearly got stuck in Rachel's cellar door today. I turned to say something to Jason. When I finally stopped laughing, I turned and backed out. Poor Jason was so embarrassed at me for laughing so hard at such a silly thing. Rachel had to know what caused the funny look on his face, so we laughed some more. I thought my sides would burst. Why is it, do you suppose, women cry and laugh at such silly little things?"

"I am sure I don't know, but I love you for it." Picking up the scriptures he read on in Micah. This time he read: "'Now gather thyself in troops, O daughter of troops: he hath laid siege against us: they shall smite the judge of Israel with a rod upon the cheek. But thou, Bethlehem Ephratah, though thou be little among the thousands of Judah, yet out of thee shall he come forth unto me that is to be ruler in Israel; whose goings forth have been from the old, from everlasting. Therefore will he give them up, until the time that . . .'"

"Stop, Joseph. Please read that middle part again." Mary's sewing fell forgotten into the basket on the floor. Her eyes afire with interest, she leaned over the table to hear more clearly.

"'But thou, Bethlehem Ephratah, though thou be little among the thousands of Judah, yet out of thee shall he come forth unto me that is to be ruler in Israel: whose goings forth have been from old, from everlasting.'"

"Did you catch that? Did you? Our son is to be born in Bethlehem—not Nazareth. We must move to Bethlehem! Joseph, we must!"

"But why, Mary? Where did you get that idea?"

Mary pushed Joseph down the bench and pulled the lamp closer. Searching the page eagerly, she jabbed her finger down. "See! 'But thou, Bethlehem Ephratah, though thou be little among the thousands of Judah, yet out of thee shall he come forth unto me that is to be ruler in Israel.' Joseph! Can't you see what he is saying there? Our son *must* be born in Bethlehem."

"I don't get that at all. That is talking about David."

"Are his 'goings forth' everlasting? No! Joseph!" Taking his robe and shaking him to get the point into his head, Mary had lost her gentleness. Now she was a lioness defending her cub. "Joseph! *Joseph!* How can I make you see? You just have to understand."

Gently removing her hands from his robe, Joseph put his arm around her trying to calm her, but Mary was not about to calm down. "Can't you see? If we moved to Bethlehem the people there would not know about us. They would assume it was your child and that would put an end to all the gossip and tales."

"Would it, now? If we just up and leave, for no good reason. We could not explain it with this scripture, now could we? That would be open admission to their suppositions. Sarah would have a big day with it."

"We could say we needed a bigger house and you needed more business." Desperation was beginning to creep into the lovely face.

"When I can scarcely keep up to the work I get now? And Reuben and the boys have offered to help build another room on before the babe is born. No, that is not the answer."

The desperation left, replaced by sorrow as her dear friends were mentioned. "Oh . . . I forgot Rachel and Reuben . . . How could I ever leave them? I would be . . . lost."

Silence allowed the crickets and night creatures to be heard. But Mary still wasn't ready to give in. She began to frown as she thought and thought some more. Joseph tried again to pull her near, but she brushed his arm away. "I can. I *can* leave Rachel and Reuben. Jesus must not hear the children's taunts about his parentage. He must be protected from them. And the taunts will come if we stay. You know they will." Stalking over to the water jug, Mary took a drink. But tense and nervous, she choked on it and Joseph had to help her catch her breath.

"Are you all right, dear? You must be more careful."

"Why?" Fire danced from Mary's eyes. "So Sarah, Miriam, and the rest can be even more cruel?" Joseph had never seen Mary like this. Here was a new side of his bride. He felt helpless. What should he do?

Mary began to shake, softly at first, then violently. Was she sobbing? Joseph couldn't tell. She was certainly making some funny sounds. Surely, she was not going to give birth—so early! Mary could hold it in no longer. Throwing her arms high, she burst forth into laughter. Tears streaming down her face, Mary tried to explain her behavior.

Joseph, relieved, just stood there with a sheepish, helpless grin on his face. Women! Would he ever understand them? He thought not. Happy, sad, vengeful, and laughing—all in two seconds time. He shook his head, hands clenched and resting on his hips, waiting to find what it all meant.

Finally, between gasps, Joseph caught the words: "First fight . . .

. . . Behold Thy Son

so silly." Then he, too, laughed. They had indeed been fighting. But the fight was over (he hoped), and they could now reason things out.

Together they reread the passage. This time Joseph could see it was talking of Mary's son. But she had to agree they had no good reason for leaving and moving to Bethlehem. As evening prayers were shared, each included a plea for help to know what to do and how to proceed.

"Do not worry, Mary dear. He is God's son, and these are His prophecies. He will provide a way. We must just have faith and wait."

"Thank you for your kindness, Joseph. You are too kind and gentle for me. I do not deserve you."

"Oh, yes. You deserve much, much more. Now, hush, go to sleep and trust in God."

Mary allowed him to push her gently into the bedchamber. She was more tired than she realized.

Fighting is too tiring. I must not act so terrible again.

But sleep did not come. Joseph listened to the tossing and turning and worried. What should he do? Should he go to her? Perhaps a cool cloth would help. As he stepped into the bedchamber, Mary sat upright.

"Joseph! Are you asleep? Joseph!"

"No, I am bringing you a cool cloth. What is it you want? Can I bring you anything else?"

"Sit down, here." Mary was sitting cross-legged in the moonlight. Her shining hair hung loose on her shoulders. "Joseph, Jesus must learn the scriptures and lessons gained at the temple. Only the priests and scribes can teach him properly."

"No, if he is to be taught by the scribes and priests, he would have been given to a woman in Jerusalem."

Mary slumped, dejected. "You are right—as usual." Silence for a minute. Joseph stood to go, but Mary caught his hand. "But, Joseph, he is to be rightful heir to the Jewish throne. No one in Jerusalem or Bethlehem is rightful heir. I am the only rightful heir."

"You are correct there. I still say *you* are to teach him. Gabriel told me we were to teach him love, respect, honor, and all the virtues a king must have. He did not say to send him to rabbinical school. He said to love, cherish, and teach him—ourselves. We are to treat him as our own son. For he is, Mary, he is ours to love and to teach."

Peace returned as Mary remembered the voice of Eloheim saying the same words to her. How could she have forgotten? His face was so kind. His hands so gentle. He had held her shoulders in His hands and told her to love and teach their son. He would help as He could, but the major responsibility would be hers. Joseph would help, but nothing—nothing—can take the place of a mother's love. Sighing deeply, Mary sank into the covers, warm and happy in her memories.

Joseph kissed her gently on the forehead, pulled the robe up to her chin, and tiptoed out, taking the cool cloth. No need for it now. Somehow (he wasn't sure how) he had said the right things and brought peace to his wife's mind. Would he ever fully understand her? He hoped not. It was exciting to discover the many different sides of his sweetheart.

As Joseph lay in the darkness, listening to the night sounds, his heart returned again and again to Bethlehem. How would they do it? What reason would they have for leaving? Surely this was when he would fail. Slipping to his knees once more, Joseph poured his heart out to his God. "Father, please help us to fulfill this prophecy. Please help us to work things out so no one will have cause to doubt the mission of Thy Son."

A warm peace began in his heart and spread through his whole being in the same way the sunlight warms the earth each morning. Why should they worry and fret? The unborn child is Son of Eloheim. *He* was in charge—not His humble servants, Joseph and Mary. He would see that things worked out as He had planned them. After all, it was His plan. Comforted and at peace, Joseph joined Mary in refreshing sleep.

Mary and Rachel were enjoying the late winter sun as they returned from early morning market. After so much stormy and cloudy weather, it was especially appreciated. "I am so grateful Ezra's cold is better. I was very concerned for a while. It came so suddenly and so hard."

"Rachel, how can I ever take care of my child? I know nothing about babies. What if he catches a cold like that? I won't know what to do." Mary's face was framed by her shining hair. She generally had it braided, but today she let it fall loose under her scarf.

"Don't worry, I will be right here to help. Mothers know quite a bit more by instinct than they give themselves credit." Rachel leaned against a gate post and looked over the valley. "Besides, my child, we have been feeding you properly so he will have a good start. You must be prepared to nurse him and you will be. I have made sure of it."

. . . Behold Thy Son

"But . . . what if he . . . bites?"

"Ha, you can bet your life on that, my dear. He *will* bite! Just pray his teeth don't come in too soon. You will know what to do. Have faith in yourself."

"If only I had been around children."

Rachel's surprise caused her to turn sharply, nearly upsetting the produce basket. "But you have, my dear. The village is full of children—all the time."

"Yes, I know that. But I have really never tended tiny babies. How do you give them a bath? And how do you keep them . . . dry? Rachel, I am so scared and, and . . . Joseph just laughs at me. What am I going to do?"

With sudden resolution, Rachel lifted the basket and headed down a steep street. This was not the way home. "Come, we will fix that situation. Michal and Matthias have a young baby and many young children. Unless I lost track, she has had one every spring since they got married six years ago. She will appreciate the help and our visit, and we will sneak in a few lessons without her knowing about it." Mary's laughter floated to Rachel's ears and she smiled, knowing Mary was happy again.

Many happy and child-filled hours later, two weary women trudged home with less produce in their basket, but much richer in friendship and understanding. "I don't see how she manages and keeps so cheerful. I just don't."

"Rachel, I just loved that redheaded girl. She is a tease."

"Yes, she put me in mind of my Michael. Has the same temper, too. Did you notice?"

"Who could miss it. I was afraid she was going to kick me black and blue before I got her to eat her lunch. She did not want to eat."

"Well, here we are, Mary. Are you sure you don't need any vegetables? You paid for some." Rachel offered the basket but Mary shook her head.

"No, Joseph will understand when I tell him what happened. I still have a bit of stew left I should heat up for our supper. Thank you. I see it will be hard, but possible if I just stay calm." Mary's face was happy but she rubbed the small of her back as if it hurt.

"Yes, and do not let the child know you are afraid of him. That is a mistake many women make so they never learn to control and teach their children. That is why there is so much disobedience and disrespect. It is shameful."

"I am sure it is. You better hurry or the men will be home and you won't have supper ready."

"Yes, my dear, you are right. Have a good evening and God bless you." Rachel's arms nearly hid the girl in her embrace.

As if trying to decide which flowers to pick, Mary wandered through the garden. Only a few of the earliest spring flowers were out. The truth was, she hated to go into the house and leave the warm, beautiful sunshine outside. Finally, heaving a sigh of resignation, Mary turned to enter the door. A voice calling up the street stopped her. Curious as to who and why, Mary stepped back to the gate and looked both ways. Running as if his life were in danger, Joseph was calling her name. All the neighbors looked and shook their heads in dismay. This was going too far! Joseph had lost all of his dignity. Mary did not care about that. She just wanted to know why he was smiling and so happy. Perhaps he had just received a new work order. Maybe from the tetrarch. But that was not it. Bursting through the gate, Joseph caught his wife in a hearty hug, then swung her up into his mighty arms and headed for the house.

"Put me down! Joseph, put me down! Have you lost your senses?" Mary's struggles only caused his grip to tighten. She wondered how he could laugh so and still catch his breath.

Pushing the door shut behind him and making sure the latch caught, Joseph slid the bolt into place. Then he sat Mary upon the table so he could look right into her face. "Mary! We have the answer! We have the answer!"

"Answer? To what?"

"We are going to . . . Bethlehem." Joseph stopped to let it sink in.

"We are *what?*"

"We are going to Bethlehem. Our son will be born there. I knew the Lord would work things out. I just knew it!" Joseph danced around the room like a boy with a bee sting on his big toe.

"Why? Joseph! Why? And how and . . . and when?" Mary stayed on the table, deciding it was the safest place to be at the moment.

"Because! Caesar has ordered a new census to be taken. We are all to go to the city of our ancestry to register and pay our taxes. We have three months to do it. Mary, if we go next week, your time is almost here and we would have to stay there until after your purification."

"Bethlehem is the place we would go, isn't it. Not Jerusalem, but to David's City." Mary's reaction was not as boisterous as

. . . Behold Thy Son

Joseph's; rather it was one of sudden relief. At times it was hard to believe all she had been told really would come true. "No Sarah and Miriam for a few weeks. I can hardly believe it."

"And, my dear, here is the rest of it." Was this really dignified, grown-up Joseph, or a little boy with a surprise to share?

"You mean there is more?" Wide eyes searched her husband's face to see if he were only teasing.

"Oh, yes. Much more! Because so many people will be coming, Herod has asked for additional carpenters to help with the building in Jerusalem. I, Joseph of Nazareth, have been offered a one-or-two year job on the building crew."

"But how? Who knew of your skill in . . . in Jerusalem?"

"Remember the Roman soldiers who went through here just before you left for Elisabeth's?"

"N . . . n . . . no."

"They had the chariots with Caesar's emblem on them."

"Oh, yes. Now I remember. A chariot broke its wheel, or am I wrong?"

"Yes. I fixed it for him. The axle had split the whole length and then it had broken in the middle. I talked him into a cedar axle and worked it a little differently. I really enjoyed the challenge after such a steady diet of chairs and tables. Well, anyway, he remembered me and when his group was assigned to bring the notice, he came to the shop and suggested I look into it. I have his seal to present to the foreman to assure me of the position."

"Oh! Joseph! Joseph! Isn't that wonderful! Maybe by then things will have settled, the village will have forgotten all about us, and we can return to our home again."

A very happy couple ate their late supper unaware of the curious stares of neighbors who all seemed to find their gardens and yards in sudden need of attention. No clue could be found to explain the strange behavior . . . just another piece of information to mull over and wonder about.

Trading stories with fellow travelers made the long, bumpy journey less tedious. Still, Mary could find no real comfort in walking or riding on the back of Jasper, their donkey. Joseph's watchful eyes caught her moments of discouragement. "Are you all right?"

The quick smile could not hide the discomfort she was feeling. "Yes, I will survive. I may not enjoy it, but I will make it."

"Joseph, is this where David fought Goliath?" a young man

asked.

Looking around to catch his bearings, Joseph smiled at the boys beside him. "No, son, this can't be the valley. We are too far from the city of Ekron. It is over the mountain to the west, there where the sun is setting."

"Well then," asked another boy, "what did happen here? Why is this valley so great?"

"This valley leads to the two great cities of Israel."

Wide eyes followed Joseph as he lifted Mary to the ground to help ease her discomfort. "Which two?"

Pointing to the southeast, Joseph said not a word. Then he moved his arm to the west a bit and looked at Mary. "The City of David is just over that ridge. Just on the other side of the mountain."

"At last! If we are this close tonight, we'll make it tomorrow—won't we?"

"Yes, if we push on. The traffic's much heavier now. The dust will be worse."

A tug at his sleeve caused Joseph to turn away from Mary. "Which two cities, sir?"

"Jerusalem, with the temple, and Bethlehem, the City of David."

"Why is it called the City of David? Didn't he live in Jerusalem? And didn't he build it as his capital?"

"Yes, but he was born in Bethlehem, as were our parents. It is his birthplace."

"Oh!" Round eyes matched his "Oh!" as visions of battles and feats of glory danced before the eyes of young and old alike.

"Joseph, perhaps we should go on to the next camp. It may not be so full and that would put us closer tomorrow."

"But the closer we get to Jerusalem, the more difficult it will be to find lodging. We better stop here and begin early in the morning. You have had a rough day. We have gone far enough. That last ride up the pass was too difficult."

Protesting no more, Mary began to set up camp. She wondered why the pain was so intense tonight. Things did not feel the same. Something was changed. She prayed earnestly that they could and would make it to Bethlehem.

Little sleep was enjoyed by Mary *or* Joseph. The crowded camp was never quiet. People kept continually on the move. A spring shower made it necessary to hastily pitch the tent. Goats and camels kept the night air full of grunts, groans, bleatings, and

. . . Behold Thy Son

snorts. Just before the sun arose, Joseph asked Mary if she would like to get started early. Her weak, tired smile was his answer. "Lie there and I can get things ready. Jasper stayed right here close by. It will only take a minute. We can stop for breakfast on the way."

"If I have to lie here one more minute, I will scream. I did not know a person could be so uncomfortable. Riding or walking will be a blessed relief."

But the walking and riding did not bring relief. Progress was very slow as Mary tried first one, then the other, to no avail. Noon found them not even halfway, so they ate bread and cheese as they continued at their slow, steady pace. Joseph knew he must get Mary to Bethlehem and lodging—soon.

Another spring shower cooled off the heat of the day but made the road slippery. Jasper stumbled as they began the climb to Bethlehem. Mary slipped off his back and walked along to give him a rest. Joseph's arm steadied the weary young girl.

"Do you suppose it will be much longer, Joseph? I can't stand this pain much more. My back is nearly breaking in two. My legs feel like mud and . . . and . . . I just don't know."

"I believe your time is near. We must make as much haste as possible. I pray we can find lodging. I do not want you out under the rain one more night. You might catch cold."

Evening found them struggling to reach the village before sundown. They must. Thank goodness the traffic thinned and they could continue without interruption. But their hearts sank as they saw the crowds of people in the streets. Tents sheltered some, but mostly, the sky and stars were the coverings for many of the people who came to the City of David. "Where did they all come from?" asked Mary.

"From all over the Roman Empire, Mary. Look at them! Old and young, rich and poor. Large families, small ones, and even people alone. Imagine what Jerusalem must be like."

"I shudder to think of Jerusalem."

"We can be grateful for the advice to avoid the main roads to Jerusalem and come by the back roads directly to Bethlehem. We could have been two more days if we had not done so."

"Where will we stay, Joseph? Where can we find lodging?"

"I don't know, Mary. I simply don't know." Even Jasper hung his head as if in despair and bewilderment.

Chapter Seven

My Son—Our Son

"No room, Mary, no room anywhere. What are we to do?" Joseph was worn out from tramping up and down the streets. He had finally left Mary and Jasper by the fountain. She had been in so much pain. But now there was a calm, serene look shining through her pain.

"Did you try the homes? Surely someone in this city would allow us to stay by their hearth."

"No luck there, either—even when I told them you were with child and your time is very near. One lady looked shocked and slammed the door in my face with 'The very idea, thinking I am a midwife! Me! . . .' Most people have been kind, but you can see for yourself, there are so many people here."

Dejected and feeling helpless beyond measure, Joseph sank to the wall and held his head in his hands. His empty stomach growled a demand for something—*now!* A gentle hand rubbed stiffness from his neck and handed him a cool drink.

"Let us pray, Joseph. God is with us. He will help. I know He will." Only someone very close by could know that this couple prayed earnestly for lodging that their son might be born in calm and quiet, protected from the spring rains and from curious eyes.

"Sir, sir." A timid voice caused them to look up, then down, at a small boy. "Sir, if you wish, Papa said you may use our stable for tonight. I have just cleaned it and laid in fresh straw. It smells fine. And I can put the animals outside."

"Oh, thank you, my child." A grateful Mary gave the boy a hug. "Leave the animals inside. We can share with them."

Grateful for this turn of events, Joseph followed meekly as Mary leaned on Jasper. Who was this child and what had touched his father's heart? Joseph had begged to be allowed to use the stables but to no avail. His surprise grew greater as they stopped at the front of the largest inn.

"Wait here, ma'am, I'll tell my parents you are here." But the boy did not get to the door before an older sister met and ushered them around back to the tiny stable the innkeeper used for his own animals. Inside, the wife was busily fixing a bed in the corner for the weary Mary. She looked up as they came through the door.

"Over here, dearie, over here. Come, let me take your robe. You must be weary. That's it, just make yourself at home."

Turning to Joseph, she scolded him. "Why didn't you say your wife was in need of a midwife tonight. She is due any moment. My! When I thought of her being out in the streets, catching cold, I thought of my daughter who is in the camp of the Zealots. She buried three babies due to exposure at birth. We can't have that happen to this pretty young thing, now can we?"

Joseph allowed himself to be fussed over and fed by the woman and her two children. Silent prayers fled heavenward giving thanks for shelter and kind friends.

Mary ate little and Joseph worried about her, begging her to eat. But the innkeeper's wife pushed him gently away saying Mary would get along better without much on her stomach. "Just see to it that you are fed and warm. Then go lie down over near the door. Gad has taken care of your donkey and Deborah has gone for the midwife. I am staying with Mary until she comes. All is well. Just don't you worry."

Joseph sank gratefully to the clean straw. How could a body get so tired? It was good there were women around. They knew what to do at such times. Mary's muffled groans of pain crept into his thoughts and Joseph became restless. A sudden, sharp outburst caused him to sit upright.

Voices drifted to his ears, bringing him to reality. "That's it, dearie. It's almost over. Bite hard on that leather strap. That's it. Once more and it'll be over. Things are going nicely. You are doing fine."

Joseph heard a deep groan and then a cry as the baby was born. "See. I told you once more would do it, dearie. And here is your son. A fine, healthy son! You did just fine. The first one is always the worst. After that it isn't so frightening. You did just fine. Here, Dorcus, take him and clean him up so Mary can hold him. I will finish here."

Should he go to Mary? Should he wait? Just what *is* expected of a new father? Dorcus answered Joseph's questions by calling his name to see if he was awake. Joseph sprang to his feet and flew to the fire to see what she wanted.

"You have a fine son. As fine a son as I have ever seen. You can be very proud of him and your dear little wife." Soon Dorcus had the baby washed and in the swaddling clothes Mary had made so lovingly.

"Are all newborn babies so . . . red? And . . . wrinkled?" asked the astonished Joseph.

"Of course, silly. But look how nice and fat he is. He will soon not be so red and wrinkled. Here, take him to his mother. She is ready to see him and you."

Trembling arms reached timidly for the bundle. "What if I drop him?" whispered the new papa. "What if he cries?" With small and careful steps Joseph carried the precious bundle to his wife. Mary smiled up at him as he hesitated, not knowing how to bend down to give the baby to her. She had never seen Joseph so awkward and uncertain—not even the day he came to seek her hand in marriage.

"Just bend your knees and kneel down. You will not drop him."

"Are you sure?" A very unsteady voice came from the unsteady man.

"Not as long as you hold him that tightly, sir. Can he breathe?" The midwife gently took the baby and gave him to Mary. "New fathers are all alike. They just stiffen up and panic. It's a good thing babies are tough at first."

"He does not *look* very tough." Mary took the baby and held him to her heart. "He looks . . . fragile . . . and as if he will break if I touch him."

"He won't. What will be his name?"

"Jesus," came from both at once.

"That's a good name, but why not David, or Solomon, or something grand? You have a fine, grand boy there." Dorcus had returned from cleaning up the area. "Jesus is too common a name."

"But Jesus is the name we have chosen," responded Mary. "His name is Jesus. Jesus of Nazareth."

Perhaps it was the early morning, perhaps lack of sleep, but as Dorcus and the midwife left, they stopped at the inn door to listen.

. . . Behold Thy Son

"Do you hear that?"

"Yes, it sounds like a chorus from the heavens singing 'Hosanna.' But I can't see anything."

"Nor do I. But I hear it. I know that much. I will be back after breakfast. She will be ready to nurse by then. I must check on another woman. They make a beautiful family, don't they?"

"Yes. It is a pleasure to have them here."

Mary looked from her son to Joseph and back again. At last! She was a mother. Finally the waiting was over and the doing had begun. "He is beautiful, isn't he."

"But . . . ," Joseph hesitated. "He is still red and . . . wrinkled. The midwife said he would not stay so for long."

"Joseph, Joseph. The babe is only a few minutes old. Give him time. Why he has not even nursed yet." Mary's laugh sounded good to Joseph's ears. She had been so miserable the last two or three days.

"May I hold him or should we let him sleep?" Joseph was still uncertain of what he should do. "What was that?"

"It sounded like a knock at the stable door."

"There it is again. I'll go see what it is. It must be a donkey trying to get in for some food." Just as Joseph approached the stable door, it began to open, cautiously. He stepped into the shadows waiting to see if it was a thief or a friend.

"But I tell you, the angels said to look for him in the stable."

"The Son of God would never be born in a . . . a stable."

"I don't care what you say. You weren't there."

"No, and I still don't believe your story."

"Go and ask Ezekiel, Gabriel, or Nathanial and the others. They were all there. They heard it, too."

"Then why aren't they here?"

"'Cause they are also looking for Him. We separated to speed things up. Whoever finds Him is to give the signal, then we are to gather and go in."

"What makes you think this is the place?"

"Oh, I don't know. I guess because it is small and clean. Come on, let's go in and see."

"But no one answered your knock. There's no one here. Come on, let's head back to the sheep. It will soon be sunrise and they will be restless."

"Go back if you want. But *I* am finding the Son of God."

Joseph stepped out of the shadows into the doorway. He noted the extra full moon and one brillant star. He marvelled at its light. Surprised to find such a young shepherd at the door, he didn't speak but stood waiting.

"Sir, is He here?"

"Who, son?"

"See, you are chasing rainbows. Come on, Isachar. Let's go back." The older youth took his arm and tried to pull him away. But Isachar was not going.

"The Son of God. The angels said we would find Him in a manger, wrapped in swaddling clothes. Is He here?"

Mary laid the baby in the lowly lamb's manger. The innkeeper's son had filled it with clean, fresh straw so her baby would have a warm, soft, snug bed. It was just the right size for him. She smiled as his face crinkled up into a cry. Was there ever a more lovely baby in all the world?

The newborn baby's tiny cry was the answer to Isachar's plea. Joseph stepped aside, pulling the door wide open. The two shepherds looked in and saw the tiny babe and his mother sitting peacefully with the moonlight shining through the door, directly on them. There seemed to be a glow about them. Isachar knew he had found the Christ Child. Forgetting to signal, he crept very quietly and humbly to the baby's side. Kneeling, he prayed his thanks for this great privilege. "May I . . . May I touch Him?" His eyes sought Mary's approval.

"Yes, then perhaps he will stop fussing." Mary's voice was soft and full of wonder. Why had this shepherd boy sought her baby? Who had sent him? And why?

Joseph started to shut the door behind the two young shepherds when he remembered the others who were also searching. Isachar had forgotten to give the signal. Joy at seeing the Christ Child had caused him to forget all else. Should Joseph go seek them? No, he must stay with Mary and her baby. I'll wait just a moment and then remind him, he thought.

But there was no need. As if by a signal, the other shepherds gathered at his door. "Did you find Him?"

"No. Let us look here. Isachar hasn't come back yet."

"This stable is so tiny."

"Yes, but have you noticed how clean it is."

Joseph opened the door wide and greeted the astonished shepherds. "Come in. Isachar is inside with the Babe. His joy has made him forget to signal you."

As the surprised shepherds stepped into the stable, Joseph took his place beside his wife and the child. In spite of the small size and crowded space, no one pushed or shoved. Even the animals stood quietly and reverently. A baby lamb wiggled between the forest of legs and laid down with his head on Mary's lap. It seemed to those in the stable that a chorus of heavenly voices was singing praises to God. Maybe it was the memory of what had happened on the hill, earlier."Isn't He beautiful, Nathanial? It is just as they said. He is wrapped in swaddling clothes, lying in a manger."

"I thought it would be a big cow manger. I couldn't see how or why."

"Nor me. I didn't dream it would be a tiny manger. It must be that lamb's."

Mary asked who they were and why they came seeking her son. In hushed voices, they told of angels who had awakened them about midnight with their heavenly chorus of praises. Frightened at first, they sought a place of hiding. But the lead angel had called, telling them to "be not afraid." He told of the birth of the Son of God and where to find Him. "So we came. We simply left our sheep and came. Something has pulled us here . . . to your stable. We know not what it is. But I do know this. This Babe is in very deed the Son of the Living God. I know it!"

"As do I!"

"And I!"

"Me, too!" Isachar reached a timid finger to touch the sleeping baby's face. He had forgotten how small babies were. His delight was shared by all as the baby opened his eyes and smiled and cooed. "Look! He smiled at me. He is a pretty baby."

As the shepherds left, the sun rose over the hilltops. Mary sat there marvelling at the events of the night. The baby began to squirm, then puckered up and cried.

"Won't he be hungry? He hasn't eaten, has he?" Mary's blush gave her feelings away. Joseph smiled, bent and kissed her, and turned to go. "I will go get some fresh water. It will take a few minutes."

Grateful to be alone for a moment, Mary took the tiny babe into her arms. Now what?

Now, silly. You have seen women nurse their babies. You know what to do. Do it!

Timidly and fearfully Mary bared her breast and with trembling

60

arms, lifted the crying baby and held him close. He nuzzled and squirmed. "He knows more than I do." Mary laughed quietly to herself as Jesus found his breakfast and began. Mary rocked gently, singing in a soft, soothing tone.

When Joseph returned with the water, Mary's smile told him all was well and he was a part of it, too. Kissing her on the forehead, Joseph sat beside her. With one arm around his wife, the other hand gently touched the soft face of her son.

"What does it all mean, Joseph? I am so . . . so . . ."

"So full of awe and wonder?"

"Yes. That is how I feel. I can't seem to grasp it all. So many strange things have happened to me—to us. The only thing I am sure of is that my son is born and is in my arms, feeding at my breast."

"Your son—the Son of God. But he is *our* son to love and teach."

"Yes, our son." Eyes shining with tears of joy, love, bewilderment, and wonder looked into Joseph's. He marvelled at how young and frightened she looked, yet how wise and old at the same time. The quiet moment was filled with the tiny sounds of the newborn baby feeding contentedly. Then came sounds of people stirring outside the stable. Panic spread on Mary's face as she looked from her nursing son to the door, then to Joseph. "Joseph, what if more people come! What do I do?"

A reassuring squeeze said, "Don't worry, I am here." Going to the door, Joseph led Jasper out into the courtyard. Brushing him gently but firmly, all traces of the week's journey soon disappeared. "I am sorry, old Sport. I should have done this last night. But my mind was full of Mary and her condition. When she was settled, I forgot all about you. Thank you for being so patient. What do you think of our new son? Isn't he something? The shepherds came all that way just to see him."

With the help of the innkeeper, Joseph found a small house, just right for a new family. He could walk to Jerusalem and work each day. Mary and her son were soon comfortable in the warm surroundings. Jesse had lent them a few things till they could get some for themselves.

In talking to Jesse, Joseph found he need not go to Jerusalem to work. Jesse was overseer for the crew at Bethlehem. Seeing the soldier's seal, he inquired as to how Joseph acquired it and why. The result—a job, right there in Bethlehem. Now Mary would not be alone so much. He could be with her and not have to leave so early

. . . Behold Thy Son

to walk to Jerusalem or be so late walking back.

One thing puzzled Joseph. Jesse said nothing about the shepherd's visit. Nor did he seem to think their son was any different from anyone else's. Joseph had heard the shepherds singing as they left. Surely they would spread the word. Yet, no one else came to see the Son of God. No one else seemed to know or care.

As the eighth day arrived and Jesus was circumcised, Joseph learned the shepherds had told all they met of the wondrous happenings. But they were told, "so marvelous a manifestation would not come to humble shepherds on the hill, but to the learned priests of the synagogue." People would not believe them. Finally, rather than be stoned for blasphemy, the shepherds locked their wonders into their hearts and only talked of them around the camp with each other.

Forty days soon passed and Mary prepared to present herself and her son at the temple. "How privileged we are to be able to do so. It is good Jesus is able to fulfill the Law," she said. Looking down at her sleeping son, Mary's smile shone with joy, happiness, and contentment. She was again riding Jasper. But this time the ride was enjoyable and she was looking forward to the return trip.

A somewhat shaken and bewildered Mary hushed her tired, hungry baby as they returned to Bethlehem that night. When would she understand it all? Why all the confusing events?

Lifting them down, Joseph brushed the dust from her hood. "Go feed him. I will bring the things in later. It takes a minute to attend to Jasper. I can fix supper when I get in. You just worry about Jesus. He will need changing, too.

"Poor dear. You are as tired and hungry and as confused as we are, aren't you, my boy." A louder, lustier wail was his answer. A gentle push started Mary on her way.

"How do I deserve such a loving, understanding husband? He is too good for words," she murmured.

Talking to Jesus as she changed all his clothes, Mary tried to soothe and pacify the baby. "My, but you have managed to soak through everything. We must start with all new clothes. Stop that squirming. How can I dress you if you kick so? Oh, I know you are hungry, but you are tired, too, and need to sleep. You always wake up if I try to change you after you nurse. So just be patient. Here. Suck on this sugar rag a minute. Rachel said to use it if you got too impatient. I know it isn't food, but maybe it will help fill that mouth a moment. There."

Lifting the clean, warm baby into her arms, Mary went to the hearth. Joseph had left a good bed of coals. She only needed to put on the kindling and stir it up a bit. With one hand, she lifted the stew pot up onto the hook. "See, we are getting used to each other. I am learning how to do things and still hold you. Oh dear, I see I better hurry. That sugar rag isn't going to work much longer."

Giving him her breast, Mary began to rock gently, back and forth. "Why did I worry so much? This is a wonderful time. I love to sit and hold you and talk to you. It isn't at all like I was afraid it would be. We are so close." Mary hugged Jesus to her, then lifted him to her face. She kissed him on his button nose. But on finding he had lost the source of his supper, Jesus let out a loud wail. "This is no time for loving. I'm hungry," he seemed to say.

The warm, spicy smell of stew warming over the hearth caused Joseph to step quickly through the door. "I said I would fix supper, but I am so starved. Thank you for going ahead.

"How's my little man doing? You act like you have not eaten for a week. Slow down there, son, or you will get a bellyache again." Laughter filled the happy home. It was so good to be home—out of the noise and bustle of Jerusalem.

"Oh! I am so thankful I don't have to go to Jerusalem each day to work. It is so crowded and dirty."

"Even the temple was crowded. The people pushed and shoved. And those priests!" Mary shuddered at the memory of the money changers. "I thought we would never find a suitable pair of doves."

"Nor I. But we finally did. I surely wish it could have been a lamb."

"Joseph! Enough! We have it all settled. Doves were acceptable and fine."

"Yes, but . . ."

"But what?"

"Your son is the Son of God. He deserved more than doves as a redemption offering." Joseph sat down beside them.

"*Our* son *is* the Son of God. But our offering was acceptable. The Lord is mindful of our humble means."

Full and asleep, Jesus was laid in his bed. Mary pulled the covers over his tiny hands. He was filling out nicely and growing more alert each day. Somehow he had seemed to grasp and understand the events of the day. "I surely do wish I did!"

. . . Behold Thy Son

"Wish you did what?" Joseph looked up, puzzled by the statement.

"Oh! Did I speak out loud?" Mary blushed. "I was talking to myself."

"What do you wish? Perhaps I can grant your wish." The teasing smile made her blush even more.

"I wish I understood what happened at the temple today."

A deep sigh revealed Joseph's bewilderment. "I, too, wish I understood."

"First Simeon, then Anna. Do you suppose they found out from the shepherds?"

"No, the shepherds did not share their story with people outside of Bethlehem. They met with too much ridicule and derision." Joseph brought Mary a drink.

"Did you understand what Simeon meant? About Jesus' mission and . . . the anguish I would suffer?"

"No, I surely did not. Nor could I follow Anna's words. It doesn't make sense. How can this tiny babe do all those things?" Joseph's work worn hand caressed the tiny soft fist.

"I don't know. I just don't know. He seems like any other baby. He eats, sleeps, grows, cries, and needs the same care. There is nothing different. He has no special powers or abilities."

"Oh yes he does. He cries louder than most." From Joseph's smile, Mary knew he was teasing.

"Just at night, Joseph. It just seems he cries louder because the night is so still."

"He surely did cry hard while we were hunting for the doves. The noise must have frightened him."

"It frightened me. I kept my hand over his ear and held his head tight to me and that helped—some."

"Just as Rachel said, 'Mothers know more by instinct than they give themselves credit.' And you, my dear Mary, are proving her right. Come. It is late and I must be off early. It is time for bed."

"Thank goodness! My arms feel like bread dough. I had no idea a tiny baby would get so heavy."

"Practice, my dear. You just need more practice. Your arms will get stronger."

"I pray so. If not, I can never manage."

"But never let them get so tough they don't know how to give your husband a tender hug." Joseph took his happy wife into his arms and kissed her. Life was wonderful.

Chapter Eight

THE FLIGHT

"Mary. Mary, darling. Please wake up."

"What is it, Joseph. Is Jesus . . .?"

"No. He is fine. But he is in danger—grave danger. I had a visitor. We must go! Quickly! We must go now—while it is dark."

"Joseph, you've most everything packed! Why didn't you call me sooner so I could help you?"

"With the child so restless with new teeth, you have slept so little. The visit yesterday was extra tiring. We are not accustomed to entertaining royalty and learned men. Here, hand me those robes and blankets. I'm certainly glad I bought Jasper back from Ishmael last week. He is a good animal and has grown stronger since being here in Bethlehem. He will carry our provisions and still be able to let you ride often enough that you will not get too tired."

"Here is the food basket. Are you sure you packed enough? It does not look like very much."

"We don't want people to realize we have left for good. They must think we are gone for only a day or two at the most. Otherwise, the king's men may come after us." Joseph's gentle hands became a prison as he held her shoulders and looked into her eyes, "Mary, this is no picnic we are going on. Herod is sending soldiers to *kill* our child. He must be protected! If we stay, the neighbors will tell of him to protect their own. We must flee, rapidly and secretly. The Lord will provide."

The terror in Joseph's eyes was mirrored in Mary's as she scurried to do his bidding. Her stomach cramped as she remembered.

Herod is sending soldiers to kill our child . . . But why? Why would anyone want to kill a tiny child? We aren't after the throne. Why would Jesus be any more of a threat to Herod than Joseph or I? We, too, are rightful heirs, but we have no plans for such activities. It will be years before Jesus can begin his work. Oh, why are people so cruel and vengeful?

But there was no time to dawdle and wonder. She must get the child ready to travel. Thank goodness his teeth were through and he wasn't so cross. Imagine, three corner teeth all at once and he was just over twelve months old.

"Poor dear. I hate to disturb you. This is your first good sleep in seven days. But we must go now. That's it, Jesus, just snuggle up against me and sleep on. Your smile is so sweet. I love it when you smile in your sleep. I don't believe it is just bubbles.

"Yes, Joseph, we are ready. See how he is sleeping? Isn't he a dear? Joseph, surely no one has ever had such a beautiful baby before, or one so good."

"No, Mary. No one ever has. We are blessed. The fact he is our firstborn helps our happy and proud feelings grow.

"But come. Jasper is ready and anxious. He seems to sense the urgency of the trip. He has not brayed once, and you know what a loud voice he has. The loading was done in record time. He usually fights every knot. Do you have all you need? Did I forget anything?"

"Yes, that lovely baby bed. It has been so precious. Will the soldiers just break it up? Can't we take it to Jesse for their newcomer? It will only take a moment."

"And have them know we are going and why? No, Mary! We cannot risk it. Besides, it would put them in danger. They would be forced to tell the soldiers where we went. Come. I'll make a new one in Egypt."

"Egypt! Egypt! Joseph, are we going to Egypt? Why? Why must we go so far and to such a wicked place? Joseph, you know how many times the Lord has warned our people not to flee to Egypt or rely on their strength. We can't go there! We must return to Nazareth!"

"No, Mary." Gently, but firmly Joseph set the trembling, frightened Queen of the Jews on the waiting animal. He would explain later. She would understand once she knew of the angel. Now he must check to be sure the house was in order.

As the door shut, Joseph thought of Jesse's goodness to let them live here and give him work on the crew. It had been a good time for them both. Yes, Bethlehem *was* home. People had been much more kind. No one to sneer, insinuate, or point. Mary had relaxed and enjoyed being a wonderful little wife and mother. She had really blossomed.

"Joseph." Mary's whisper caused Joseph to start. He must not look back now, only ahead. There was no time to spare. No one must see them leave. The sun would soon be up. The dogs would soon be roaming. Haste was essential.

"Yes, Mary. I'm coming. Has Jesus stirred? Look at that face. Surely, it is meant for us to go tonight. There is no moon, the storms are past, and we can catch up to the caravan that left yesterday. We must not go all the way alone. Easy, Jasper, I'll get that gate."

They paused outside the city for one last look. Mary took Joseph's hand and realized that he, too, was frightened and trembling.

"Goodbye, dear home. May you shelter others who are as happy as we have been."

"Yes, and may you be spared the bloodshed other homes will feel if we stay. Oh, Mary. Why must Herod be so cruel and wicked?"

Again at the top of the hill, Joseph stopped. He looked over the City of David—blessed with the birth of the Savior within its humble walls. Jerusalem seemed proud and haughty, he thought. It is no wonder Jesus was born in gentle Bethlehem. Would they ever return? Only God knew.

The first rays of sun found the family far from Bethlehem. Once they had to hide behind a hillock as mounted troops thundered by. Hearts in their throats, they wondered how Herod had learned of their plans. Surely, they had been careful. No one knew where they had gone. As the dust settled, their hearts returned to almost normal and they began again. Now, other travelers joined them on the road. Many were families, but some were single individuals. Where were they all going? Were they, too, fleeing from the wicked Herod? Why were some of the groups so large?

"Oh, we are out for a short visit . . . No, our journey began in Nazareth. My wife and I are both from there," Joseph would reply when questioned by other travelers.

"Joseph," Mary touched his shoulder, "even here people look on Nazareth as just a step above Samaria. Why don't we just say we are from Bethlehem? Then they won't shun us so. I am afraid to travel alone."

. . . Behold Thy Son

"Think it through, Mary. Herod doesn't know we came from Nazareth. He is looking for a family from Bethlehem. Besides, for a few days, we are better off alone. The Lord will protect us.

"Come walk beside me. I will carry the child. Then we will be able to talk. You have not asked who told us to flee or when he came. You have just trusted and obeyed my wishes. It is time you knew. See, Jesus is still asleep. Your arms and legs must be very tired and cramped." Joseph took the child from Mary and helped her to the ground. "Jasper could use the rest, too. Whoa, Jasper, no need to pick up speed. Give Mary's legs a chance to get limber."

"May we have a drink at that well? There is a family already there. Surely that young boy would draw us some water."

"Yes, Jasper needs some. The smell of water is probably the cause of his sudden burst of speed."

At the well, the two families greeted each other cautiously. Neither asked the usual questions: Where are you going, how long have you been on the road, and where did your journey begin? Rather, all talk was about water, the beautiful day, and would the newcomers have some salt they could share. Not even names—just guarded pleasantries were exchanged. Mary didn't offer to show off her baby and they showed no interest. Joseph thanked the young boy for watering Jasper. Only Jasper and their donkey acted friendly and normal. They brayed and talked as if they had a great deal of gossip to share.

"Well, our animals seem to be friendly enough," spoke the stranger. "Maybe you would like to join us for an hour or so. Two families together would be safer and less noticeable."

"Yes, please do come with us," urged his wife.

Joseph reached for the rope. "Here, Jasper, we are ready to go and you can talk to your new friend as we go."

"Dear, my arms feel better. Should I take the baby?" asked Mary.

"No, I am fine. He will soon be awake. Let's not disturb him any more than we have to."

Mary was grateful the precious face was hidden. Joseph was so kind and wise. But if they went with this family, she must still wait for him to tell her why and who. They must act natural.

That family surely doesn't act natural. It is almost as if they are flee-ing, too. I wonder why. They seem to be a devoted and kind family. However, the parents are not young. I wonder if this child was born to them in their later years, as I was to my parents?

The way did seem less dreary as they traveled together. The

miles were slipping away a little faster. Jesus awakened and enjoyed the ride on Jasper's back. The boy had suggested they tie him on and things had gone more smoothly. The boy seemed to yearn to touch or hold Jesus. Mary's heart went out to him, and she asked if he would like to carry the child on his shoulders. No need for words. Eyes and smiles gave his answer. Pulled hair only brought squeals of delight. The woman's eyes were glistening as she watched her son's joy.

"We love him so much, we just could not give him up. We had to flee. Egypt is no place for us. But perhaps we can return in a few years," the woman explained.

The words echoed Mary's thoughts. She could understand the tears and worry.

Thunder on a clear day? No! There is dust on the road. See— back there! Fear came to the five faces as they watched the troops come closer. Were they Roman . . . or Herod's? Why were they traveling so fast? How many of them? Or was it robbers? Too much speed to be a caravan.

"Come, we must act natural," urged Joseph. "Look, there is a well. We can stop there and eat our noon meal. If they are looking for either of us, they will not be expecting two families traveling together." Joseph was right, as usual. Mary gave silent thanks for such a wise helpmate. Truly he was chosen for his wisdom and courage. The boy began to draw the water without being told. Certainly he was loved and well taught. If only Mary could remove the fear from the mother's eyes.

"Would you please hold my child? He is too eager to play in the water. I will be fixing the cheese and bread. We will share ours and eat yours later. Joseph, would you please get us a robe to sit on? And, sir, your donkey seems to have a rock in his hoof. No, the other back hoof. That's it. It is probably a small one. It will take a while to find it." Joseph's chuckle brought a warm smile to Mary's face and she began singing a little song.

By the time the soldiers drew up, a happy family picnic was in progress. Trembling hands and hearts seemed to be caused by the joy of sharing good stories and good food. The dust swirled around as the soldiers drew up, seemingly uncaring if they trampled the folks or not.

"Hey, you there. Yes! You! Where'd you come from?"

"Nazareth. We are natives of Nazareth."

"How long you been journeying?"

. . . Behold Thy Son

"We got an early start this morning. That is why we have stopped for an early lunch. Say, can you tell us something? Are the wells like this one every half-day's journey to Beersheba?"

"Yeah. That's where you are headed?"

"Yes. We plan a visit at Beersheba. Could we ride with you? We have heard of bandits along here." Joseph seemed so calm.

"The earlier troops went after them. We are after a runaway family of three who are stealing a young boy. About his size—there. Only not so tall or old. They don't have a young child either. Hey, you there, Grandfather, would you mind looking at my horse? It has a rock in its hoof."

Mary offered the hot, hungry soldiers a drink and some bread. The smiles and grunts softened their tense faces and she realized they were a group of young men, barely sixteen years of age. It must be a new detachment training under a tough sergeant. Soon even he had relaxed and all eleven of them were sharing their provisions with the family and each other.

Joseph caught his breath as mention of the wisemen and Magi of the East drifted to him. Maybe it wasn't the other family they were after! Suppose that was a trick to catch them. How could he warn Mary? "Oh, Merciful God, please help us!" he silently prayed.

Mary was enjoying the young soldiers. Would Jesus be as handsome and as tall? Would he be kind and gracious? Surely, he will not have to serve Rome as these young men are serving. One especially took her eye. He seemed to be far away—thinking of something different and special. Such a peaceful look in his eye. "Would you care for more cheese, sir?"

"What? . . . Oh, no. No thank you, maam. I've had enough."

"Don't mind him. He is still way out in the stars," jeered his companions.

"Yes, he has been no good since he talked to those wisemen."

"Which wisemen?" Mary really didn't need to ask. The look in the boy's eyes told her which wisemen. She had seen them, too.

"Maam, being a Jew, you would understand more than these fellows. Remember your prophecies of a Savior or Messiah? Well, my mother is Jewish and she has taught me of your ways. She's always talked of Him as a King—a grown man. Well, yesterday we met some wisemen who had seen Him. Imagine that! They had seen the King and Savior. Only He isn't a man. He's a baby and will have to grow up just like I did. I pray I'll be able to serve in

His army. If I can only live long enough for Him to grow up and become leader, I'll be the first to join His troops. I'm going to train and work and be prepared! While He is learning to walk and talk, I'll be learning to be a good soldier and to take orders."

"Yeah, but remember there is Herod to deal with. He will not hear of anyone taking *his* throne. I'll bet he'll hunt that baby down and slay him—quick! Just wait and see." The sergeant spat into the dust. It was evident he had no love for Herod, either.

Thank goodness Jasper brayed right then and no one saw Mary's face or heard her gasp. "But," said the young soldier, "if God could call the wisemen from their own countries and lead them with a star to the baby's home; and if they could find Him when Herod couldn't and in fact didn't even know of Him then God will warn the parents and the baby will be protected. If He is the Messiah, all will be fulfilled."

"Yeah, *if* he's the Messiah. And *if* there will *be* a Messiah, which there won't.

"Okay, men, mount up and let's go. We've got to catch that family if we expect to split that reward."

"Oh, is there a reward?" The grandmother spoke for the first time. She had been busy with the young child.

"Yes. The couple have been raising the boy while his mother hunted for a husband. Now she's found one and wants the boy back. But the old couple feel they own him now. They've had him for ten years. I can't see why anyone would want an eleven-year-old. They are not old enough to work and eat enough to feed four horses. Hey, Kid! Bring my horse over here. Good luck on your journey.

"I would advise you to catch up with a caravan. You never know just who you'll meet on the way."

"Thank you. We will do that. You have been most kind." Joseph patted the young soldier's horse. The boy Jesus came tottering closer. As Joseph picked him up, the horse turned, neighed, and touched him gently with a soft nose. The young child squealed with delight.

"Who knows, son. Maybe you *will* serve in His army. Don't lose that dream. Keep it bright." Smiles and laughter failed to bring a blush to the soldier's face nor did it wipe away his faraway look.

As the dust faded, smiles returned to the old couple's face. Even the boy managed a laugh as his grandmother hugged him. "Aw, I'm too old for that," he said. But he didn't push her away.

Without a word, they began preparations for leaving. The women gathered things and handed them to the men. "You must

. . . Behold Thy Son

love him dearly. I can't begin to realize your feelings. Jesus has been ours for just over a year. Yet when Joseph said we must flee for he was in danger of his life, I felt as if a dagger had been driven through my heart. No wonder you were frightened at our approach. Come, let's go on together. We will lean on each other and help."

"Oh, thank you. Jesus. Is that his name? He is such a sweet child. Jason has taken to him. See how they get along."

"Jason. That was Rachel's boy's name. He, too, was so good and considerate. The name fits. My name is Mary and my husband is Joseph."

"Mary, Joseph, and Jesus. Good Jewish names. We are of Benjamin, from Ramah. How wonderful we are all going to Beersheba."

Joseph guided Jasper onto the road. "Beersheba is a good place, but we must go on. Our errand takes us farther into Egypt."

"Prisca, surely the Lord has preserved us. Joseph, thank you for helping us. I am Philip of Ramah. I guessed you are from Nazareth, but your speech has been softened as if you have spent time elsewhere."

"Yes, we have spent time at Bethlehem."

"Bethlehem," Prisca's face lighted even more. "Then you must have seen the men from the East, too."

"Yes, we did."

"We, also, talked to them of the Messiah. To think we were so near the town where He was born. If we had not the need to flee, we would have sought Him out and given Him a gift." The tribe of Benjamin was eager for a savior, too.

"Indeed, you have given Him a gift. You have helped guard His life. I heard tell Herod was sending soldiers to kill Him. And you have caused the soldiers to pass through on another errand."

"You mean, Joseph, the soldiers won't go back?"

"No, my dear Mary. They will come again, but the Messiah will be safe."

Philip, Prisca, and Jason found it unnecessary to talk as they thought of how perhaps they had helped to save the precious child. Finally, "Do you think we will ever get to see or know him?"

"Yes, Jason." Philip had not answered—Joseph had. "Yes, Jason. You will and will love Him, too. Remember the Messiah is for all of us of the House of Israel."

Motherly thoughts took over as the men discussed the coming and mission of the Messiah. Somehow, Mary couldn't think of that just now. She had too much to be grateful for. Jesus was safe. When would Joseph tell her how he had learned of their danger?

"God of Jacob, We thank thee for our safety and for the family who so lovingly shared with us. Surely Thou art mindful of thy humble servants. May we teach this, Thy Son, to know, trust, and love Thee as his Father. Please continue to guide and protect us. For we are in Thy hands, as Noah and his family were. We know Thou wilt aid and preserve us. Amen."

Mary's heart was full and eyes moist as she added her amen to evening prayers. Yes, God had preserved them. Three days alone with Philip, Prisca, and Jason had been gratefully enjoyed. Nights had been peaceful, clear, and warm. Once, robbers had approached, but seeing their poverty, they merely spat, cursed their luck, and rode on. Jason had mentioned his father's wisdom of traveling as poor folk and not as they might have. "Besides, we would not have been able to play with baby Jesus if we had stayed in our fine clothes."

The provisions, food, medicine, and tent acknowledged the gratitude felt by Philip and Prisca. Joseph's humble "thank you" stilled the questions in Mary's mind. This was how "the Lord will provide." Yes, Mary was feeling more at peace. Still, it would be nice to know how he knew and where his assurance came from. Six people in one small tent did not invite confidences. She just had to wait patiently.

But now she would find out! Lachish was a good place to avoid. Herod's soldiers were there searching for Philip's family. By taking the lower, eastward road, they found another caravan heading toward Egypt. Other Hebrew families were already with the caravan, so it was natural they, too, would join. Philip found a family who was near their journey's end and in need of lodging money. A short bargaining session found Mary, Joseph, and baby Jesus in their own little tent. The sudden rain showers gave more reason to rejoice in the shelter. Yes, God was good. Two days to clean up and rest were so welcome.

"Is the boy asleep?"

"Yes. His gums are swollen, but that ointment Prisca gave me seemed to relieve them." She snuggled closer.

"Perhaps it was the rubbing that brought relief."

"No . . . I'm sure it was the . . . Oh! Joseph, there you go, teasing again. I just don't know. Fathers are supposed to be serious."

. . . Behold Thy Son

"Not all the time, dear. We get to enjoy life, too. Besides, you might forget to laugh and smile if I didn't tease."

"Thank goodness you don't let me forget to laugh. Did you see Jesus' reaction to the camels? I had not realized he hadn't seen them up close. That baby one was so pushy and nosey. He knocked the boy off his feet. Puckering up to cry, Jesus looked my way to see if I'd run to help. I pretended to be busy and not pay any attention so he just whimpered and tried to crawl out of the way. The camel kept booting him along faster than he could go. Finally in exasperation, Jesus turned around, put his arms out and tried to give the camel a hug. It snorted and ran off."

"Yes, I watched from across the square. You were even more fun to watch. Trying to pretend to sort the washing. My! It feels good to have clean clothes. That bath was wonderful, too. Philip has been so good to us.

"Imagine their joy if they knew they had helped the Messiah—the baby the wisemen found. It is so hard to not tell them, Mary! His safety is so important. We must be very careful. Now is *not* the time for the world to know who he is. Danger is everywhere—especially in Herod!"

At last, Mary was to learn why Joseph had seemed so weighted down and sad. Knowing, sharing the burden would make it easier for him. Hadn't his learning of the "Visit" lessened and relieved her burden?

Softly, tenderly, quietly—almost whispering—Joseph unfolded how he had been awakened by a soft touch on his shoulder. Thinking it was Mary returning from caring for a teeth-troubled boy, Joseph had rolled over, smiling in contentment and joy.

"Joseph, awake and arise. Quickly! Make haste to leave this very night. Jesus is in grave danger!" the Angel had whispered.

Danger? Leave—tonight? That wasn't Mary's voice. Nor was it Mary's gentle hand. Eyes wide open, Joseph had seen the same messenger who had told him of Mary's purity. There was no glorious light—only enough so he could see without Mary being disturbed.

He was told to arise quickly—let Mary and Jesus sleep until the last possible minute. He must pack only enough for one day. That way the neighbors would expect them to return by nightfall. Do take extra clothing that wouldn't be noticed. Jasper, the usually contrary donkey was waiting patiently at the door. Joseph's query had revealed Herod's wicked plan. "He wants the wisemen to tell him where to find Jesus so he can slay him as he has his heirs."

"Slay . . . our precious baby? Oh, Joseph!"

"Shh! We are obeying the commands so he will be safe."

"Go on, what happened next?"

"Well, after giving me the instructions again, he admonished me to be very quiet—no lights. No one must suspect. It was then I realized we were whispering. As I followed the instructions I turned to see him watching the baby as he slept. Tears were in his eyes. I could not tell if they were for joy, sorrow, or pain.

"It made me realize again, that we—you and I—do not fully understand what it all means. We cannot know how, why, or when the prophecies concerning that precious child will be fulfilled. We do not understand His mission or our part in it. Going to the messenger, I started to ask the questions in my mind. He told me we must love our God, trust Him, doubting not, but go forward—always striving to be faithful. We must search the scriptures and teach them to Jesus. Ways would be provided. 'And remember, always, you have been entrusted with the Son of God.'"

Sobs shook the manly frame. Mary's arms held him tightly. She waited quietly until he could go on. Once again Mary felt restored and able to go forward and face—what? Only God knew what would come. With Joseph, a worthy son and king of Israel, able to receive direct revelation—with him as her companion and guide, how could she falter?

As he was able, Joseph told how he asked where, how, and for how long? "Jasper is ready. He is a good donkey if you use a firm hand. Go quickly before dawn, along the south road, then by the back road to the crossroads. Proceed as quickly as possible on the main road to Egypt."

"Egypt!"

"Yes, Egypt, and be still! Do *not* awaken the child yet. Here, this is a sack of figs."

"But Jehovah has warned and rewarned us not to trust Egypt or to seek refuge there. This is in direct opposition to His instructions!"

"I know it, you know it, but more importantly, Herod knows it. He will never think to look for a devout Jewish family in Egypt."

"Oh! So we simply must go forth, trusting and accepting direction as it comes."

"Yes. That is exactly right. Here is the baby's bundle. Mary does love him so. Feel the softness of his clothes."

. . . Behold Thy Son

Mary felt warm all over at the compliment. The extra effort was worth it. "Go on. Did he help pack all the things?"

"No, only those for the baby. It was as if it were a special privilege to be serving Him in this humble way. He went on to say, 'Let your heart rule your head. You are so practical and observe the Law so strictly that you may miss the promptings of the Spirit.' This troubled me but I let it pass. When we met Philip's family, my head said, 'Don't speak. You are fleeing. They are danger.' But my heart said, 'They, too, are in danger. See the fear. Perhaps we can help.' Then I remembered the angel's words to let my heart rule."

"Joseph! What if we had passed them by! I am so grateful you listened and obeyed."

"Yes, my dearest little wife. And now my heart says it is time to sleep. We start off at dawn. Goodnight." He kissed her lightly on the cheek.

"Goodnight. Thank you for being you." The night sounds filled the tent. Camels snorted and groaned.

"Joseph . . . Joseph, are you asleep?"

"Mmmm? . . . Not now. What is it?"

"How long did he stay? The messenger, I mean?"

"As I completed the preparations, he corrected a knot, then told me to wake you and hurry. Time was fleeing. As I went to wake you, he moved again to the baby and wept as he watched him sleep. I turned to wake you and he was gone when I turned back."

"Oh . . . Joseph, even the angels are watchful and rejoicing for our son."

"Yes, for *our* son. He has been loaned—entrusted to us—to teach and guide, but above all to *love*."

Silence again revealed the night sounds. Both parents listened to the steady, even breathing of *their* precious son.

Dusty and hot, the caravan gratefully stopped for the noon meal. Could it be they were only two days out? With all the dust, noise, and confusion it seemed a month. Traveling with Philip's family had been so quiet and pleasant.

Only Jesus seemed to enjoy the extra sights and sounds. He would ride Jasper and look and look and then turn to look again. Thank goodness Jason was there to help. He seemed able to know just what Jesus was interested in and would take him to see, explore, taste, or hear the new things. Mary knew he was safe with Jason. The two boys had completely captured the hearts of all the caravan. Even the cranky camels stood to let the children pet their soft noses. The young kids with the milk goats would nearly push him over in their eagerness to be petted and loved. They were nearer Jesus' size, but the young camels were more gentle with the unsteady child. Jesus seemed to prefer them to the frisky kids. Perhaps he didn't like the eager bunting and nuzzling which inevitably pushed him down.

A commotion at the well caused Mary to look up. As her gaze drew to the well, she saw a look of horror on the face of Prisca. Going quickly to her, Mary asked, "What is it? Why are you so frightened?"

"Look! The soldiers are returning! Oh, Mary! What can we do? Where are Philip and Jason? Oh, God of Abraham, Isaac, and Jacob, please preserve us again. Please don't let them take Jason!"

Mary clasped the praying hands and drew Prisca to her feet. "Come. Don't act afraid or give them cause to look our way. Joseph is talking to the sergeant. Come to the donkeys and wait for Joseph." They withdrew from view behind the donkeys but kept watchful eyes on the group at the well. Suddenly, both caught their breath as they watched Jason lead the child Jesus toward the soldiers. Both their precious sons were going right toward danger!

The sergeant turned and saw the two boys and his face broke into a smile. "Say, I don't know why it is, but the sight of those two brothers warms my heart through and through. Not many older brothers are as warm and gentle as the oldest son. You can be proud of him."

"Indeed, I am," said Joseph, the fear leaving as he realized they were once again receiving the protecting hand of God. "Indeed, I am."

"Sons of different mothers? I noticed your wife is too young to be the lad's mother."

"Yes, sons of different wives. What brings you this way? I thought you were going to Beersheba?"

"We received word the rich lady no longer wanted her son back. She decided he would be an expense and a burden. Besides, she has begun a new baby and feels one will be enough to care for." He drank long from his cup.

"Are you headed to Jerusalem?"

"How I wish we were!" He spat angrily at the ground. "No, we are going to Bethlehem to correct Herod's mistake—if we can."

"Herod's mistake?"

"Yes, the fool! Here, son. Here are a couple of coins for you and

. . . Behold Thy Son

your brother. Be sure you don't squander them. Naw, no thanks needed. I enjoy watching you."

Turning to Joseph he continued. "He seems such a beautiful child. Speaking of beautiful, where did you find your young wife? She is the most beautiful woman I have ever seen. Those eyes, that mouth, and that shining hair. Truly, she is a gem. How did you get so lucky? I didn't know Jewish women were ever so beautiful or so striking."

"She is the daughter of Jacob, my father's brother. Her father wished to keep the inheritance within the family so she was given to me. Yes, she is 'most fair of all virgins' and as wonderful as she is fair."

"It's no wonder the child is so extra comely. What is his name?"

"Jesus." Would this information give them away? Fear caused Joseph's heart to beat so hard he could hear it beating madly in his ears.

"Jesus. That's a common Jewish name. Why didn't you name him Samuel or Sampson. Or even David. I understand they were of extra beauty and heroes to your people. Why the common name of Jesus?"

"Jesus means 'God is our help' and surely we as a people need all the help we can get."

"Yes, that is true. That is true. You are a haughty, stubborn people. Maybe that is why Herod wreaked such bloodshed on Bethlehem." Again he spat angrily into the dust.

"Bloodshed . . . in Bethlehem?"

"Yes, that fool, foulmouthed, evil . . . I can't think of the right words to describe him. He is beyond comprehension. Anyway, some learned men from the Eastern countries came through Jerusalem looking for the 'newborn King of the Jews'. They asked everywhere. Perhaps you got to see them. You couldn't miss their fine trappings."

"Yes, we saw and talked to them."

"Did they ask you about the baby king?"

"Yes," Joseph replied.

The soldier waited to see if Joseph would tell more but he realized that was all Joseph felt inclined to say. "Well, news got to old horn-toad Herod. He invited them to the palace, wined and dined them, and asked why they searched for a king when he was king and the only rightful heir. They were too polite to remind him he was Rome-appointed and not rightful heir to the Jewish throne.

Instead they told of seeing a new star and following it this far and how they were certain they were close to the new child. Herod asked how long they had seen the star and was told it was over a year ago since they had first seen it.

"Herod called in all the stuffed poppin-jays *he* calls wisemen and had them dust off the old scrolls and search until they found where and when the babe or child should be found. After a night of frantic reading and searching, it was decided that Bethlehem—City of David—was to be the spot. So the wisemen were duly informed. Herod then told them to go, find the child and return to tell him so he might, also, worship him."

Another puff of dust arose as he let his anger show. "That is not what he wanted. Remember—I told you before that he wouldn't let the child grow. Didn't I?"

"Yes," grimfaced, Joseph nodded. "Please, go on."

The young boy whose mother was a Jew broke in, "But he didn't find the child! I tell you! Somehow that family got away. I'll bet the wisemen warned them and they fled to Jerusalem, Dan or Beersheba, anywhere! I say Herod didn't kill him!"

"You mean they tried?" asked Jason with a horrified gasp.

"Oh yes!" The sergeant could not go on for a moment. None of his troops seemed willing to talk of it either. When the explanation did come forth it was as explosive as thunder. "Babes! Can you imagine—soldiers commanded to slay babes! Men, even women and older children I can see, but *babes*? Herod became suspicious when the wisemen didn't return by the next night. The third day he ordered a regiment to Bethlehem to slay all male children two years and under. He wanted to be sure he didn't miss. I'm glad I wasn't on that detail. Can you see me killing babes? I'm hardened but how could I order these young men to do so? *Never!* I understand he had to finally send his personal guards to do it. No one else would obey. They are used to giving out horrible punishments. But this! I understand some of the men even lost an arm rather than obey that order." A shudder added emphasis to his disgust.

"How many did they slay? Was there resistance?"

"Rumor says eighty to ninety babes, ten to twenty fathers, and fifteen to twenty mothers, and about that many older children. But I've learned to cut rumors in half, at least. After all, Bethlehem is a small place. If eighty to ninety babes were to be found under two years, every woman from age twelve to fifty would have had to give birth in the last two years . . . all of them boy babes. Now, you

. . . Behold Thy Son

Jews are a hearty bunch, but that is expecting too much from such a small town."Joseph smiled at his reasoning. He agreed. Eighteen was more like it. Unless they killed the older ones, too.

"Anyway, they hit during a town meeting so the men would be away. They did not want any foul-ups. They hit and left as quickly as they could. I'm glad to be on this wild goose chase. It could have been our group. Now, I just have to go back and try to restore peace. Men from all the areas around have gathered and a rebellion is brewing. Herod's neck isn't worth much. I understand many of the guard deserted rather than return to him."

"Poor Bethlehem. The City of David has been bathed in blood."

"But I tell you the child escaped! I *know* He did! You do, too. I see it in your eyes." The young soldier looked hard into Joseph's face.

"Yes. I, too, believe if He is the Messiah, His life would be spared." Joseph spoke softly as his eyes fell on the child Jesus.

"You can be glad you hadn't stopped over at Bethlehem. That child would have gotten it for sure."

"You are right. We can indeed be grateful."

"Well mount up, men. Time is fleeing. Say . . . Do you suppose Jesus would like a short ride?"

Watching from the distance, Mary cried out as she saw Joseph lift Jesus into the open arms of the sergeant. Horrified, she watched as they galloped off up the road. She didn't notice the young soilders had not followed. "Oh! Jehovah, please! Please! Protect our son and return him to us unharmed!"

Prisca's steadying arms kept Mary from rushing out. "See, Joseph isn't worried. He is laughing and so is Jason. Surely your child is in no danger. Wait. Trust Joseph. He is the child's father and loves him, too."

Unable to control her sobs, Mary sank to her knees, burying her face in her hands. She did not hear Joseph's return. But the gleeful squeals and tender arms of her son brought her face into view.

Immediately Joseph realized what he had just put Mary through. Dropping beside her he wiped her tears and explained why he had let the sergeant take the child. "He is drawn to him and would protect him at all costs, Mary. He is not like the soldiers you have seen at Jerusalem." To a wondering Prisca and Jason and a worried Mary, Joseph related all he had learned from the soldiers.

"Poor Hannah! Her son would be slain. He was but three months old. And Sarah's child—after all these years."

"Yes, and I thought of Benjamin's boy who is just two and finally well enough to walk on those crippled legs. And Dan's son, at last, after all those girls."

"Deborah, poor Deborah. Hers is just one-and-a-half years old. She loved him so much more since her first three were dead at birth. How can they stand it? Oh, Joseph, how can they bear their losses?"

Tears glistened on their faces. Again a cry of pain. "Little Reuben was with his grandparents while his parents sought work in Jerusalem. And Isaac and Rebecca had just been given Nathaniel to raise as their own . . . Oh, Mary. Truly, the Lord has blessed and protected us."

Philip had slipped quietly into the group soon after Joseph had begun. Now he asked a question. "I thought you were from Nazareth? Yet, you seem to know quite a bit about the people of Bethlehem." Prisca's face mirrored her husband's question.

"Yes, we are from Nazareth. But remember, we said we had spent some time at Bethlehem."

"Ah, yes." Philip relaxed and smiled. "You mentioned seeing the wisemen." Turning to leave, he stopped—suddenly—turning a white face to Joseph, Mary, and the child Jesus. "You left Bethlehem just the day before the slaughter. Just *one* day ahead! The child would have been slain, too. He is under two. How fortunate you have been." Puzzlement again appeared in his eyes. "Were you warned . . . somehow? Perhaps by the wisemen? How did you know to flee?"

Joseph's face was calm as he answered, "Yes, we were warned. And it was because of the wisemen. Jehovah has truly blessed us. His plans cannot be stopped." Although Philip and Prisca waited for more explanation, none came. The move-on signal caused them to hurry their preparations.

Mary was now composed but sobs would break forth now and then as she thought of the losses of her dear friends. They had been so good to her. Why did such cruelty have to come to the birthplace of the Son of God? Why? One more question to be tucked away and the answer sought in days to come.

Day upon endless, dry, dusty day finally brought them to Beersheba, just within the border of Egypt. Tears mingled as final farewells between the two families showed the love which had grown between them. Even Jason, young man though he was,

. . . Behold Thy Son

wiped away a few as he 'allowed' Mary to kiss and hug him. But it was the child Jesus who really tugged at his heart.

For a few short days, Jason's dreams of a little brother had been fulfilled. A brother to teach how to catch and throw a wad of weeds. And wasn't it Jason's skill and patience that enabled Jesus to ride Jasper without the tie and to guide him with the bridle? Yes, Jason had even been able to show him the many people of the caravan. Together they had listened to the strange words and songs and thrilled to the dancing around the campfire.

But the best part had been the baby animals. Jesus had finally gotten brave enough to touch the baby camel. He had even begged to ride him. The goats and kids were their special delight. Mary would ask him to go for the meal's supply of fresh goats' milk. Jason had been allowed to milk the black she-devil, Shasta. It was only natural for him to aim and fire on the laughing Jesus who was trying to pick up two kids at the same time. The herders' rebukes never came as they all laughed at the surprised look on that dear little round face. Jesus never did figure out what had hit him. Even though Shasta had turned around and bunted him, Jason had enjoyed the moment to the fullest. Nor would he ever forget the first time the parrot whistled at them. Being so 'old and wise,' Jason could not let Jesus know he was so scared his teeth were chattering. Even his knees lost their strength as that piercing whistle came again, followed by a horrible, terrible laugh. Expecting to find a madman or a crazy woman, Jason did not see the parrot on his perch atop the camel's pack. The men's laughter at his expense made it even worse. When Jesus puckered up and cried, Jason became angry. He had started toward the men to demand an explanation, but Jesus' arms were wrapped tightly around his knees and his face was buried in Jason's robe. Which had shrieked the loudest, the bird or Jesus? That boy surely did have a set of lungs. Jason had been sure Mary would hear him and come running.

But it was Joseph's tender, firm hands which had loosened the child's stranglehold. His gentle coaxing soon brought an end to the tears and wailing. Holding the sobbing child tightly, Joseph had asked the camel driver to bring the bird closer so they could see him. Jason had shrunk behind Joseph as the driver brought the ugly, screaming bird nearer.

"Not too fast, please. Let them see it and approach on their own."

Ugh! . . . Who would want to go close to that, thought Jason. Joseph told them of the parrot, telling how he, too, had been frightened the night before as he searched the caravan for the cheese seller. The driver had told of its value as an alarm to alert him if strangers or thieves approached. He had not used his dagger once since he had traded for the green bird.

"Why do you keep the thong on him? Does he fly? He looks too awkward and fat to fly." Jason found himself in front of Joseph now. The bird had quit screeching and was smoothing his feathers with that huge, curved beak. He was pretty when the light hit him just right.

"Yes, he flies. Not great distances—but far enough to get away."

"Ffwwyy?" Jesus held out a hand to pet the bird. Thank goodness the driver was alert. He pulled his arm back just as the huge beak snapped at the tiny fingers. Jason shuddered thinking of the strength of that beak. Joseph had stepped back a step. Neither of them tried to touch the parrot again. Now Jason knew why no one had stolen the green bird.

Yes, it was fun to explore and learn when you have a little brother. Why were they not going on to Alexandria with them, Jason wondered. Many Jews had found refuge in the big city. Why couldn't Philip persuade Joseph to go that far.

"Are you sure, Joseph? Tahpanhes hasn't nearly as many Jews. If your enemies search for you, they will find you quickly."

"No, Philip. Our enemies won't search for us. We only need a place for a short time. We soon return to Bethlehem. You must begin a new life, but we will soon resume our old life with old friends. We must again express our thanks and gratitude for your kindness. Surely the God of our Fathers sent us to you. How can we ever repay your kindness?"

"Oh, but it is we who are in your debt." Prisca handed yet another small parcel to the protesting Mary. "Here is a new belt. Jason finished it this morning. He is too bashful to give it to you himself. Joseph, your very presence and friendship saved us from the necessity of lying to the soldiers. They weren't even aware of us. And that precious babe of yours has given Jason a new reason for living. You have been so very kind."

Mary's tears said more than words could. Thanks passed wordlessly between the two of them as she tied the new belt around her robe. Who cared if it wasn't as colorful or as smooth as her old one. This one had been a labor of love, and she loved the givers.

Farewells over, Joseph led the quiet Mary and the puzzled Jesus toward the city walls. The clerk had spoken of a carpenter shop

. . . Behold Thy Son

that needed skilled help for a few months—nothing permanent—just a short time. Perhaps they would find a small house to use, also. That was probably why Philip had insisted they take the sack of coins. It was more than enough to cover rent and food until work was found. Such goodness! Surely, Jehovah would bless such good people. He sincerely prayed so.

Chapter Nine

BETHLEHEM OR NAZARETH?

The moon seemed close enough to touch as they looked out the window. Jesus was asleep—at last. Afternoon naps meant he stayed up late in the evenings. Today he had fallen asleep in the morning, too. Mary had not let him sleep over an hour, knowing Joseph would be anxious to finish packing early and get to bed. They wanted an early start for their journey.

"If it were safe, nighttime travel would be better this time of year. No heat of the day, less dust and insects, and that full moon to guide us." Joseph was tired but excited.

"Think of the mosquitos near the swampland." Mary took her husband's arm, gently pulled him away from the window, and headed him towards the bed.

"They are out twenty-four hours a day, seven days a week, rain or shine. No way to escape them. But you want to know something?" Joseph lifted Mary's chin and looked lovingly into her eyes.

"What?" softly, expecting to hear how much he loved her.

"I can take mosquitos any day to those dread sand fleas. At least you can see the mosquitos and they don't hide in your clothing."

"Oh, Joseph! How unromantic!" A playful punch was aimed toward him. "Here I thought you were ready to tell how much you love me, and you talk of mosquitos and sand fleas. Really!"

"But I told you this morning that I love you. Isn't that enough?"

Joseph's eyes betrayed his teasing mood. His tender kiss shared his love and feelings with his wife. "Yes, my darling, I do love you, more each day. I keep thinking if my love grows any more I will burst. Yet, I find I just expand and find room for it. Pretty soon I will look like old Melhor and have to be carried around in a chair, too."

"Oh, silly, you don't get fat from love. You just get better. I am the one who gets fatter from love." A sudden frown caused Joseph to search her eyes, seeking the reason for her sudden change of mood.

"Why the sudden change, my darling?"

"Oh . . . it's nothing. Really." Mary tried to turn away but Joseph's hands held her firmly and she had to look into his eyes.

"If it is nothing, why the sadness? And so suddenly?" Mary sank sobbing into his arms. "Goodness. 'Nothing' surely has you upset. Now remember, we have no secrets. So come on, tell me what is wrong."

"Joseph, I . . . I . . . I have not grown fat . . . from our . . . love." Sobs shook her slender body. A puzzled look covered Joseph's face.

"You have not grown fat from our love? For goodness sakes, what do you mean by that? Pray tell me."

"I thought at last I was with child—your child. But no. Do you realize how long we have been married and no new babies? Jesus is nearly two years old. I should be with child by now."

"Is that what you are worried about?" Lifting her into his arms, Joseph carried Mary to the bed. Kissing her gently he sat her down, loosened her arms from around his neck, and sat down beside her. "Mary, we will have children, in the due time of the Lord. Until then, our concern is for Jesus and teaching him.

"Besides, I am very grateful you are not with child for this journey. Once should be enough for you. We will be much longer on the road than before Jesus was born. It is wisdom on God's part that we are not awaiting a child."

"I guess you are right." The twinkle in her eyes and the love in her voice softened her next words. "Why are you always so right? What would it hurt if it were *I* who was right—just once in a while?"

"But my dear, you were right when you chose this home. It has been so warm and cozy."

"Do you think Jesse would let us have his little home again?"

"Perhaps. But then again, he may be angry at our sudden departure. I am so grateful his child was not born yet when Herod

86

sent the soldiers."

"Yes, oh my yes." Mary sat up suddenly as if shot from a bow. "Soldiers! What if they are just waiting for our return?"

"I know they aren't. My dream left no doubt that we are to return—now. The danger is past."

A shrug and resigned smile, "Then I will just have to trust you, my always-right-husband."

"Yes, you will, my pretty, teasing wife." Their tickling and playfulness caused Jesus to stir in his sleep. "Hush, my dear. We do not want him awake now. He would never go back to sleep."

"Besides, Joseph, it is time for prayers and sleep for us. Morning is too close."

"Mary, those soldiers said Herod is dead but that Archelaus is even more cruel and wicked. I feel Bethlehem is still too dangerous for us to live there. We must choose somewhere else."

"But where, Joseph? What did your dream tell you?"

"Only that it was safe to return to Israel. We no longer need to stay and hide in Egypt."

"If we return to Bethlehem, Jesus would be the only man-child his age. People would become jealous because of him." Mary gathered her wiggling child into her arms.

"I hadn't thought of that. It is a very real possibility. They could put two and two together and turn us in."

"Bethlehem cannot be our home." Mary was sad. She loved the little town.

"The other soldiers, the ones who have been in Egypt, said an epidemic is sweeping through Egypt. Many people from Takpanhes have died from it."

"What kind of epidemic?" Mary held her son tight. He squirmed but could not get away. Nor could he understand the reason for such a tight squeeze. When squirming got no results, Jesus tried crying. But his mother simply held him tighter so he gave up and listened.

"It starts with a headache, then stomach problems, and then high fevers. Coughing and sneezing get worse, and finally they simply die."

"How awful! How blessed we have been." She put Jesus down, holding his hand so he could not run away. "I surely wish Jason were here to help with him."

"He was a good friend. I, too, wish Philip and his family were

. . . Behold Thy Son

here. This big caravan is slower and noisier. But the thieves have become so bad, the only safe travel is in large groups. Have you noticed the absence of small parties on the road?"

"Yes. Perhaps we will stay at the next camp long enough to wash and dry some clothes. Jesus needs them worse than we do. He is constantly in the dirt. He also loves to play in the animal troughs. Maybe I will just have to wash his clothes out and let them dry on the pack as we travel."

"Yes, son, you are quite a handful for this little mother of yours." Joseph had swung the boy up over his head and held him there, squirming and squealing in delight. Father and son loved such moments. "Keep it up. Keep her busy and happy. Do you hear?"

"Hey! Mister! Don't hold us up! Keep moving! There's no time for such foolishness!" Those behind were impatient at the delay.

"Oh, yes. There is always time for love," smiled Joseph to the man as he sat Jesus on Jasper and started walking once more.

The steward came back from checking the camels and their loads. His horse pulled up beside the family. Something always drew him here. Wish I knew what it is, he thought. I don't like Jews, yet I keep coming back to visit again and again. The troubled thoughts caused the frown to grow deeper than usual.

"Something troubling you, son?" Joseph was drawn to the young man. Surprised to find he was very learned, yet so young, Joseph had inquired and found he was the son of a wealthy Greek who had lost all his money. The man sold his sons and daughters to pay the debts. This young man had nearly earned his freedom.

"Not really, sir. Not when that young child is around. I ought to keep him around all the time. When he rides the rounds with me the people aren't so ornery. They enjoy trying to get him to talk and forget to lie to me. Babies add spice to life, don't they."

"Yes they do. And Jesus is learning more words all the time."

Mary broke in, "Thank you, sir, for seeing he is not taught the bad words. I heard the camel driver trying to get him to use profanity. I did appreciate your rebuking him and taking Jesus away." Mary was learning to trust this young man, even though he seldom smiled.

"Will you be going all the way to Jerusalem, or will you turn off and go to Bethlehem?"

"That is what we were just discussing. We aren't sure. Are you familiar with that area? Do you know the roads and conditions?"

"Yes. I spent two winters in Jerusalem, traveling out in all directions. Terrible place, that Jerusalem. The friction between Jews and Herod, and the Jews and Rome is really something." The young man sighed.

"Can we go somewhere else . . . Juttah, perhaps, and not go through Jerusalem?"

"Juttah!" Mary grabbed her husband's arm. "Do you mean it?"

"Hush, Mary." The rebuke was gentle, but firm. They must not give themselves away.

"Why are you so excited about Juttah? Nothing out there but goats, sheep, and hill people." The steward made Juttah sound almost as distasteful as Samaria.

"My wife has family there. Perchance you know them. Zacharias and Elisabeth? They are elderly, but are prominent in that area." Joseph watched his reaction carefully. Had he said too much?

"Oh yes. Very prominent indeed. He's the old man that went deaf 'till his aged wife gave birth to a son, isn't he?"

"Yes. The son's name is John and is just six months older than our son. They waited many years for his blessed coming." Joseph felt reassured he had found a true friend.

"I would be careful when you call it blessed. They have had nothing but trouble since that child was born. When Herod ordered the blood bath in Bethlehem, he got to thinking of the birth of John. It was Zacharias' turn in the temple again, so the soldiers were sent to find his son and kill him."

"Kill him! John? Was John killed?" Mary grabbed Joseph's arm to steady herself.

"No, someone warned the old man so he sent word for his wife to take the child and hide." The steward stopped to hand Jesus a fig. It was fun to watch the boy try to spit out the tiny seeds.

"Thank God he was saved!" But Mary's relief was short-lived. The answer to Joseph's next question cut as a knife through her heart.

"Where are they now? Are they in Juttah?"

"No." The young man hesitated, realizing the pain he would inflict. Very slowly the words inched out. "The wife fled with the child, but Zacharias was not so lucky."

"What happened?" Mary nearly pulled him from his horse.

"The soldiers charged into the temple demanding to know where the child was. When the old priest refused to tell them, he

. . . Behold Thy Son

was struck. He looked surprised but still refused to talk. My friend was with the detail and said the captain became obsessed. 'Speak, old man, speak! You can talk. Don't try to pull that trick on me. *I* know you can talk.' The priest answered he didn't know where John and his wife were. He had sent word that they were to flee. Then with a smile he straightened and said, 'Thank you for the assurance that they got away. I have been praying for their safety while I completed my work here.'

"The enraged captain struck him again, so hard he fell back, hitting his head on the altar. He seemed to be dead, but to be sure, they worked the old man over good."

Joseph steadied the shaking, sobbing Mary. Unable to understand why his parents were so upset, Jesus reached out and patted them as they had so often comforted him.

"I am truly sorry to be the one to relay such sad news."

"That's all right. Thank you for the information." Joseph gave the young man's arm a gentle squeeze.

"Joseph, we must go to her! Please, let's go to Elisabeth." Mary had lifted the bewildered Jesus from Jasper and was holding him tightly to her heart.

"Yes, my dear, we shall." Turning again to the young steward, Joseph pressed for more information. "Do you know where she is now? Can you direct us to her?"

"I know where she was last month. Because of the tales of witchcraft and such, she is never safe for long."

"Witchcraft! But why!"

"Because she birthed a son in her old age."

"But Sarah gave birth to Isaac in her old age, and it was not called witchcraft." Mary hugged her son until he squealed.

"You know people. Willing to believe anything. Well, some gossip got the story going, and it grew until Elisabeth has to continue to hide for the boy's safety. Besides, people were afraid Herod's soldiers would repeat their actions in Bethlehem."

"Do you know where she went? To which area?" Joseph's worry lines had returned. If his elderly cousin was in danger, what of the boy Jesus?

"Yes. If you wish I will show you the turnoff and draw a map so you can find her. You will miss Jerusalem traffic and can double back to Bethlehem on a back road, if you decide to go there later.

"Here, take this seal. It will warn the robbers and thieves to leave you alone. You are part of our group and we will track them down if you are harmed or troubled." Joseph noted its curious workmanship. "It is the master's. He is the wealthiest trader to use these roads. His armed guards are feared by all. You probably noticed we have no trouble? Well, you won't either if you keep that seal in plain sight."

"Thank you, my friend. Thank you. We do appreciate your help."

"Here, Jesus, have another fig. Then I must be on my way."

All boy and always hungry, Jesus stretched out an eager hand. As he ate it quickly, Joseph watched worry lines grow on Mary's face. "Come, little mother, one more fig won't spoil the child's lunch. Surely you remember his appetite."

"Indeed, I do. That's what worries me. We have let him be too free. If Zacharias was killed and Elisabeth and John are in danger, then Jesus could be, too. We must not teach him to trust everyone so completely, but to fear and be wary of strangers."

"My head agrees with you, but my heart says, 'Let him learn trust and love. He will be protected.' Therefore, in keeping with the angel's instructions, I struggle to do so. As you saw, the steward would not let him learn profanity. Jesus is protected."

Sighing heavily, Mary shook her head in dismay. "Trust again. Trust in God." Looking into her husband's eyes, her anxiety was written on her face. "Sometimes that gets very hard to do."

"I know, my dear. It is hard for me, too. But when I try to figure out a time He has let us down, I have to admit the answer is never. So, I shrug and go on."

"Please help me, Joseph! Please help me have more faith."

"I will, my darling, I will. Now we better hurry on before we get yelled at again. We have been going pretty slow."

"Gid-ah-up!" squealed Jesus as he kicked at Jasper to speed him up. "Gid-ah-up!"

The steward's map was accurate in every detail. The seal also proved provident. Two groups of robbers had approached, but on seeing the seal hanging from Joseph's neck, they scowled, saluted, and rode on. "Blessed again. See, Mary, God is watchful of us. We should be in Elisabeth's home by nightfall."

"I can hardly wait. To see Elisabeth again and to share with her the happenings of the past two and a half years will be very good indeed."

"Yes, perhaps she can help us understand it all."

. . . Behold Thy Son

"**STOP!** Stop where you are! You are trespassing! Why are you here?" Looking on all sides, they could not see who was talking to them. Mary grabbed her son. For once he did not fight her embrace but held on tightly.

"I said, why are you here?" Again there was no face to go with the voice which seemed to come from all sides at once.

"We are peaceful. We seek family who has been reported to be in this area." Joseph spoke loudly, turning all the while to see if he could see who would respond.

"Who are you? Whom do you seek?" Joseph noticed a small hill to the left of them. A few small bushes were struggling to grow on it. It stood slightly apart from the other hills. That must be where the man was.

"We are Joseph and Mary of Nazareth seeking Elisabeth and her son, John. They are our first cousins. My wife stayed with Elisabeth and her husband just prior to their son's birth." He spoke directly to the small hill.

Sure enough, the bushes wiggled as the loud voice came again. "Why do you seek them?" Joseph thought the man must be using the Roman horn to speak through. He had watched troops working with one of them.

"To renew family ties and love. We have been told Elisabeth is in hiding in this area. Can you direct us to her? We would be very grateful if you would."

The bushes parted and a young man armed with bow, arrows, sword, knife, and Roman horn stepped into view. "Yes, I will take you there. Follow me." He handed the horn to a hand in the bushes. "We must be very careful who goes on from here. They have received much persecution. Elisabeth is not well. She has spoken often of you. Perhaps your visit will raise her spirits."

They found the old woman in a dark cave with few comforts. Mary cried out when she saw the conditions. Elisabeth was resting near the entrance of the cave. Hearing someone at the entrance, she turned to see that her son was still asleep and safe in the back of the cave. Only then did she look to see who was coming in so boldly. "Elisabeth, can it really be that you are forced to live in such a manner?" Mary's arms were outstretched, seeking her beloved cousin. Elisabeth could not see their faces but Mary's voice stirred warm memories. "Elisabeth, it is Mary, Joseph, and our son, Jesus. Have you forgotten us?"

"Mary! Mary!" The aged woman struggled to her feet, but the

younger Mary moved faster and helped her. "Oh, Lord God of Abraham, Isaac, and Jacob be praised. Is it really you? Or am I dreaming? Zacharias! Zacharias! Did you hear that? It is our dear blessed Mary. She has brought Joseph and her son. We get to see the Son of God! Again we get to see the Son of God!"

Joseph and Mary aided the sick woman as she struggled to stand. Mary sobbed as she saw how weak and ill Elisabeth was.

"She often speaks to her dead husband as if he were here." The guide had followed them in, making sure they really were friends.

"Mary, Mary. Thank you for coming. I wanted to see your son again. Where is he? Bring him closer."

Where was Jesus? On seeing the struggles of Elisabeth, Joseph had hastily set Jesus down and rushed to help. The watchful Mary had also forgotten her son for one brief moment. "Jesus. Jesus. Where are you?" Thinking he would head back to the light and Jasper they looked to the entrance, but he was not there.

As panic swelled in their hearts, a squeal of delight followed instantly by a scream of terror sprang from the back of the cave. Jesus, finding the sleeping John, had stretched forth a hand, touching his face to see if he would wake up and play. John, used to rats and other creatures of the cave, awoke with a howl of terror, sure that once again he had a rat on his face. The laughter and comforting arms of his mother soon stilled his fear. Before long the two boys were rolling and tumbling together as only little boys can.

The visit did revive the ailing Elisabeth. Joseph helped her into the afternoon sun. A blanket shelter shaded her eyes but allowed the sun to help heal her body and spirits.

Once again the exchange of stories and happenings continued far into the night. The two boys were delighted to have the extra time to play. Once in a while Mary or Elisabeth had to separate them for a time until ownership or authority was reestablished between them. Finally, they were put to bed.

"Who would guess that he is the Son of God? He seems like any other child. Have you told him of his parentage?"

"No, he is too young yet. But we will when the time is right. When do you suppose we should?"

Elisabeth leaned forward. "As soon as possible. His is an important mission. He must be prepared."

"Why do you suppose we were sent to Egypt?" Mary still did not understand it. Surely they could have hidden in some small town in Israel.

. . . Behold Thy Son

"Last night Elijah read a passage to us. We wondered how it would be fulfilled." Elisabeth turned to look out at the young man who had become her constant guard and companion. He stood now at the path to ward off any intruders. "We were rereading Hosea which has a reference to calling 'my son out of Egypt.' I pondered at length as to how that could ever be accomplished.

"Zacharias and I enjoyed your visit when you came from Bethlehem. Just when we could see our way clear to return your visit, we heard of Herod's order to kill the babies. Then Zacharias sent word for me to flee. Only after many days of prayer did I receive peace of mind that you had somehow escaped. But I did not dream of Egypt as a possibility."

"That is where we were directed to go. So we went."

"Thus another prophecy has been fulfilled." Elisabeth settled back on her bed. "It is all so marvelous, is it not?

"Now, I can be at peace. I know he is safe and well taught by loving, obedient parents."

Mary's gentle hands smoothed the covers and pushed the white hair out of her cousin's face. She bent and kissed her, then began preparations for bed.

"Zacharias' death saved both our sons, Mary. His death was not in vain." Mary's grateful smile glistened with tears of sorrow.

Joseph counseled with Mary and Elisabeth as to where they should live. All feared the new tetrarch and his wickedness. Bethlehem was too close to Jerusalem. After three days of discussion, it became apparent that Nazareth was the best answer. "Perhaps things have settled down and the old stories and feelings forgotten." Joseph tried to relieve the anxiety on his wife's face. "Rachel and Reuben will be glad to see us."

"Do you really think they will? We haven't kept in touch. And we left with such haste."

"We left to work for a short time, due to the census. Remember?" Joseph lifted her chin and kissed her on the nose.

"Will the people come back to your carpenter shop? Will you have enough work? How will they feel about our stay in Egypt?" Mary was still uncertain.

"Don't tell them. Of course you must not lie, but only answer questions. Don't volunteer information. Your son must not suffer what mine is suffering." Elisabeth seemed much stronger this morning.

"But what excuse do we give for escaping Herod's evil decree?"

Mary still had questions.

"You were visiting friends so missed it. And that is the truth. You were visiting with Philip and Prisca." Elisabeth had grown wise in evasive but honest methods to protect her loved ones. "No need to tell anything more."

Mary and Joseph laughed softly. The look passing between them spoke their delight in the elderly woman's behavior. Yes, it was good they had come to visit. Elisabeth's grief for the loss of her beloved husband had been eased by their visit. Once again her sense of humor was helping to lift the gloom of the dark cave. She firmly declined their offer of a home for her and her son. "No, I must stay here in hiding and protect John's life at all costs. Our presence would endanger your lives."

John could not understand why they had to move to yet another cave. But as the men who were helping to guard and protect the little family led them to the new place, John and Jesus forgot their troubles for a time and enjoyed riding on the donkey. When comfortably settled in her new hiding place, Elisabeth encouraged Joseph and Mary to be off to Nazareth. "You must go. You would be in danger here. I only wish I had gifts to send with you."

With tears streaming down her face, Mary hugged her dear cousin. "But you have sent gifts. I now understand about Egypt and have peace of mind about it. And, thanks to John, Jesus knows how to catch lizards and toads."

"And we now know where to go to live." Joseph lifted the protesting Jesus onto Jasper. "Thank you so very much. Mary is once again ready to face Nazareth—thanks to you."

"But, Fawthaw, why can't John go wiff us?" Jesus did not want to leave his friend. Nor did John want to be left.

"He must stay and help his mother, son. His place is here."

"Why don't we stay heah, too?"

Mary hugged him and laughed, "Because, Jesus, with *two* such mighty hunters here the lizards would soon be all gone."

Farewells were saddened further by the knowledge that they might not meet again in this world. "Come to the Passover in Jerusalem. We will come each year. Meet us there."

"We will when we can do so safely. Our sons must remain friends. The crowds will be so great the people may have forgotten about us—for a time." So a place and time was set.

In Nazareth Rachel and Reuben welcomed them with open arms. And they did not pry but waited for details as Joseph and Mary volunteered them. Yes, Joseph's shop was available. The new man had quit last month and left town. His work was so poor that people went to the next village rather than have him do their work. Ezra would be glad to let them have their old house. He was doing very well and was ready to buy Nathan's house. "Remember the one he built for you, Mary?" The blush showed she remembered, only too well. "His wife wants to go to Capernaum. Nazareth is too small for her."

"Zeke and Miriam are no longer in Nazareth," Rachel told them. "Zeke was found by a husband who beat him to death in his lover's arms. The council released the husband from all blame. Miriam fled to her mother's home in the next valley. Nor is Sarah such a problem anymore. Jeremiah has turned to drink so often that he is constantly drunk. She has her hands full providing for her family. She has no time left for gossip and trouble."

Jason did not agree. "Oh yeah! Sarah still gossips."

"How sad! They were both good women." Mary would not condemn them.

While preparing the beds, Mary expressed her worries about no new babies coming. "I keep thinking—maybe. But no, I'm always mistaken."

"Now, don't you worry your head about that! Your time will come. In the meantime, you have done a fine job teaching Jesus. He is very obedient and good. Still, he is all boy. That's good. He isn't spoiled—much."

"Aw, come now, Rachel. He's not spoiled at all." Joseph and Reuben were bringing in extra fuel for the fire.

"Oh, no? Then why did he get extra pieces of nut cake at supper?" Rachel's eyes twinkled as brightly as Joseph's.

"To keep up to Jason. But Jason isn't spoiled, either, is he?" The friends laughed together, enjoying the chance to visit and tease once again.

"Oh, hush!" Rachel threw a pillow which Joseph caught and sent right back.

"Mary is afraid the women will say it serves her right to be barren after entering the marriage bed already carrying a child. I tell her not to worry. What do you think?"

Reuben answered, "I think those stories all died down when Miriam left and Sarah no longer had anyone to gossip with. I've not heard them now for some time."

"Nor have I," agreed Reuben. "Someone did ask last week if we had heard from you. I never told anyone you had stayed at Bethlehem and not gone back to Jerusalem. Speaking of Bethlehem, how did Jesus escape Herod's decree?"

Looking at her husband for support and confidence, Mary sighed, then began. "Well, we were visiting friends, so escaped it."

Rachel looked at Reuben and shrugged. He spoke for them both. "Look, you two. Many things have happened with you which we do not understand, nor have you explained them. But we decided if you ever chose to return, we would ask no questions. We would just be grateful for the chance to have you close again. Maybe someday you will feel free to tell us. Until then, we will just love and trust you."

Mary's tears and Joseph's handshake spoke their gratitude. "It is good to be home. You are true friends. This much we can share with you." Then Joseph told of their visit with Elisabeth and John. Reuben and Rachel already knew of Zacharias' death. Now perhaps these good friends can understand our behavior, Mary thought. Joseph prayed so.

Chapter Ten

TWELVE YEARS OLD

"Mary, the trip here and the excitement of returning and moving into your old home would naturally upset you. Of course things wouldn't be normal. You could be sick from the change of water." Rachel hoped she was wrong, but experience had taught her caution in such matters.

"Rachel, I *am* with child. I *know* I am. I have been sick every morning for four weeks and those herbs have been all that would help."

"Have you told Joseph?"

"No, he told me—this morning. He has been silently praying for children, also. This morning in our prayers he said, 'We thank thee, Father, for answering our prayers and sending seed to our household once again. Now please help us prepare thy Son, Jesus, for the coming of a brother or sister.' I could hardly remain on my knees. Oh, Rachel! It was so beautiful."

"See, the Lord has a timetable for us all. He knew when it would be proper and when you would be ready for another child. I wonder if it will be a son or a daughter."

"I would like a daughter, but Jesus needs a brother. He and John got on so well together."

"We must begin now and make clothes for him. You have few of Jesus' left. We mustn't be caught unprepared."

"Rachel, Rachel." Mary laughed at her friend's eagerness to begin preparations. "You were just telling me not to be in a hurry or too anxious and now *you* are."

"Oh hush, and give me those shirts. Honestly, Mary, that son of yours must climb every hill and tree he can find. He's worse than any of my boys were."

"You have just forgotten. But it does seem he is anxious to learn about everything. I noticed him sitting quietly in the garden last week. When I thought of him again, he was still there. He had scarcely moved at all. When I called to him, he didn't look up. Just put his finger slowly to his lips to tell me to be still. So I went to him. A butterfly flew off and over the wall. His shoulders drooped and he looked up and said tearfully, 'Mother, that's the first time I ever got that close to a butterfly. He was coming out of his cocoon. I got to watch the whole thing. It was beautiful. But his wings are still damp. He can't fly very well yet. Something might hurt him before he can fly to safety.' I was so amazed, I just stood there."

"Yes, he is more interested in the animals and plants than most boys his age, and he seems to understand them."

"It frightens me. I cannot give him all the answers he seeks, nor can Joseph."

"I really believe he figures them out for himself. He was telling me about why bees visit the flowers. I asked how he knew so much about it. 'Oh, I just watch, ask questions, and think about it, then watch again to see if my ideas are right.' He is very observant."

"Too observant at times. This morning he asked why I was getting sick all the time. Joseph just snorted and buried his head in his bowl. I stammered and stuttered and could not find words, so I told him to eat his breakfast. The look of pain in his eyes made me realize I had been too abrupt. But I could not bring myself to talk to him about it." Mary stood to stretch her tired muscles. Settling herself once more, she once again took up the never-empty mending basket.

"Now, Mary, it is nothing to be ashamed of. Childbearing is a beautiful, normal happening. Let it be presented so for Jesus, too. Let him share in the excitement and preparations. I always told my boys that when two people love each other as their father and I do, God plants a seed right here near my heart. That seed grows and grows until the baby is ready to come into the world. They loved to feel the baby kicking. When the hiccups started, squeals of delight were shared by us all."

"Is that all I would need to tell him?"

"Sure, he is not ready for a 'father-to-son talk' yet. But he is old enough for a 'mother-to-son talk.' Don't be afraid. It is a beautiful time for you both. Pray about it and the right moment will come."

Mary shared the conversation with Joseph as they lay in bed that night. "Is Rachel right? Should I tell him those things?"

"Yes. I believe that is the right thing to do. Then he can look forward to a new brother or sister and be more ready to share with them."

An opportunity to share this wonderful knowledge with Jesus did arise. Mary realized he was staring at her as she rubbed her back. Hiding her embarrassment, Mary sat on the bench beside him. His eyes searched hers, but he did not speak his thoughts. Not wanting to be scolded again, he returned to his play with his wooden blocks.

"Son, you asked why I am getting sick so often, and I was cross with you. Please forgive me." Jesus climbed onto her knees and kissed her nose. "I am getting sick and will grow fat because of a new baby. Your father and I love each other very much. And we love you, too. But we know how lonely you get all by yourself. Do you remember the fun you had with John?"

Eyes wide, Jesus nodded his head. He did not speak but waited to hear more from his mother.

"We prayed long and earnestly that God would send another child to us. And He has." Putting a hand on her stomach, Mary looked down, then up into his eyes again. "God planted a seed right here, next to my heart, and that seed is growing into a new baby brother or sister for you."

"Really? For certain?" Jesus could not believe his ears. Mary nodded.

"Did I grow in there, too, by your heart?" Here was something new to think about.

"Yes, Jesus, you did. Put your hand right here. Sometimes you used to kick me—hard, right here, till I was sure you would break my ribs."

"Did I really kick you? And . . . hurt you?" Remorse at the pain he had caused his mother filled his eyes. When she nodded, he hugged her, begging her to understand. "But I didn't mean to, Mamma, I didn't mean to hurt you! Honestly I didn't!"

"I know, son. I know." Hugging and kissing him, Mary looked into his eyes. Her heart melted. Why had she been fearful of this beautiful moment? "You were just growing and needed room. You became impatient at being trapped in such a tight place. But God knew you still needed time to grow, so you just had to be patient."

"Will our baby be as tiny as Ezra's? He is really too little to do anything."

Mary's laughter filled the happy home. "Yes, my dear boy. Our baby will be tiny at first and too little to do anything except eat, sleep, cry, and wet for awhile. But he will grow—just as you did. Then you will have someone to play with." Jesus joined his mother in happy laughter and merriment. This was exciting!

Mary's preparations for supper screeched to a halt when Jesus came running to ask yet another question. "Mom, can we name our new baby, James?"

"What if he is a girl?"

"A . . . a girl! Like Prissy? Oh, no!" Mary nodded smiling. "Not a girl!" and he ran outside. Supper was late, but Joseph joined in the laughter as he helped Mary finish preparations and put the food on the table.

Mary's mending went slower and slower as she thought through her dilemma. Finally a very soft, faraway voice came from somewhere near the mending basket. "Joseph, I just realized you could take . . . another . . . wife."

"I could *what*?" exploded from the hearth.

"I said," she faltered then gathered up her courage and began again. "I said you could take another wife. The Law says you can."

"What would I want with *another* wife? I barely keep up to you!"

Joseph came and knelt by his wife. His hand lifted her trembling chin so he could look into her eyes, but Mary refused to look at him. If she did, her tears would spill out and she was determined to hold them in. "My darling, has the Lord not provided for all our needs and wants?"

A nodding head said yes, but fearful eyes said no. "But, Joseph, you are doing well in the shop since we returned. You . . . you could . . . support another . . . wife." Tears began to spill, just a bit. A hasty hand wiped them away.

Joseph's big, warm, steady hands were gentle as he took her small, trembling hands and kissed them, always looking into her eyes. "Mary, I must enjoy every minute with you. There is no time to share you or our family. Jesus needs careful training and guidance. He is growing and learning fast. And now he will have a brother or a sister. My hands are full. You and our family keep me pretty busy.

"I know I could take other wives. But it is not necessary or good that I do so. Unless directed by the Lord, I will not take another wife."

Relief spread over her troubled face as Mary realized Joseph was being honest. Then, fear returned as she voiced her thoughts. "But . . . but what if . . . you are commanded to do . . . so?"

"Don't worry your pretty head about it. The angel said you were to be 'my wife' . . . not my first wife. Our lives will be full teaching Jesus."

Mary melted into his arms as the tears spilled freely. "Joseph, Joseph. I could not bear to share you with another woman. I just couldn't."

"There, there, darling. You won't have to."

Pulling away, Mary looked deeply into Joseph's calm eyes. "We have to a lot, don't we."

"We have to what a lot?"

"Trust in the Lord. We must have faith every minute of the day and night." Mary returned to her mending.

"That we do, my darling, that we do."

Three years passed before Joseph and Mary were able to meet Elisabeth and John for the Passover. Impending motherhood and added responsibilities made it wise to wait.

Joseph marveled at John's wisdom and maturity. He seemed very old for his five-plus years. Still, Jesus and John spent many carefree, happy hours sharing secrets and boyish fun.

Mary's heart cried out to the aged, bent Elisabeth. Time was not being kind to her. The hot desert sun and winds were aging her even faster. But Elisabeth did not complain. "Life is as good as we make it. We have sufficient. And . . . ," she looked around the room, "and once again we meet and enjoy being together. What more could I ask?"

John could not understand how Jesus could say that a little sister tagging a fellow around would be any fun. "But isn't she always in your way?"

"No, Rachel isn't in my way. She has learned to sit quietly for a minute or two and watch the animals, too. She would have loved the ride to Jerusalem. But Mother was afraid she'd get sick again, so we left her at Ezra's house and brought baby James."

"I'm glad *I* don't have a sister."

"Aw, you'd like Rachel. She doesn't cry much anymore. And

. . . Behold Thy Son

she loves to pick flowers."

"Wish we had flowers. Mother would enjoy them. She really misses them." John slumped. "Wish I could help more. She is always so tired."

Children in bed, the parents chatted in front of the fire. "Have you told him yet?"

Joseph looked at Mary. She looked into his eyes, then dropped her head and looked at her hands. Blowing out his breath, Joseph got up and poked the fire.

"Well, have you?" pushed Elisabeth.

"No, we haven't. We tried several times, but the time did not seem right." Searching Elisabeth's face for understanding, Joseph went on. "The Spirit seems to keep us from doing so. Sometimes we read a scripture and I go to tell him it is speaking of him, but I . . . I can't. The Spirit always stops me."

"Well, then," practical to the end, Elisabeth smiled, "it must not be the right time. The same has always happened with me. John will find out sometime, but I wonder when."

"Yes," murmured Mary, "I wonder when."

A broken piece of pottery bumped down the narrow street. Squeals of delight punctuated the pushing and shoving as each boy tried to be next to kick it along. "Whose turn next? Mine?"

"No, goofy, it's mine. You're after me."

"Wrong again, Dan. It's my turn." Jesus kicked hard—and missed. Laughs and pokes were shared in great fun. Dan took advantage of Jesus' grinning embarrassment and the pottery flew. Several more attempts and misses found the boys at the well.

"Anybody got a cup? I'm thirsty!"

"Me, too!"

"Jared has one. Can we all share, Jared?"

"Sure, Dan. What are friends for?" The cup found its way out of his robe and into the eager hands.

"Hey, where did you get this thing, Dan? Looks like it's part of something expensive!" All the boys crowded around Zeke to look more closely.

"Yeah! What is it?"

"You're right. It is from something expensive. Mom got mad at Dad again this morning. She grabbed the vase his aunt had sent for their wedding. Mother hates Aunt Phillipia. Dad's always quoting her as the authority on everything. Well, Mom let fly. Dad ducked, and the vase hit the wall. Boy, did Dad yell when he saw what she'd thrown!" Dan looked down at his sandals. The rest came more as a murmur. "Thought sure he'd kill her if he caught her, but she ran to the neighbors and got away."

"Wow! That sounds like my parents!"

"Mine, too. They are always fighting and throwing things." Simon handed the cup to Dan.

"Do you ever get scared?" Dan asked Jared as he handed the cup back.

"Sure do. Especially last week when Mom threw the knife. I'm grateful she's a poor aim."

"Yeah. I get scared, too. I'm sure glad it only happens once in a great while. Hope things have calmed down by supper time."

"Wanna eat at our house?" Zeke kicked the shard to Jesus. "Say, Jesus, don't your parents ever fight?"

"Never."

"Not *ever*?" Wide eyes betrayed the disbelief of the others.

"Not ever." Jesus stood his ground.

"Aw, come on. All parents fight sometimes." Simon took a threatening step forward. But Jesus didn't give way before the bully and continued to shake his head.

"Ya mean they don't argue or quarrel either?" Dan picked up his pottery. "Come on, fellers. Let's head to the hills."

"Okay, last one's a swine herder!" Squeals of laughter followed the racing boys through the sleepy town.

Out of breath and thirsty again, the boys flopped onto the grass. "You know, I can't remember ever seeing anyone in your family fight or quarrel." Dan poked Jesus to let him know he was being spoken to.

"Mother says she didn't bring us into the world to fight and quarrel." said Jesus.

"What?" This sounded fishy to the boys. No one talked like that—and made it stick.

"I said, Mother says she did not bring us into the world to fight and quarrel." Jesus repeated and rolled over, tucked his arms under his head and watched the clouds pushing each other through the sky.

"Don't you ever get mad at Rachel or James? Doesn't Simeon ever get into your things?"

"Oh sure. But we just talk it out and go on our way."

"I don't believe it!" exploded Simon. "I *don't* believe it!"

. . . Behold Thy Son

"I do!" Levi sat up. "I spent three weeks in their home while Mother and Father were gone. Not once did I hear any quarrelling and fighting. If things got sticky and cross words started, it was just as Jesus said. His mother would look the cross person in the eye and say 'I did not bring you into this world to fight and quarrel.' Then she'd find out the trouble, help solve it, and we'd go on.

"Once I got so lonesome I thought I'd die. I kicked Rachel hard so Mary would have to punish me and I could cry. Rachel screamed like a peafowl. Mary came running. She asked what the trouble was and Rachel told—just like a girl. I stood there waiting for her to strike me. But she didn't. Mary just kissed Rachel and told her to hush and go pick some flowers for the supper table. Then she put her arm around me and led me into the house. She talked so lovingly and softly I knew she wasn't going to punish me, and I started to bawl. I couldn't hold it in any longer. She just led me to the bench and sat with her arms around me till I quit. She kept saying, 'Go ahead and cry. You have a right to feel lonesome. I get that way, too.'" Levi looked around to see if the boys believed him. Encouraged by what he saw, he went on, "Well, she had me do something in the house so no one would see my red eyes, and at supper I got extra dates. It was lots easier to bear the lonesomeness after that."

No one said anything for a long time. While each boy sorted through his feelings. Simon summed it up for them all. "You're lucky, Jesus. You're one lucky fellow."

"I know," said Jesus softly. "I know."

The clouds pushed and jumped, then sped onward. Nine pairs of eyes were aimed at the clouds, but only one saw their antics. As the ninth stood to go, he called to his friends, "Come. It's nearly supper. We don't want to be late again. Remember last week?"

"Yeah, I sure do."

"Me, too!" echoed the others as they followed Jesus down the hill.

"Say . . . Jesus."

"Yes, Zeke."

"Don't your parents *ever* quarrel? Bet they don't agree about everything."

"You're right, they don't agree on everything. But they talk it over when we aren't around. They simply hold their peace when we are there, then discuss and settle it when we aren't."

"Wish my parents did that."

"Me, too. Sometimes I think they use us to hurt each other."

"Mine fight less than they used to. And I'm sure glad."

"You're lucky, too, Gad. Mine used to never fight, but they do now." Dan waved his goodbye and headed home.

The weaving loom hummed as the women visited over their mending, weaving, and sewing. "Where is Mary? Why isn't she here?"

"Didn't anyone tell you? Her baby came last night. They have two girls now."

"Another girl. Won't they be pleased?"

"Speaking of Mary, have you seen how Jesus has grown?"

"He has shot up this past year. He will be ready to go to Jerusalem in the spring, that's for sure."

"Who does he favor? I can't tell if he looks more like Mary or Joseph. Some days I can almost see Joseph's eyes, but the next day I see Mary's expression in his face." Sarah inspected her sewing in the light.

"He doesn't look like either Mary or Joseph. He has his own look. I've always considered him good looking. But then I have always liked him and enjoyed his company." Esther, too, held her sewing up to inspect.

"I still remember that day when everything was going wrong. Supper wasn't started, water wasn't fetched. It seems as if those are the days the kids pick to cut teeth, stub toes—one thing after another. I had four screaming, fighting children who even got the animals upset. Just as I was ready to melt into tears and give up, Jesus came to the gate with a bunch of flowers. He wasn't much more than five or six at the time. There he was all smiles and sunshine. I almost told him to stop it, there was nothing to smile about. But he asked if he could come play with Paul and his brothers and sisters. Not waiting for an answer, he climbed over the gate, gave me the flowers and went to the squalling kids. They still hadn't seen him. He put his hand gently on Paul's shoulder and said, 'Paul, look what I found. I thought you would like him.' The noise stopped instantly and became oh's and ah's. Curiosity got the best of me so I peeked over their heads to see what had caused the change. There was the biggest toad I had ever seen. I nearly screamed it was so ugly, but those kids were fascinated. Paul took his prize and showed it to his brothers and sisters.

"'This is a magic toad.' Jesus said. 'He brings sunshine into

. . . Behold Thy Son

your home. But only if there is no quarrelling and fighting. That frightens him. And he needs some water. So you better go fetch some.' Now remember, Jesus was only five or six. Still, such wisdom. We received further instructions that music and laughter would keep the toad there. We had that toad till it slipped away to sleep. It *was* a magic toad, for we all wanted to keep him."

"Yes, Jesus is different in so many ways. You know, he won't fight. He always backs away."

"I have noticed the same thing. He is like my Sam. Sam will take only so much, though, and then watch out!"

"Your Sam is different, too. I always say if a boy hasn't sense enough to defend himself, he is useless." Sarah went to the water jug.

"Didn't you hear what happened last week?"

"No, what?"

"Simon was acting like a bully and teasing Mary's Rachel and her friends in the yard. He soon had them all crying but Rachel. She warned him to behave, but it was no use. Jesus came home about then on an errand for his father. He found them all crying. He, too, warned Simon to go and leave the girls alone.

"Simon's answer was to pitch a clod at a smaller girl's head. Jesus tried once more to reason with him, but when he clearly refused to listen, Simon was suddenly eating dust. Jesus would not let him up until he promised to never tease little people again. When Simon finally promised, Jesus still didn't let him up. My Zeta said Jesus stayed right there while he explained *why* Simon must not pick on others. Then he helped Simon up and cleaned him off. Last of all, Jesus brushed himself off."

"Yeah, just like Joseph would have done."

"Blood sure does tell. He is more like Joseph every day."

"But he doesn't *look* like Joseph! I still say the old stories are true." All eyes turned to Sarah.

But her wagging tongue was stilled by the next comment. "So? Your Philip doesn't look a bit like his father. He is the spitting image of Jeremiah's brother, Dan. Does that prove you begot Philip by Dan and not Jeremiah?" All enjoyed the discomfort of their friend. Rachel had successfully squashed that old story—forever.

Rachel and James were most unhappy to learn they did not get to go to the Passover this year. "This is an important year for your brother—his twelfth year. In order for us to take care of all that must be done in Jerusalem, you will stay with Jude and baby Leah. Grandmother Rachel will need your help. She is getting pretty old and tired." Crying and begging failed to change their parents' minds, so farewells were said as the boy Jesus left Nazareth with his parents to return from Jerusalem a young man—fully accepted as a member of the Jewish city of Nazareth.

Mary's thoughts kept drifting back to her journey twelve years before. She had certainly changed since then. The quiet little girl of Nazareth had been in Egypt for awhile. That first two or three years after they were married had been unsettling and eventful. But things finally settled to a routine. Mary became an accepted wife of Nazareth, doing the usual, expected things. Mother of five beautiful, obedient children, she was kept very busy, feeding, caring for, and loving them. Yes, life was good.

She wondered again if they should talk to Jesus about his birth. But Joseph was probably right. They should wait until after they returned from the Passover. Then it would mean more to him. Besides, memories fade and become fuzzy.

"Mother, do you suppose John will be there? It's his twelfth year, also."

Mary's face softened as she thought of John. He grew older and more quiet at each visit. His letter telling of Elisabeth's death had been too grown-up for his years. "He said he would. You know how he always follows the Law. Yes," Mary's arms went around her son, "I am sure we will see him there."

Jesus was twelve all right and just a shade shorter than his mother. They looked more like brother and sister than mother and son. Joseph's heart warmed as he watched them. It would not be long until Mary would be looking up to her son.

"May I go ahead with Dan and his parents? I'll be back for supper." Jesus' eager face looked from mother to father.

"Certainly, son. Go ahead. But get some goat's milk on the way back."

"Okay, Father," and he was gone.

"Joseph, that was such an impressive Passover. Jesus seemed to grasp and understand its meaning more than any of the boys there."

"Except John. He seemed to understand, also. But you are right. Jesus seemed very impressed by the proceedings." They walked in silence thinking about the things which had taken place. "I, myself,

... Behold Thy Son

have not always understood what was said and done. Many things became clear only as I explained them in answer to Jesus' questions. Yet he seemed to have the answers and was trying to help *me* understand."

Mary sighed, "I know the feeling—only too well. He explained some of the scriptures to me yesterday. I believe it was one of Moses' books. Yes, it was about the creation. It was astounding to hear his reasoning. I could not keep up with him."

"We must talk to him, Mary. Tonight we must tell him of his heritage and his birth."

"How it frightens me. Will he believe it? Will he become arrogant?"

"No," Joseph's arm went around his wife's shoulders. "He is not likely to become proud. I think it will cause him to withdraw and become more quiet and concerned. That is his way—not pride. Remember how he took the news of our royal lineage?"

"Joseph! Joseph! Have you heard the news?" came from behind them.

"What news?" Joseph pulled to the side of the road to await his friend's arrival.

"The Zealots are planning to drive the priests from the temple next month. They are furious at what is going on there."

"I, too, am dismayed. But I doubt that is the way to do it. Force will get us nowhere."

Mary's thoughts turned to her children at home as the men discussed the Zealots' plans and position. Politics and wars were for men. Only homes and families were for women to worry about.

Someone in the group shouted ahead. "John, John, speed up! You are too slow. Speed up or turn aside."

John. Mary's heart was saddened at the memory of the sad John. All alone and trying to stand unafraid. "He has had to grow up too fast. I wonder if he can come out of hiding now."

"Who, dear?"

"Am I talking out loud again?" Mary hid her face with her scarf. She must stop this habit.

"Come now, tell me. Who is too old?" Joseph gave her a playful poke in the ribs.

"John. He is too much alone."

"That he is. That he is. I asked where he was going. He said 'Back to the desert. I know its ways. The desert is where I belong.' I couldn't persuade him to come with us."

"I tried, also, as did Jesus. I am afraid we will never see him again. He didn't say 'see you next year.'"

"I noticed that, too." Joseph checked the pack.

"Ah, they are stopping for the night. This is the best well. The water is cooler and more plentiful. Where do you want to make camp, Mary? Close in or near the outside of the group?"

"It really doesn't matter."

"If we are going to talk to Jesus, it better be where we have a bit of privacy." Joseph turned to the left.

"Ohhh, yes. Talk to Jesus. What do we say? How do we go about it?"

Joseph had no chance to reply because a friend called to invite them to set up camp near the date trees with their small group. It would be a good place, close enough for protection, yet far enough away for the needed privacy.

"Where is that son of yours?" inquired the friend. "He set our tent up for us on the way down."

"Visiting with friends in the group. He started out with Simon's family, then probably went to Dan's." Joseph kept his voice steady to keep Mary from realizing how worried he was becoming. This was not like their son. Jesus was very dependable and seldom gave them cause to worry.

"Joseph, have you see Jesus since we left?" Mary's face revealed her concern. "He is always here at camp time—unless he tells us ahead of time where he will be. I just talked to Dan and Simon. He left their group soon after we started. We were with the first group and they came later."

"Were they the last group from Jerusalem?"

"No, there was one group after that. But no one his age was in it. It was Rabbi's group."

"Well now, no need to worry, darling. He may be with Rabbi, asking all kinds of questions. They should soon be here. Let's eat supper." Joseph wanted to keep Mary from worrying.

"Joseph! Aren't you concerned? He may be in danger!"

"Calm down, Mary. I *am* concerned, but I know our son. He is very obedient and careful. You will see. Now come on, I'm starved!" For a starved man, Joseph ate little and very slowly. Mary watched and smiled faintly. Joseph *was* worried.

Just as they finished, the rabbi's group joined the camp. Joseph excused himself to go find his son. Mary saw him start, half turn, then turn back and ask again. Panic-stricken, she ran to him.

. . . Behold Thy Son

"Joseph! Joseph! Isn't he there? Haven't they seen him? Are they sure?" Joseph never could hide anything from his wife. She read her answers on his face. "Joseph, what are we to do?"

"Break camp. We must start back immediately. Rabbi said he disappeared soon after they left the city walls."

"What's the excitement? Why all this disturbance?" The burly voice belonged to the caravan leader. His word was law. Mary always trembled in fear when he came around.

"Our son is not with any of our groups. We must return to find him."

"How old is your son?"

"Twelve years."

"A young man, now, aye. Well, he's probably just proving he's a man and can do as he wants. Don't worry, he'll come soon."

"No, he is not with the last group. We must go back now and find him."

"Oh, no you won't! None of *my* caravan is going to start out after dark. Not on your life!" His feet planted firmly, he folded his arms and stood in their path.

"But we have to! Jesus may be in trouble. Perhaps thieves or . . . or worse." Mary stood her ground, too. Joseph could not help his amusement. When her children are in danger, Mary becomes very brave, he smiled to himself.

"Jesus. Is he your son? Bright lad, that one. Very bright. He walked a full day with me coming in. I enjoyed talking to him. He is not the usual boy. Very responsible, too. No, he won't be in danger. Too smart. Go to bed. He'll be here by morning. If not, you can start back then. No sense your getting into danger unnecessarily."

Two very uneasy and upset parents did go to bed, at last. However, sleep did not stem the rush of worried thoughts. As the sun peeked over the hills, they turned their faces to Jerusalem. A final search of the camp had brought no reassurances. No one could help.

Traveling against the massive exodus from the city made their progress slow. Besides, each group had to be questioned. Only once did they get any help or encouragement. An old man had visited for an hour with a young man of Jesus' description—just inside the city walls. Jesus had declined the invitation to travel with the group.

"Said something about his father, his house, or something. I didn't catch it all. A fine son you have there, a very fine and bright son. Very respectful, too. You can be proud of him."

"Thank you, sir. We *are* thankful for him." Joseph pulled Mary away and they headed on again.

A return visit to their Passover lodging yielded no clues. No one had seen or heard of him since they had all left. "We will stay here. If Jesus is lost, he may return here. Come Mary, you look exhausted. A warm bath, supper, and good sleep will make you feel better."

Dawn found the worried parents searching again. Friends joined in the search. Still there were no answers when they returned at nightfall. Joseph insisted Mary stay and rest while he went forth again. Mary had slept so fitfully she was worn out from sheer exhaustion and fear.

"What if he has been taken by John's enemies? What if he has been . . . killed?" Joseph caught the collapsing Mary. She voiced his silent and deepest fears.

"Now, now. Remember how God has protected him before? Surely he is safe now. We just have to find him."

Mid-day brought the same negative reports. Joseph could see Mary would not stay behind again. Friends worried they would both drop with exhaustion. "This isn't like him. Jesus isn't irresponsible. I don't understand it. I don't!" Mary sobbed and sobbed. Weakened from lack of food and sleep, she felt she could not take another step. But she *must*! She *must* find her son.

"Surely God is watching over him. Our prayers have been heard, little mother." Joseph's head dropped and rested on hers. He prayed, "Oh, Lord God of Abraham, Isaac, and Jacob, please guide us. Please help us. Thou knowest we have tried to do as we were commanded. We have done our best to teach and love Jesus. Please help us find him!"

Mary looked into her husband's haunted face. He had aged in these three days. She had never seen him so tired and upset—not even when he learned she was with child before their marriage.

"Where else do we look, Mary? Three days! It's been *three days!*"

"Let's go to the temple and pray. Perhaps there we will get the help we need."

For the first time in three days, Joseph's face brightened. "Yes! The temple! That's it! Why didn't we think of it before? Come, let's go!"

"What's it? What didn't we think of?" Mary grabbed her shawl as Joseph pulled her out the door.

. . . Behold Thy Son

"The temple! Jesus will be at the temple. You know the questions he has been asking and asking then asking again. He said he hoped the priests would answer some of them. There was little chance during the Passover for many questions, so he went back."

Mary ran behind her husband. Too out of breath to speak, she let herself be led by the hand. The other hand was busy holding her scarf around her head and face. People stopped and stared but no one tried to stop them or get in their way. Rushing up the steps, Mary stumbled and fell. Joseph picked her up and started to carry her, but she made him put her down. "I'm all right. Just let me catch my breath. We must be dignified." But it was Mary who rushed through the door calling, "Jesus! Jesus! Are you here?"

A surprised priest stepped forward to block their way. "Why are you so upset? He said you knew where he was."

"He's here? My son is here?" Mary grasped the old man's arm.

"Yes, if Jesus is your son, he is here. Has been for three and a half days."

"Where! Where do you have our boy?" Joseph grabbed the other arm, nearly upsetting the priest.

"Boy! You call *him* a . . . a . . . boy? A *man* is closer to the truth. So wise and learned. Where did he get such schooling?"

"He is only twelve. He has been in the schools at Nazareth." Joseph let go of the priest to steady Mary. She looked ready to collapse at any moment.

"Nazareth has such fine schools? That is hard to believe! I know the rabbi there. A good man, but slow in the scriptures. This lad should be teaching *him!*"

"We study the scriptures . . . in our home." Mary was puzzled. Jesus had not seemed particularly gifted to her, just quick.

"Aw, a good Jewish home. Hard to find them these days." He turned to lead the way down a dark, hollow hall. The slapping of their sandals echoed and reechoed in eerie voices. "Most folks are more worried about keeping their bellies full and fancy clothes on their backs than studying the scriptures. 'Rabbi can do that. That is his job,' they seem to say."

Mary clung to Joseph's arm as they made their way through unfamiliar halls and rooms. "Where is he taking us?" she whispered. Joseph patted her hand and smiled. Surely their son was safe if the priest spoke so highly of him. But where were they keeping him? and why?

Stopping at yet another closed door, the priest turned to look at them. "You really did not know where he was, did you. I can't understand. The lad kept assuring us you knew." A pause, then a smile. "No, he did not say you knew. What he said was 'They *will* know where I am. They will know where to find me.' And you did. Come, he is in the library. He has spent his time here questioning and teaching the priests. Even the great High Priest has been no match for him."

Voices poured through the opening door. Hesitating, the worried parents looked upon a strange scene. It was as the priest had said. Their son, just barely over twelve years of age, sat in the teacher's chair answering questions from the priests. The High Priest sat on a stool at his feet, where the boy should have been. Jesus was answering with authority, yet in a humble way—not arrogantly. It was as if he knew he was more learned but wished very much to share his knowledge with them—the learned men and leaders of his people.

Motherly instincts soon won over the feelings of awe and fear. Rushing to her son, Mary called his name. "Jesus, Jesus, why have you done this? Your father and I have searched sorrowfully. Why have you dealt with us this way? We were so worried! Why didn't you let us know?" Her reproach and scolding were stilled as her son turned. Mary fell back toward Joseph's protecting arms. Was this her son? Where had he gained so much . . . maturity . . . and authority?

There was a moment of profound silence, then Jesus responded—this new, grown-up Jesus—"Why have ye sought me? Wist ye not that I must be about my Father's business?" Seeing the bewilderment and shock at such an answer, Jesus smiled a boyish smile. Another moment of silence. What did he mean, "my Father's business," wondered parents and priests.

Silently begging understanding, Jesus searched first his mother's face, then Joseph's. Joseph's showed pain, then relief as the meaning of the words sunk in. "My Father's business." Jesus knew! Joseph was not his father. The temple, the priests and rabbis belonged to Jesus' Father, and Jesus knew it. But how? When and by whom did he learn of it?

Mary's relief after all the worry took her breath away. She swayed—ever so slightly, but Jesus sprang to her side and led her to the chair he had been sitting in. "This is my mother, Mary, and" turning to her husband, "this is Joseph of Nazareth." Joseph stayed back. He did not belong. Jesus stretched out his hand. "Please,

. . . Behold Thy Son

steady her and I will go get some water for her."

"I will go," came from many priests at once. Food and drink soon appeared and the reunited family was ushered to a table as questions were tossed back and forth. Joseph hesitated but Jesus was, as before, obedient to his earthly father. Mary marvelled but could not understand what was happening. As she had done so many times before, she trusted Joseph and his judgment. He would explain it all to her later.

"But, Joseph, we agreed to talk to him. You know we did." Mary pushed the bedding into place. Too tired to sleep, but too exhausted not to sleep, she thought only of accomplishing what must be done, and then heading to bed. A gentle voice caused her restless movements to halt. She turned to ask, "What? What did you say?"

"There is no need. He knows. I don't know how or why, but Jesus knows." Joseph sank wearily to his bed.

"How do you know that?" Sometimes these two men in her life were just too much to comprehend, and this was one of those times. Joseph had agreed to Jesus' sleeping by the animals. He had not hesitated a minute. Nor had he scolded the boy. Instead, he had made sure she did not get a chance to scold him, either. "Just what makes you think he knows?"

"Did you not hear what he said in the temple?" Joseph pulled Mary down beside him and pulled the covers over them. This would be a cool night. Maybe he should take Jesus another robe.

"What did he say? He told them we were his parents."

"Are you sure that is what he said? Think on it a moment. He said, 'This is my mother, Mary, and this is Joseph of Nazareth.' Do you remember?"

Mary stiffened as she remembered. She had been too excited at finding him to notice. But she had wondered at his words, 'Wist ye not that I must be about my Father's business?' Joseph had no business at the temple. Joseph waited quietly as Mary sorted through the events of the day. When she began to sob, Joseph knew she was beginning to understand. Would they ever fully understand?

"I wonder when he knew and who told him."

"You said he had spent more of his spare time alone, with the scriptures lately." Joseph wondered if he hadn't better take that robe to the boy; it was becoming more chilly.

116

"That is true. He has been quieter lately. I thought he was just getting prepared for the opportunity to study with the priests."

"Yes, we should have thought of that right off. He had so many questions and was looking forward to the chance to ask them. But the crowd of young men was so large he only got to ask one question each day. Of course, that is where he would go. And he would naturally think we would know where he was."

Footsteps outside their tent brought their conversation to a halt. The footsteps stopped at their flap. "Mother, Father," came a soft whisper. "Are you awake?"

"Yes, son, we are. Come in."

The boyish face looked a bit sheepish in the moonlight. "It is cold out here. Is there an extra robe?"

"Yes." Mary sat up and reached for the extra robe and handed it to him. "May I have a kiss, or are you too old for that now?"

An awkward peck landed somewhere between her nose and ear as he picked up the robe. "Goodnight, Mother, Goodnight, Father. I love you both. Thanks, Father, for not being angry and . . . and for understanding."

"Goodnight, son." An outstretched hand was clasped in two growing ones as father and son looked into each other's eyes. "I love you, very much."

Jesus missed the door flap as tears clouded his vision. He fumbled through, hesitated, then turned back. "Father?"

"Yes, son?"

"I've chosen my vocation."

"Good. It is time for that. You are now a citizen of Nazareth."

"May I . . . May I continue to work with you . . . in the shop?" Jesus looked down at his hands. His father was an expert carpenter—the best around—and he was aiming very high desiring to study under him.

Joseph found a lump in his throat. Had he heard right? Did Jesus really want to study under him? *Knowing* he was not his father? "Are you sure that is what you want?" choked the humble man.

Jesus looked up and there was no doubt about it. His feelings were very visible in his countenance. "Yes, Father, more than anything else. You are the best carpenter and I love the work. But most of all," tears flowed down his face. He ducked, wiped them away with his sleeve then looked up and began again. "Most of all, I love you very much and want to be like you. And if I spend my appren-

. . . Behold Thy Son

ticeship with you, I will learn to be more like you."

Salty tears mingled as father and son embraced and wept together. Words were inadequate for such feelings. Mary wept tears of joy as she watched, marvelling. Then two arms pulled her into the circle of love.

Chapter Eleven

JOSEPH! OH, JOSEPH!

Rachel was blushing as she set the table. Joseph watched his eldest daughter, wondering why. When she tripped and spilt the stew into the lap of their guest, melted into tears, and ran into the bedchamber, Joseph understood. Their guest was Dan.

A frequent guest, Dan was accepted as Jesus' best friend and treated like one of the family. The two seemed inseparable when work, chores, and schooling were over. Teasing Rachel seemed his favorite pastime if Jesus was not around to stop him. But lately the teasing had changed in tone, and Rachel did not seem to mind it so much.

Leaping to his feet, Dan spilled the hot stew onto the floor. Yet his main concern seemed to be Rachel's tears, not the loss of his supper. Looking from the bedchamber door to Joseph and back again, he silently begged permission to go to her.

Joseph and Mary understood the message but played dumb. "Oh, dear. Jesus, please help him clean up that mess. Joseph, please go to Rachel and calm her down. I will get a fresh bowl for you, Dan. There is plenty."

Realizing he might as well do as he was told, Dan helped Jesus clean up the mess. "See, I told you so."

"Told Jesus what, Dan?" asked the ever-present James. He was in the awkward position of being too old to play with the babies, but too young to join in all of Jesus' and Dan's games. So he stayed as close as he could—hoping.

"Boys' secrets. And they can't tell." Mary ruffled James' hair as she sat the fresh bowl down. "Here, Dan. Thank you for your help."

"Thank you, Mother," said Jesus as he smiled at her.

Rachel came out after the men of the house left for the town meeting. Red eyes spoke eloquently of how she had spent the time alone. Mary smiled as she gave her some stew. But Rachel was too miserable to eat. "Oh, Mother, why am I so clumsy? And why do I hurt so?"

"Because you are a growing girl with feet and hands suddenly bigger than you are used to. Also, a new feeling is growing inside you. Dan is no longer only Jesus' best friend. He is exciting and fun to have around. His teasing has become gentle and of a different nature. Have you noticed, his voice is now almost as low as your brother's?"

Rachel nodded—gloomily. Where did all this get her? Her twelfth birthday was next week. Then her father could, and would, arrange her marriage to one of the older young men of the village. They were so poor it would have to be someone who was not concerned about her lack of dowry.

"Why the long face, my dear? It was only a bowl of stew."

"It was only my whole life! That's all it was!"

"Your whole life?" Mary knew what was meant but she wanted Rachel to speak her feelings—to get them out into the open.

"Yes!" Rachel cried. "What does it matter if I *do* like Dan. Maybe I even love him! It won't make any difference. I'll have to marry some old man with money." Sobs tried to surface, but Rachel was *not* going to cry!

"Marry some old man with money? But why, daughter? Why do you think that?" Mary slipped an arm around her daughter. But Rachel pulled away.

"Because! Because I don't have a dowry! We're poor! I'll have to take anything that comes." Melting into a heap on the table, the girl gave in and sobbed, seeking to ease her broken heart.

A gentle hand smoothed the beautiful reddish hair. A lighter shade than Jesus', her hair sometimes looked copper in the sunlight. Mary's eyes glistened as she thought back to her own twelfth birthday and remembered the same feelings shared with her pillow. Mary had not told her mother her concerns, especially after her special friend Salome had been married to the rich Zebedee and moved to Capernaum, never to visit again.

"Rachel, Rachel, have you heard your father say anything about matchmaking?"

"He keeps saying I will make some man a fine wife," blurted out between table and arms.

"Yes, but does he ever say a name? No. He has not. Do you forget that he chose me? That my father and mother let me say yes to whomever I wanted?"

Rachel looked fearfully into her mother's face. This was too much to hope for. Surely they would not let her . . . Mary smiled at her daughter as she took the troubled face between her hands and kissed the red, swollen nose. "Mother, are you . . . are you saying?" Rachel could go no farther.

Mary nodded. "Yes, my child. Your father and I decided a long time ago, long before you were born, that you would be free to choose your mate as we did. We have never regretted our choice. We have been trying to teach and guide you so your choice will be as wise and . . . and wonderful."

Grabbing her mother and holding her tight, Rachel cried once more. "Oh, thank you, thank you! That is the best news I have had all year!"

"We both like Dan. He is a good, fine, hard-working young man. He has an excellent record and treats his mother and sisters with respect."

Wide-eyed, Rachel searched her mother's face, unbelieving. "You mean . . . you mean you and Father have discussed . . . us?"

"Yes, my dear, many times."

"But how did you know?"

"By watching and listening. Dan has been in love with you for nearly a year, now. You have been slow to respond. We have been wondering if you would. Your eyes seemed to be only for Zeke or Simon." Mary's teasing brought a blush to her daughter's face.

"Oh, Mother! Zeke is nice, but . . . but. Oh, I don't know. And Simon is too much a bully yet. He doesn't even like himself." Rachel turned very serious. "Do you really think Dan . . . likes . . . me?"

"I do. Indeed, I *know* he does. Ask Jesus if you don't believe me."

"Jesus?" A girl does not ask her brother if his best friend likes her.

"Yes, Jesus. Talk to him. He can help you. He has been inventing reasons to have Dan over here so Dan could make you notice him." Soft hands smoothed the hair back into place once more.

. . . Behold Thy Son

Rachel had one curl that insisted on hanging down into her eyes.

"Really? No. You're teasing me! Jesus has really been helping Dan?" A toss of the head brought the curl right back down.

"Really. Jesus is not yet interested in girls. But he has been a most willing helper to his friend."

"I just can't believe it," Rachel said wonderingly.

"Believe it, my dear. Believe it. Now come help with the dishes. I am very tired."

With the dishes gathered and in the water, Rachel stood looking far into space. "Is it the same for the others?"

"Is what the same for whom?" Mary was struggling to get the sleepy Leah ready for bed.

"For Jesus, James, Jude, and Leah? Do they get to choose, too?" Mary nodded. "Does Jesus know?"

"Yes, your father talked to him last year. He explained many things to him and told him to choose wisely." Lifting the sleepy child, Mary slipped into the bedchamber. Closing the curtain as she returned, Mary started, then smiled at Rachel still standing, holding the same dish. "Rachel, you look like a Roman statue. At this rate we will not get the dishes done till next week."

"Did Father have a father-to-son talk with Jesus like you had with me last month?"

"Yes. Jesus knows all about men, women, and babies, too." A sudden back pain stopped her in her tracks. Holding her back, Mary slumped to the bench. "Speaking of babies, I fear this one is not going to make it. Nothing has seemed normal since the start."

"Babies! Mother, are we . . . are you going to have another baby?" Rachel was at her mother's knee looking intently up into the troubled face.

"I pray so. But I fear we shall lose it. It is too much like the time Deborah lost hers."

Mary was right. This baby was not to stay with them. Twice she lost her babies. The first came too early and was dead at birth. The second died of the fevers within a week. Reuben's and Rachel's loving care helped the family in their crises. Assurances from kind, well-meaning friends helped somewhat, but an aching void—not her precious babies—filled Mary's arms.

Daughter Rachel proved as wonderful a nurse as the woman for whom she had been named. "How can I remain ill long with two such choice and loving Rachels to wait on me and care for my family." But Mary remained sad and quiet. Joseph worried about her. Mary's joy in living seemed to be fading.

Seeking to fill the void, Joseph brought Joses to the family. "His mother and father are both gone. He is left all alone. Is there room in our hearts to welcome him?"

Jude especially welcomed his 'twin brother.' "We are the same age. We can be twins," he said. People soon forgot that Joses had not always belonged to the family.

"Mother, you were sort of adopted by Reuben and Rachel's family. Now we get to adopt." Mary smiled as she ruffled Jude's curly hair.

Still, Mary was very melancholy. Not even Joses' eager efforts seemed to cheer her up. Then Rachel's first baby was laid in her arms. "Look! I am a grandmother! Now I have a baby to love again!" Once more their home was happy and brimming with love, health, and happiness.

"Dan, you must bring Rachel and our grandchild over often. Mary is much happier when you are here." Joseph seemed exuberantly happy tonight. He was like a schoolboy with great news to share.

"Joseph! Joseph! Calm down. Do you want the neighbors to wonder?" Mary pulled her husband's arms around her.

"What do I care what the neighbors think? This is too good to keep any longer." Mary found herself swinging through the air.

"What, Father?" Jesus had been in the shop when the message came, but Joseph had shared it with no one.

"I am to supervise the building of the new rooms for the synagogue." Joseph paused to listen to the oh's and ah's and congratulations. "And . . . "

"There is more?" What could be added to this good news?

"And . . . Jesus is to be my first assistant." Joseph's hand clamped Jesus' shoulder.

"Did I hear right, Father?" Jesus could not understand this good news. When Joseph nodded he blurted, "But why, Father? I'm still an apprentice and only seventeen."

"But you are the best man in the village for the job. You are intelligent, quick, and very accomplished. Better yet, you take orders well. And you know Rabbi. He'll be there, giving orders and more orders."

Mary imagined she could hear Jesus thinking, "Father called me a *man*!" and laughed softly as she watched him sit taller, straighter. Jesus would do his very best. Joseph was a wonderful

. . . Behold Thy Son

father and teacher.

"Do we get our new room before you start? We really do need it." Mary cuddled Rachel's tiny new baby to her face.

"Yes, we will start it day after tomorrow. We should be done about the time the work begins on the synagogue."

The work went well. Rabbi, true to form, gave many orders, only to change his mind again and again. Joseph and Jesus were able to keep the men working in spite of him. Any excuse to watch the men work was gratefully accepted. James helped grudgingly; gardens and flocks were his first love. Mary's heart warmed at the gentle yet firm way Joseph worked with his sons. James was good at the work, but Jesus was gifted and loved it. Yet, there was much James could learn from working with his father.

"Here is the warm drink you asked for. My, but it is cold here. Is there no way to heat up your work area? Your fingers must be very cold." Mary and the children had jars filled with the precious warmth.

"Yes, my dear, they are. But there is no way to heat it. We have tried everything. Work seems to be our answer until the roof is on. Rabbi wants it finished by the beginning of summer. We must push on."

Jude, Joses, and Leah wandered at will among the workers, sharing the warming drink with all. Leah was almost five and was spoiled by all but her father and Jesus—or so they said! Her dark hair and snappy eyes mirrored her father's coloring.

"May I see the new altar?" asked Mary. "Jesus was so pleased with your work last night."

Taking her hand, Joseph led the way to a room in the old part of the synagogue. Converted to a workroom, the small bedchamber's fireplace enabled the men to do the fine fitting needed on the new altar. It was beautiful work. "Jesus has a way with people. No one seems to mind taking orders from him. He managed to pin Rabbi down to a final plan before they started on it. We are behind because of his constant changes. However, Jesus is learning how to work around Rabbi's ideas in such a way that no offense is given."

"He is a good son. But I do wish he would marry. He is the right age. Dan and Rachel have a child, Jonah is marrying next month, and Zeke and Simon were married last month. Why doesn't he get excited about marriage, also?" Mary was especially pretty when she had that look on her face.

Joseph kissed her tenderly. He didn't care if the workers saw them. He loved his beautiful Mary. "Give him time, Mary. They are all a year older than Jesus. He has plenty of time yet. His thoughts are seldom of girls. He fills his hours and minutes with scriptures and people. And there *is* his Father's Work."

Locating Leah and the boys, Mary sat on a stone that lay rejected in the sun. "Why isn't this stone being used?"

"See that large crack down the middle?" Joseph pointed his finger to a tiny line.

"*That* is a large crack? What, pray tell, is a *small* one?"

"You cannot see a small one." Joseph gently nudged Mary over and sat with his arm around her.

"We must get the garden in. Jude can spade it when we get back. Joses has hauled the fertilizer. I want to sell the extra produce like we did last summer."

"Mary, Mary, there you go again. Getting anxious too soon. The cold is still in the air. Jude probably won't be able to get the spade in the ground. What's your hurry? Afraid Deborah's garden will outdo yours?" Joseph playfully flattened her nose with a cold thumb.

"No, Deborah's garden can never be as good as ours. She doesn't have James to tend it." She looked into Joseph's eyes then away—over the valley.

A yell from the crew sent Joseph running with Mary following after him. Accidents had been few and minor on the job. But with so many men working on so many things, Joseph worried. A sudden sickness hit his stomach when he saw Reuben's youngest son, Jason, lying motionless on the ground. His crumpled body resting under the scaffolding told the tragic story.

Rachel answered Mary's knock. Seeing her tear-stained face, Rachel knew something was wrong. Thinking it was Mary's lot to again suffer loss, Rachel pulled her into the house, an arm lovingly around the sobbing woman.

"Come, sit down. Reuben will soon be here. I will send him to Jason's home with the stew. Their baby is so cute. Spitting image of his father. Mary! What is the trouble? Tell me."

"I . . . can't, dear Rachel, I simply can't. It's too . . . sad."

"Have you lost another child?"

"Yes, but not my own. I loved him as my own. But . . . he . . . he

. . . Behold Thy Son

is yours," finally poured out of the sobbing woman.

"*Mine?*" Rachel's hand flew to her throat.

"Yes. Ja . . . Jason . . . is . . . dead."

"Jason? . . . How? . . . Why?" Rachel held Mary captive as she searched her face for the answers.

"Down at the synagogue. He . . . fell from the scaffolding." The two grief-stricken women held each other trying to give comfort.

"Oh, my dear, dear, Jason. My baby! My baby!" Rachel pulled away and walked to the hearth. Absently she pulled the pot off the stove. "His new baby. His wife. His family." Panic-stricken, she turned to Mary. "How will they live? How will they survive?"

The loss of an unborn child is different from the loss of a grown child. Even the grief and pain of losing two babies could not match the sorrow Mary read in her friend's eyes. Rachel had been so kind and good so many, many times when Mary needed her. But Mary did not know how she could help now or what she should do. Words were inadequate.

Because of Jason's new baby, Joseph had the men bring his body to Reuben's home. Mary saw to the necessary preparations. Reuben stayed with his wife, searching for solace in their grief. Jesus helped carry the body home, then stayed to help his mother.

"Mother, do you suppose I should go talk to them?" Jesus asked.

Mary looked at her son. Taller than his father, well-built with work-hardened muscles, Jesus was trying to fill a man's shoes. Perhaps he could help. She smiled, nodded, then squeezed his arm before returning to dress the body with spices. A bewildered, saddened young man came back into the room. "I tried to comfort them, Mother, but I fear I only made it worse."

"Probably because you are alive and Jason is dead. I felt that way for a moment when I learned of your sister's new baby." Handing him a basket, Mary started him toward the door. "Please go fill this with white cloth from the big chest. Rachel seems to have none and we need it soon."

Rachel needed others to be there, to listen, and to take over the necessary arrangements, as Mary was doing. Grief had been her lot so many times, but Rachel had been spared until now. Jason was the first child she had lost. Rachel had been truly blessed.

Jesus watched his mother help the couple face the reality of what happened. After the burial, he saw them turn to Jason's wife and young family to give what help they could. Ezra was the oldest and best able, so he took the young widow as his wife to raise his brother's children as his own. Jesus watched as the first wife welcomed the new responsibilities, sharing her blessings—willingly.

One evening when he was alone with his mother, Jesus asked, "Mother, would you remarry if something happened to Father?"

The mending halted, then began again as Mary sorted her thoughts. "No, I am too old to try to please another man. Life has been too wonderful with your father. Besides, nothing is going to happen to your father. We have too much to do. You are still unmarried."

Jesus dropped his eyes. Marriage was discussed too often for his liking. No girl or woman had stirred his heart for long. Couldn't they see he must choose with extra care? Searching his mother's face, Jesus realized they did know his responsibility.

"Besides, your father is needed to help raise his family." Her eyes dropped to her mending as her face flushed.

"What do you mean, Mother? Why are you blushing?" Curiosity whetted, Jesus leaned forward eagerly seeking the reason for his mother's unusual behavior.

"I have news to share with your father. He has been so busy he has not realized the changes in me." Mary could not bring herself to look her son in the eye.

"Changes?" Jesus found no answers as he looked his mother over. "Say, is that tiny shirt for Rachel? Or is Ezra's wife expecting?"

"She is expecting. But this new shirt is not for her or for Rachel. I will be needing this shirt about the same time they do." There, it was out!

"Oh." Shrugging, Jesus picked up the toy he was carving. His hands were never idle of late. Even as he searched the horizons for answers to his many questions, his hands found the carving knife. Toys seemed to find a ready home faster than he finished them. A sudden realization flooded over him as his mother's words sank in. "*You*? You will be needing it? Mother, are you, are you . . . ?" Tongue-tied, Jesus got no further.

"Yes, I am with child. And I feel this time all will be well."

"Does Father know?" Chips flew from the speeding knife.

"No. He has been too busy and tired. But the extra work will soon be over and he will only have the shop's load to carry. Then I can tell him." Mary looked at her firstborn son. He had grown even

. . . Behold Thy Son

more quiet since Jonah's and Dan's marriages. "Jesus, why the frown? I am well. All will be well."

Jesus looked deep into his mother's eyes. Should he burden her with his worries? Perhaps she was aware of them already. "It is Father I am worried about."

Mary's reaction confirmed Jesus' fears. "Yes, he is working too hard and such long hours. That cough will not go away. Nor is he eating properly. I fear for him." Mary suddenly looked old and very tired.

"I try to get him to slow down, but he pushes on. Rabbi is not satisfied, so the work must be pulled out and done again. He got soaked in that shower when he tried to protect the work. I had to go pull him under the roof."

"Please watch over him, Jesus. Please see that he is more careful. I need him." Mary's hand held his arm very tightly. "We *all* need him. Please do what you can," Mary implored her son who did his best to reassure her.

"But, Joseph, the push is over. Surely you can take *one* day off. I want to take Leah to the hills. You must come with us. I have a secret to share with you."

Joseph kissed her, pulled on his cloak, and started for the door. "There is no secret. I am not as dense as you think."

"Then you know?" Mary ran to him.

"Yes, my lovely wife. Ezra's efforts to hide his joy only serve to spread the news faster. You, my dear wife, are getting two new babies to fuss over this fall. And now, I *must* be off." But not before he kissed her again.

Mary's chuckling followed Joseph as he hurried out the gate. He knew nothing of *her* secret. Joseph—the wise man—was not aware he was to become a father again.

The chuckles turned to worries and worries to fear when Jesus helped his father home early in the afternoon. Feverish, Joseph gave no resistance to their ministrations. Never had he felt so sick in his entire life. A sudden spring rain had caught him unaware. Weakened by exhaustion from finishing the synagogue on time, Joseph's body fell victim to the cold and fevers common this time of year. The fever refused to leave. Instead it climbed and got worse. Rachel and Reuben came, but even they could get no results. Jesus stayed, watching first his father and then his mother. Mary seemed to lose strength along with her husband. Dawn

128

found Joseph worse yet. He had not recognized anyone since suppertime. Somehow, Mary knew he never would again. She must prepare herself for his death. But how? Turning, she saw Jesus sitting there quietly, tears slipping down his face. Mary's heart went out to him. Joseph had been so close to his son. They seemed so much alike. What would Jesus do without his father's guidance?

Jesus looked up, saw his mother's face, and came to her. "Mother, what can we do? Why can't we help him? I am afraid he is going to die!"

"Yes, son. He is nearly gone. He doesn't have a chance. His resistance got too low this winter." Mary pulled Jesus down onto the bench beside her. Tenderly she wiped the tears from his face. But more kept coming.

"I should have done more. I should have watched more carefully." Jesus found comfort in his frail mother's arms. Tears mingled as they tried to strengthen each other. "Did he know of the new baby? He never mentioned it."

"No. I never had a chance to tell him. He was already working too hard. I was afraid he would work even harder if he knew. The child will never know his father."

"*His* father? What if it is *her* father?" Jesus was rewarded by a faint smile. "You were so sure Leah was a boy."

"Oh, all right. So I don't know. But whichever, it will not know its wonderful father, which will be a terrible loss."

The family said goodbye to Joseph at sundown, but he did not respond. Mary fell across his heaving chest, sobbing. Joseph's feeble arms lifted and gave his dear wife one last hug, then fell back. Unable to bear her sorrow, Mary fainted. Loving arms lifted her limp body and carried her to Leah's room. Torn with grief for their mother and their father, Jesus and James stood helplessly in the doorway, hearts breaking.

Seeing little Leah crying in the corner, Jesus went to her. She backed deeper into the shadows. Kneeling beside her, Jesus put a hand on her dark hair. Leah pulled away, sobbing. What could he do? Settling himself beside her, Jesus began to talk very softly of the things Leah had done with her father. After a long moment, Leah's sobs began to subside. Encouraged, Jesus continued to speak softly. When Leah turned to look at him, he knew she was listening. "You see, baby sister, all of us have to die sometime. That is the plan."

"Will we live again?" Leah searched her brother's face for

. . . Behold Thy Son

reassurance.

"Yes, we all will. Everything will live again."

"Even my duck we ate last week?"

"Yes," chuckled the amused elder brother, "even your duck."

"Good." Leah accepted the outstretched hands and crawled into the loving arms of her brother. "But, Jesus, how do you know?" Jesus' head rested on the dark hair and his eyes closed in silent prayer. Leah tried to turn to look into his eyes. "How do you know everything will live again?"

"The scriptures, little sister, the scriptures. I have read and studied them many hours. They promise this great blessing."

"But how do you know the scriptures are true?" Jesus' eyes seemed to look beyond the walls of the humble home, beyond the walls of the city, far beyond the horizon. Becoming restless and impatient, Leah squirmed around and looked into his eyes. She tugged at his robe. "How do you know, Jesus?"

"Because I have asked my Father and He said they are of Him."

"Our father said *that*?" Leah's eyes were wide with wonderment.

"Yes, our Father, but not the one lying on the bed." Busy with Leah's questions, Jesus had not seen or heard Mary's approach. "But our Father in Heaven who loves us all very dearly." Jesus turned toward the group at Joseph's side. Seeing Mary sitting quietly near his side, he spoke to her. "He has a plan for each of us, Mother. We all have a work to do. Father's work must be finished. He has done so much and worked so hard." He searched her eyes seeking assurance that she understood.

"I know, my son. But the pain and sorrow are still there. I loved Joseph so very much. He has been so good to me. And . . . the younger ones need his guidance as much as you did. It is for them I sorrow, not your father."

"Maybe that is why I have not yet found a wife, Mother. Perhaps I am to take Father's place for a time."

Mother looked at her son holding his sister, giving comfort and guidance. She found peace beginning to grow in her troubled heart. "Yes, we do have you and you are so like your father. So very much like him."

"He was a good man. There is none finer, anywhere."

"Mother, Jesus, come, we must prepare him for burial." James' young face was twisted with grief, tempered with determination. An outstretched hand helped his mother and then Leah, to their feet. Jesus accepted the help, then hesitated. Two brothers embraced, giving each other solace and comfort.

Mary watched as they embraced.

I must be brave. I must have faith. Oh, Joseph! Please help my faith to continue to grow. Please! Wherever you are.

The little family council lasted far into the night. Mary's news of her forthcoming child helped ease the sorrow. Jesus told of his plans to assume the place his father had left. "There is still plenty of time for me to marry. I can keep the shop going and provide for you, James, Joses, Jude, Leah, and our 'baby brother.'" Mary answered his teasing with a grin. "We will make do."

"Yes, we can. James has already planted the garden for us. Joses and Jude have done well with it. Leah's ducks and hens are doing very well. So I think we can manage."

"You mean I can still stay?" Joses had prayed long and hard that he would not be asked to leave this good family.

"Of course. You are one of my children, my very own. What would I do without you?" Mary's hug was received and returned—tenfold.

Knowing he would come did not calm the discomfort in her heart as Mary opened the door for Joseph's brother.

"Mary, I came as commanded by the Law. My business is doing well in Capernaum, and I can support you and your four children. Jesus would then be free to marry as he should." Benjamin was a handsome man, but not as large as his elder brother, Joseph. He was a "big city" man.

"Sit down, please. I thank you for your kind offer. I have been expecting you. Benjamin, you are a good, kind man. But you are not Joseph. I loved him deeply. No one can ever take his place. He provided well for us. We have no debts. The house is in excellent repair. The children are well taught. We can provide for ourselves; our garden is doing very well, as is the shop. I do extra sewing and weaving for friends and neighbors. Even Leah helps with her ducks and hens. And, you see, there will be another baby." Mary placed the plate of fig cakes on the table. She seemed compelled to move about constantly.

"But what of the unborn child? He must know a father's love."

"Jesus is so like his father. He will see to it the child is not neglected." Mary brought the cheese, offering it to her guest.

. . . Behold Thy Son

"Thank you, again, dear brother. However, Joseph has seed, so under the Law, I am not required to remarry. You have a wife and many children. We need not add to your burden and responsibilities."

"Then here, take this." Benjamin pulled a heavy sack from his belt and laid it on the table. "We suspected you would feel this way, so my wife and I want you to have this money. Please take it. Let us help this much. Joseph was good to us after our parents died. He put off his marriage plans until we were all married. This is the very least we can do."

"Bless you, dear Benjamin, bless you." Mary's gratitude glistened through her tears.

After their jugs were filled, the women had time to visit. One subject had been favored the past few days. "Now Mary'll *have* to let that young man get off his pedestal. Really, the way he has been treated one could think they were in the royal palace and he was the crown prince."

"Well, he is, Sarah. Jesus is the heir to the throne. With Joseph gone, he is not crown prince any longer—but king. I say he would be a good one. He is gentle with all and shows great wisdom."

"Gentle? You mean weak. I say a firm kick in the right place is best for kids. You don't see me putting my arms around my children when they are naughty. They have to earn my love and affections!" Sarah's nose went even higher into the air.

Yes, Rachel thought, and they are so unruly so much of the time. You have kicked too often and loved too little. She wisely decided her thoughts were best not shared.

"He is not so good looking, either. James—now there is a good looker. He has Jesus beat all hollow. Even Jude has more looks than Jesus. He doesn't look the part of a king at all. Joseph was very good looking. Mary is a beauty. You'd think he would have gotten some looks from somewhere."

"But, Deborah, he is fine looking. There is a good, clean cut to him." Rachel couldn't believe her ears.

"Oh, Rachel, you always were partial to him. I agree he is fine looking. But our king should be exciting and handsome!"

"Still a romantic, are you? Even at your age?" Rachel laughed as she picked up her jar and started up the hill.

"Well, so what? You never get too old to dream." Esther set her jug down, then replaced it on her head. It didn't want to balance this morning.

"Speaking of dreaming . . . Mary is still such a beauty we better all watch our husbands. They may start dreaming." Sarah looked as if she knew something pretty juicy.

"Whatever do you mean?" All eyes were on Sarah.

"*You* must be dreaming, Sarah. Do you think Mary would want your drunken Jeremiah after her life with Joseph? Really!" Esther was revolted by Sarah's suggestion.

"Elisabeth, you better watch out. You are right next door. I understand she calls on your husband for every little thing." Sarah's face was not kind. She was still trying to dig and hurt.

"Sarah! That is a *lie*! We went over together and told her to please call when she needs help. She thanked us graciously and said with Jesus home and Leah's good help, they could manage fine. Not once have they sent for help. Instead, she came and helped me make soap the first part of the week. Mary is a fine neighbor, Sarah. I have no fears from her. And I trust my husband."

Esther took Elisabeth's arm. "I am stopping off on my way home. May I walk with you, Elisabeth? Mary promised a new recipe for a poultice for bee stings."

"And that is another thing," screeched Sarah. "Why is Jesus still home? Why isn't he married? It is not natural, I tell you, it's not natural!" Sarah found herself alone with her unkind thoughts and miserable ways.

. . . Behold Thy Son

Chapter Twelve

THIRTY YEARS OLD

James was excited. This was his big year at the Passover. Jesus would take Father's place. Mary warned him she wanted no repeat of the problem Jesus had caused them in his twelfth year. "I could not bear it. Not so soon after your father's passing. Do you understand?" she had asked. But then, James was not as free with people as his older brother. Shy, James would rather people speak to him first. Then, if he could control his shaking, James would speak back. Maybe now he was accepted as a man in Nazareth, it would be easier for him. Mary hoped so.

No amount of persuading could sway Mary from her plans to go. "I must go and make one final sacrifice for your father. He was a good, righteous man and I owe it to him."

"But the baby, Mother. What about the baby you are carrying?" Rachel and Dan were to keep Leah, Joses, and Jude. Leah would be a big help with Rachel's babies. The boys could carry the water for the two gardens.

"Rachel, all is well this time. We are going one day early so we will not have to push quite so hard. I can ride or walk. Remember, I made the trip before Jesus was born. I am not nearly so far along and large as I was then." Mary continued to pack, unpack, and then start again.

"You were younger then, too, and hadn't had four babies and lost two more. You know you would never forgive yourself if anything happened to this baby." Rachel took the bread from her mother's oven. She loved to bake here at Mary's home. Her own oven was not as good and she burned things too easily.

"That is why we are going slower and why we borrowed the donkey from Reuben and Rachel. They are going with us so it will be a most pleasant trip, I feel sure."

And it was. They had fine weather, good friends, and a spiritual feast. Reuben and Rachel added much pleasure to the familiar trip.

"With Jason and Joseph being called to the other side, we decided we better put our lives in order so we would be ready, too." Reuben pulled his robe a bit tighter. The flies were biting too hard for his liking.

"But who would be better prepared than you two? No one does more for the stranger or friend than you. No one is as quick to follow Rabbi's bidding." Mary could see no reason for them to feel inadequate.

"We must not just *be* good, we must *do* good."

"Reuben, that is what I said, no one *does* more good than you two." Reuben had aged more than Mary realized.

"What he means, dear, is that we must strive to live the Law completely. The Law requires all able-bodied Jews to visit Jerusalem for the Passover. We have let first one excuse and then another keep us from doing so." Rachel hesitated, ashamed of her record. Jesus spoke carefully. "Jason was concerned that you had not been back since his twelfth year. He was going to insist you come this year."

"He got his desire, didn't he?" Reuben's wry smile betrayed his feelings. "It is sad how complacent one can become; sliding a little here, not going quite far enough there, all the while thinking we are doing great. Then along comes the death of a loved one and we realize how short we have fallen."

"Reuben!" Jesus stopped dead in his tracks. "Reuben, you don't blame yourself for Jason's death, do you? You cannot take responsibility for that! It was an accident! Reuben, it was an accident!"

Reuben's head dropped. He could not look Jesus in the eye. "I feel . . . responsible . . . somehow."

"Things do not work that way. We each work out our own plan. You had taught Jason well. He was the best, most skilled and dependable man on that crew. He was living the Law as well as any man can." Jesus walked on. He hands clenched into fists, relaxed, then became fists again as he searched for words. The silence hung heavy over the little group.

Mary marvelled at the wisdom of her son. She realized he was trying to find the words that would help *her* find peace, as well. Many nights had been spent crying her heart out, trying to see where she had failed Joseph. She should have forced him to rest. Perhaps if he had known of the baby, he would have slowed up a bit. Perhaps she had been unwise in her cooking and hadn't fed him properly.

"Our Father has a plan for each of us. We are not told what it is to be. We must go on faith. Some will die young. Others will suffer many hardships and be tested to a greater degree. Our reward will depend on how well we accept and use those hardships and tests." Jesus paused to see if he was making progress.

"What you are saying is that Rachel and I have been so blessed. We have raised all our sons to manhood. All are such fine young men. Now we must face the test of seeing one taken in his prime, leaving his family to struggle alone without him." Reuben still had many doubts.

"You are getting the right idea. Ezra took Jason's family under his protection and care. They are being well cared for and loved. Jason will have more seed, thanks to the kindness of his brother. Also, he has gone to his reward. We can be sure of that. He was humble and honest and lived the Law to the fullest extent possible." Shifting the load a bit, Jesus eased the donkeys' burdens. He made sure neither of them got sores from improperly balanced loads.

Rachel slipped her arm into her husband's and looked into his cloudy face. "Reuben, what if he had been sick like your brother? Would you have wanted to watch him suffer so?"

Reuben winced as the words hit home. "If it had been Mordicai, I would have worried. He is having a very hard time with tithing. It gets paid only because his good wife insists on it."

Mary's arm slipped into Reuben's free arm and she gave him a squeeze. "See, Reuben, it is as Joseph told me so many, many times. We must have faith and continue on, striving to do our best each day. He was right. Only if we keep our faith can we smile and go on as we should. All things work out in the end. We just can't see them clearly now."

Jesus flashed a warm smile at his mother. It was as though he had said, "You are going to make it, Mother. Father has trained you well."

James did not allow gloomy thoughts to stay for long. His questions kept them all busy and laughing. "Philip said they made his

. . . Behold Thy Son

group go without food and drink for five days. I can't take that."

"James, James. You have been there before. You know that is not done. Why are you so gullible? Have we not taught you?" James ducked the hand set to ruffle his hair.

"Just leave my hair alone. I'm not a kid anymore. I am twelve and know what's what." Ducking quickly, James ended up on the other side of the donkeys.

Jesus leaned over. "James, anyone who believes Philip's tall tales needs to be reminded he is still a kid once in a while.

"See that stream over there? How about a swim? There is plenty of time to catch up afterward. Is that all right, Mother?" Although he had assumed much of Joseph's responsibilities, Jesus looked to Mary as head of the family.

"All right. But do not tarry too long. We are going fairly fast." Watching the boys scamper to the water, the three friends waved then started on. They must not get too far from the main group.

"You certainly do give Jesus a lot of freedom." Reuben was frowning slightly.

"Yes, but he has never disappointed me, so I am able to continue to do so." Mary prodded the pokey donkey in the ribs.

"Joseph helped me to see that Jesus is different in that way. He senses responsibility more than most children. He has never made a child cry with his teasing. Instead he helps them see themselves as they are and they laugh, too."

"He has certainly learned from his father. At times I have to take hold of myself and say 'that is Jesus—not Joseph.'" Reuben shook his head in amazement. Rachel nodded in agreement.

"I know," murmured Mary, "I know."

"Mother, did you notice how John has changed?" Jesus took the bundles from his mother and tied them onto the donkey. "Whoa, there. Hold still. This is not going to hurt. Did I hurt you on the way to this fair city?"

"Yes, he seemed so quiet and far away. He must not be eating properly." Mary returned to get yet another bundle. The extra bundles came from taking advantage of the many shops at Jerusalem. She had saved for months to be able to splurge—just a bit.

"You really spread your resources well, Mother. What is in all these bundles?"

"Oh, I got some soft cloth for baby clothes and some spices I can't get in Nazareth. We used up most of our herbs for your father. And a few odds and ends." Mary had a pat for the donkey's soft nose. Then she made a return trip for another bundle.

"Could you believe John? He said he had learned to prefer locusts to fish. I can see eating them if that is all you can get. But by choice?" Jesus shook his head.

"Now, just because you have had a life of ease and luxury." Mary's finger waggled at her son, but her eyes twinkled merrily.

"Ease and luxury?" gasped Jesus.

"Yes. Ease and luxury," repeated his mother. "Compare John's lot to yours and you have ease and luxury. Here, this is the last one."

"I guess if I look at it that way, you are right." He checked to be sure all was secure and balanced. "You know, Mother, I won't be a bit surprised if John is called to be a prophet. He is certainly preparing for it."

"It certainly seems so." Mary gazed toward the desert regions. "That was what his parents believed was his destiny."

A whirlwind of energy flew around the house and stopped in front of them, cutting off Jesus' questions. James had forgotten his 'grown-up manners' and was enjoying boyish games with new-found friends. "Aw, do we *have* to go today? Couldn't we wait till Lish's parents leave tomorrow? Please!"

"Come on, my dear little brother, we promised Rachel we would be home to take Leah and the boys so she could go to Capernaum with Dan. Or have you forgotten?" Jesus smiled at his brother. He seemed so grown up one minute, yet so young the next.

Downcast eyes and slumped shoulders showed that James had not forgotten. Mary shook her head in amazement. "And to think Rachel was married at this age."

"Married!" James jerked upright. "I'm not getting married! No sir, not me!" Fleeing from the laughter of his mother and brother, James ran to tell Lish "Goodbye, see ya next year."

"Meet us at Reuben's camp in one hour, James," gasped Jesus between gales of laughter.

"Has he told you his plans, Mother?" The final check had been made and they were moving towards Reuben's lodging place.

"Yes. He has chosen wisely. Plants and trees are his love so he must be allowed to choose his own way. He can help you evenings as needed. Also, there will be times in winter when he will have more time." Mary shut the gate behind the donkey.

"I spoke to the steward at the orchards. He agreed to teach

. . . Behold Thy Son

James and help him fill his apprenticeship. I felt he was a kind man—firm but kind."

A smile lit Mary's face. "Just what James needs—firm but kind. I do wish he would work more with you. He has the makings of a good carpenter."

"His heart is not in it. He lives to be with his plants and trees. It would be unfair to insist he work with me."

Two brothers returned for supper, each carrying the marks of his chosen trade. Laughing, Jesus brushed the leaves and dirt from James' robe. Then James took the broom and removed the sawdust from the back of Jesus' robe. James had grown and was nearly as tall as his brother. Both had to stoop to avoid bumping their heads on the low door frame. "After you, dear brother."

"Oh, no. How naive do you think I am? You just want a chance to 'dust off my seat' when I stoop to go through the door. Besides, you are the elder. Age goes first." The broom settled back into its place. James stepped back.

"The eldest must be polite. You go first." Twinkling eyes confirmed James' guess. Jesus stepped back, bowing low to beckon his brother to go ahead.

"So, be polite and take your place as you should." A poke in his ribs and a flip of the wrist sent James whirling like a top. When he regained his balance, James found his brother safely in the house. "I forgot about that trick."

Joining his brother and mother in the spicy smelling kitchen, James saw Jesus poking his nose into the stew pot. Mary popped his hand with a long spoon. She disliked lids lifted. "Lets all the smell out," she said. Supper would be great again tonight.

"I passed Sarah hobbling down the street. I took her scowl and 'Humph!' to indicate she had been here, trying once again to help you see the wisdom of your 'fine, upright son taking my sweet little granddaughter, Sarah, to wife. Why, she is the spitting image of me. No finer beauty or wife could be found.'"

Laughing at James' imitation of her departed guest, Mary found it hard to scold him. Jude popped up with, "'And don't forget, my dear Mary, I have been your son's most loyal supporter all his life.'" Holding their sides, the family laughed till tears ran down their faces.

"Won't she ever give up?" gasped James. "She has tried on every one. You would think she would realize it is Jesus who will choose, not her." His sleeve served to wipe the tears of laughter.

"I keep telling her, and the rest, that he will choose in his own good time. Until then, I will enjoy having him as head of our household." Mary pulled the lid from the pot, allowing the smell to fill every corner. Tasting the stew, she pronounced it ready. "Wash up and get ready for prayers. I will dish this up so it will be cool enough to eat."

James ate and then left to visit friends. Joses and Jude accepted his invitation to accompany him. Jesus declined the invitation; he wanted to study. The shop was keeping him pretty tied up. Training young men was harder than he had supposed. His three apprentices were obedient, but one really had more thumbs than fingers. Young Simon knew more than they did.

Mary was also reading. She poked the fire and added another log. Straightening, she looked at her son. Scroll in his lap, Jesus was staring out the window at the stars. Smiling, she went to him and brushed the hair out of his eyes. "You really should marry, Son. You are twenty-six. Even your father was married and a father by that age."

Startled back to reality, Jesus looked questioningly at his mother. "What did you say?"

Gently repeating her words, Mary watched the bewilderment and concern grow in his eyes. "Is there a reason you have put off marriage? Leah has a fine husband and home. James is waiting for you to set the lead. Joses has his eye on Naomi. Jude will soon be ready to look around. So you see, there is no need to worry about us anymore. Rachel and Dan have invited Simon and me to live with them." Her hand rested lightly on his drooping shoulder.

"Mother, Mother. If only I *could* understand," groaned Jesus. "There is so much I don't understand and this is one of the things that bothers me most. I have tried. But it does not seem to be right."

Helpless in the face of her son's anguish, Mary realized for the first time how troubled he was about this matter. All she could do was wait and listen.

"Please! Help James to see he must not wait for me. He really loves Esther. She would make him a good wife. Isachar has his eye on her, too. James better hurry or he will lose her. I have talked to him, but it hasn't helped. James feels I should be married first." Searching his mother's face for understanding, Jesus went on.

"The last thing father talked to me about was the importance of choosing a wife who would support and understand me. I have important work to do, so my wife must be strong and above reproach."

"I see. Then I shall let you do as you feel you must." Mary cradled her son's head in her loving arms. He would always be her son no matter what else he became. "Certainly you have never given cause to distrust your judgment." Kissing him on the top of his head, Mary returned to her spot. "We will be grateful for your help and guidance.

"And . . . ," she flashed a smile at him, "I *did* talk to James. Yesterday. I believe he has gone to ask for Esther's hand tonight. I, too, heard of Isachar's plans. James was too busy planning to be aware of the competition and the danger of losing her."

Running steps. Then the door burst open with a crash. "Mother! Mother! She said *yes!*" James was breathless from excitement and running up the hill. First Jude then Joses collapsed against the door. "She really did! I can't believe it!"

"Who said yes to what?" Mary winked at Jesus.

"Esther said *yes*, she will marry *me*." James grabbed Simon up and threw him high into the air. The noise had awakened the sleeping child and he had staggered out to see what was happening.

"Careful there, boys. Someone is likely to get hurt." Mary set the scriptures aside. "So you finally asked her, did you. And she said yes. We are happy for you."

"She thought I would never ask for her hand and nearly said yes to Isachar last night. But then she talked her father into saying no. I nearly lost her!" Wide-eyed, James wiped his brow in relief. "What if she had said yes to Isachar?" He sank to the bench, sprawling backwards on the table.

"See, I told you to go your own speed and not wait for your brother. His mind is full of other things. We are just going to have to go on living around him." Mary started back into the bedchamber with Simon.

"Well, *I* am not going to wait." Joses announced. "Naomi is not going to slip away from *me*. Jude, will you come with me tomorrow?"

"What? Another one?" cried Jude in mock despair.

"Mother, why do you cry when we read of the King?" Simon set the scriptures aside to give his mother a comforting hug.

Jude took them up to continue reading. He was helpless in the face of women's tears. "Because we are the royal house and Jesus is the King."

"Oh, I know all that. But it shouldn't make Mother cry. That is an honor."

"But with honor comes responsibility. And in this case, great and grave responsibility." Mary wiped her eyes and kissed her youngest on the nose. "I am so worried about your brother. He has always been so steady and dependable."

"How long has he been gone? It seems like forever." Simon went to the water jug.

"Forty-eight days. I marked the door frame with an X the day he left and every day since. I counted the X's this morning. There are forty-eight of them."

"How long did he say he planned to be away?" Jude drank the drink Simon had brought him, smiling his thanks.

"He didn't know. He said he felt restless and in need of peace. He said, 'I need some time to myself. Maybe if I talk to John he will be of help to me. The reports of his preaching speak well of his wisdom.' So I suppose that is where he went." Mary wondered if now was the time to tell of her son's mission.

Slow, dragging, deliberate footsteps seemed to be coming up their walk. Mary started, then threw her arms around Simon as Jude took the broom, ready to do battle if need be.

"Mother, are you still up?" Soft, yet firm and steady, that voice belonged to her eldest son. Mary flew to the door, fumbling to get it open.

"Jesus! Jesus! You are back! Come in, son. Come in."

But when the door opened and Jesus stepped inside, the family shrank back. This was not the Jesus they knew. Here stood a man shining with inner strength and purpose. A man who knew what he must do and where he must go. Jesus was no longer just their elder brother, carpenter for Nazareth.

"Mother, is there some food prepared? I am weak and hungry. Since entering Nazareth, the memory of your stew has pulled me on." Jesus sank to the bench, cradling his head in his arms on the table.

Should she get the stew warmed up or care for her son? Torn, Mary stood rooted to the spot. Jude sprang to heat the stew. Simon brought a cool, fresh drink of water.

Taking the dripping cup from his brother, Jesus drank slowly, thirstily. "Thank you, little brother, thank you. It tasted sweeter still

. . . Behold Thy Son

because you served me without me asking for it."

"Would you like more?" Simon's face was alive with joy at having his big brother home again.

"One more, please. I am dry enough to drink the Sea of Galilee." This time, Jesus stayed sitting upright. The water had given him strength.

Mary shook herself to action. "Here, let me wash your feet. No. First, wash your hands and face. You look simply awful!"

"Thank you, Mother." Jesus obediently washed his face and hands. "Looks like you will need clean water. I was pretty dirty at that."

"I am so glad you are home. It has been forty-eight days and long nights." She wiped his feet then slipped fresh sandals onto them.

"Forty-eight days? Are you sure?" Eyes wide, Jesus watched as his mother went to the door frame and counted the X's. "No wonder I am so starved. I could eat a camel."

"Here, big brother. This stew was still a little warm from supper so I did not get it boiling. You can eat it right now." Jude had their biggest bowl full for him. "Eat it all up. You know Mother's feeling about those who do not finish their supper."

"I will try. But you may have to finish it for me. That is another of Mother's rules, remember?" Jesus sighed long and deep. "It has been so long since I ate and drank. Simon's water has nearly filled me up." Jesus smelled the steaming spoonful. "It is so good to be eating your cooking again."

Mary beamed. "I love to care for my family. But why have you not eaten? How long has it been?"

Eating as he figured in his head, Jesus stopped suddenly, spoon in mid-air. "Forty days and forty nights. It has been forty days . . . if you are accurate in your calculations."

"Forty days? But why? Didn't you have money? Were you robbed?" Mary's face was ashen. What had her son been doing? Why?

"Forty days and forty nights without food and water? I *don't believe it!*" Jude shook his head gleefully. "Mother, I do believe we just caught Jesus in his first lie and is it a whopper!" He slapped his knee in delight.

"But it is true, Jude. I can prove it. Remember I told you I might go look up John? Well, I did. All along the way, I met people who had listened to him. All talked of his baptizing and teaching. I knew we must all be baptized to become members in the Kingdom of God. Rabbi has refused to do so, and I knew that was wrong.

"So I went to John to seek baptism of him. The Spirit whispered that I must do so. John was in his rough desert attire, standing in the River Jordan. Spring rains had swelled it to about waist deep. I observed John immersing the people after saying a brief prayer. One young lady stuck her toe up and he baptized her again, fully immersing her this time.

"I knew he was the right person. But did he have authority to do so? No one in the crowd questioned him. But John's teaching was so positive and forthright, few could dispute him. John had not noticed me, so I slipped away, found a quiet spot, and thought things through. It was the eighth day since I had left home. I remember because I ate the last of the eight pieces of cheese Rachel had sent. 'One each day,' she said, 'or you will get fat with all that wandering and no work.' As I ate the cheese, I felt my restless feelings grow stronger. Only when I thought of John would they go away. Kneeling, I asked my Father if John had the authority to baptize in His name. The answer came swiftly and surely: 'Yes, go be baptized by your cousin, John.'

"Rising, I went directly to John, asking for his services. He refused, saying I was without sin. He was baptizing for the remission of sins and *he* had need to be baptized of me. I assured him I must have the blessings of his calling. Our Father requires it of all His children. So he baptized me.

"On rising up out of the water, the heavens were opened. A dove floated gently in the still air. All nature was hushed. No one stirred. Drifting to us, the dove settled on my shoulder, quietly folded its wings, and nibbled at my ear. Hearing John gasp, I looked at him. His eyes were wide and his face ashen. He could not speak. I wondered if he had been struck dumb like his father. But he took me into his arms, wept, and cried out in a loud voice, 'Behold, the Son of God!'

"People watched, then some turned away. A few knew we were dear friends and cousins so felt John was just prejudiced. Others believed and pressed him to explain himself. I slipped away. The old restless feelings were back, worse than ever. Wandering all night, all day on and on, I found myself in the wilderness. No food or water has passed my lips since that cheese I ate before going to John. I have stayed in the wilderness until today. I have found peace and direction. Finding myself very weak, I headed for home.

. . . Behold Thy Son

Here I am."

"I cannot believe it!" exploded Jude. "No man, no matter how fit, can go forty days without water. Food, yes, maybe. But water? *No way!*"

"Moses fasted forty days and forty nights. The writer tells us very plainly he had neither food or water." Jesus seemed to be searching for something deeper than the questions at hand in Jude's face.

"But Moses was a prophet, talking to God. *You* are no prophet." Jude gave him a poke in the ribs.

"Are you sure?" Jesus spoke softly, wistfully.

"Of course not!" exploded Jude in laughter. "You are Jesus of Nazareth, my elder brother. A dreamer perhaps, but no prophet."

Jesus slumped against the table. "Well, little brother." His eyes were sad. Was this the way it would be from now on? "It *is* the truth. Never has a lie passed from my lips. Even in teasing. If your faith is not sufficient to believe me in this, then I fear for you." Eating slowly, Jesus stared into space. "Here, Jude. I really cannot finish it. By Mother's rules, you must." Standing, Jesus handed the nearly-empty bowl to Jude.

"Here. Let me have it, Jesus. No need for either of you to eat so much you become ill. Come, Simon and Jude, time for evening prayers. Jesus can lead us since he is with us again." Mary quickly tidied the table. She looked worried and upset.

When the snoring assured them both boys were asleep, Mary questioned Jesus further. "What happened? How do you know?"

"Remember what John said?" Mary nodded. "A voice came down from heaven as the dove settled on my shoulder. Some—those who believed John's words—heard the voice say, 'This is my beloved Son, in whom I am well pleased.' The peace, joy, and comfort those words gave to my heart! I had been so troubled and restless. I had not been able to receive any answers lately. But, Mother, Father is well pleased! I know for sure. I heard Him say so!"

"A dove. I offered doves at your birth, Jesus. We were too poor for a lamb." Mary's eyes dropped, seeking to hide her tears.

"And, as you said it would be, your offering was accepted. I wandered, full of joy, yet still wondering and wanting to know what I must do. As the sun rose one morning, I found myself in the presence of angels. They taught me much. So many of my questions were answered. I learned the full meaning and purpose of my birth, my heritage. The scriptures were opened as never before and

I saw their meaning. The feelings of restlessness and bewilderment were pushed aside as I was taught and shown the way." Again, Jesus' whole being seemed to glow and shine with inner strength.

"Mother, it will not be easy. Most will not believe me. Jude doesn't. But my way is clear. I know what I must do. My time has come. Please! Please continue to believe in me. You know of my birth. But. . . ," he looked into the dark night trying to push in through the window, "but, thank God, you know not of my death."

"*DEATH!*" gasped Mary.

"Yes, gentle mother." Jesus took her trembling hands, raised them to his lips and kissed them gently, tenderly. "My death. It is part of my work. It must come. But not before the time set for it. So, please, be assured I will be safe and protected until then."

Frantically searching his face, Mary realized Jesus was at peace, so her fears began to melt—slowly. "Must you work alone? No wife, no friends?"

"I will have help. Some will believe and become faithful followers. As for a wife, I cannot say. I have no answer for that."

"When do you begin?"

"On the morrow," he said softly, trying to ease her fears and pain.

"On the morrow?"

"Yes. It is time. My work has begun. I am thirty years old and can legally preach as I have been commanded to do."

Mary slept very little. Her heart was troubled. She heard the smooth, even breathing coming from her son's room. "He is at peace. Why can't I be?" she asked herself.

Chapter Thirteen

RUMORS

"Why has your son closed the shop? Where is he? When will he be back?" Sarah's impatience had grown with her years.

Ushering the angry woman to a chair by the hearth, Mary searched for words to satisfy her guest. "The shop is not closed. Jude is doing fine. He has learned well. The work is going on."

"Going on! You call that going on? Jude will never be the carpenter Jesus is. He is slow and clumsy." The old tongue had not dulled over the years. Sharp and quick, Sarah frequently cut unnecessarily deep with her words.

"Oh, you old hypocrite! You never did like Jesus until he fixed that broken-down old bed for you." Simon's eyes flashed fire and indignation. "He couldn't fix it so he had to practically rebuild it and you only paid the price of fixing it."

"Simon! Simon! Apologize at once! You know we do not talk that way." Mary's surprise was equal to the shame she felt for the conduct of her son. "You have been taught differently from that."

"I will *not!*" Simon planted both feet firmly. Clenched fists on hips, he looked squarely into Sarah's hateful eyes. "I heard what you told Rabbi yesterday. He asked me to clean the trays for him. Neither of you knew I was behind the chest working with the polish rag. It was all I could do to keep quiet. I made up my mind, then and there, that if you *ever* came to our house again, complaining about Jesus, I would tell everyone the truth."

Sarah shrank back into the chair, her conscience stabbing her. Mary stood transfixed at the courage of her young son. She was bewildered by the mixture of pride and shame raging within her breast.

"You told Rabbi you knew on good report that something was definitely wrong with Jesus. He has repeatedly begged for the hand of your granddaughters, yet each has refused him and for very good reasons. You know I have been in this very room eight or nine times and heard *you* begging Jesus to marry your granddaughters. Rabbi knew it, too. Yet you lied to him. Knowing Rabbi knew the truth gave me the strength to keep quiet. Besides, I wanted to hear the rest of your lies. And were they big ones! They took my breath away."

Simon looked at his mother out of the corner of his eye. As long as she was quiet, he had courage to go on. "It was Mother's idea that Jesus fix the wine at Jude's wedding in Cana. She, not Jesus, had the idea. I don't know how he did it. All I know is I helped fill the jars with fresh water. Then I helped serve it to the guests. It was the purest white wine ever served in Cana."

Mary's face burned in memory of that day. The guest list was longer than planned. Food had been prepared in abundance, but she had neglected the wine order. Jude was too happy with his new bride. James was seating the late guests. Joses was nowhere to be seen.

Because of the health of the bride's parents, Mary's family had done an unusual thing. Rather than carry his bride's invalid father over the steep, winding roads to Nazareth, Jude had suggested that the wedding be held in his bride's home instead of at his own. Mary knew none of these strangers. Searching the crowd, Mary's eyes fell upon Jesus. "Yes. He now has power from his Father. He can help." Never would she forget his rebuke, nor the kind look in his eyes. "Woman, what wilt thou have me to do for thee? That will I do; for mine hour is not yet come." Face burning in shame, she had obeyed his instructions.

Here was one more mystery to store away in her heart. Jesus was no longer subject to her wishes. His was a greater work. From the results of his instructions, she knew she had not been mistaken. He did have power. But *He,* not *she,* was to decide how and when to use it. His power was not to be used for the gratification of appetite or passion.

Why had she even thought to have him help? Oh yes. He had shared with her his experiences with Satan during his forty days of fasting. Satan had known of his ability to change stones into bread. But Jesus had not done so—even when in such dire need for himself. There were natural means to provide such needs, so he must not use his special powers to do so.

I understand it a bit better—I think.

"Mary! Are you going to stand there and . . . and let this . . . this child talk to me like this?" Sarah was standing, white and shaken in the face of the truth.

"But, Mother, all I have spoken is the truth. You know it. I know it. And. . . ," he shook a finger at Sarah, "and *you* know it, too, if only you will be honest with yourself." Simon was not going to give in until directed to do so by his mother.

Praying for guidance, Mary went to her son. Putting an arm around him, she began to speak in a soft, trembling voice. "Son, you are right *and* wrong. You are right to defend your brother and his honor. But this is the wrong way. Please apologize for your lack of manners, not for defending your brother."

Eyes downcast, knowing his mother was right, Simon tried to speak the words of apology. But they seemed to stick in his throat, halfway up and halfway down. Swallowing hard, he began again. "I . . . I am . . . sorry for disgracing my mother this way." As Simon looked up at his opponent, his flashing eyes caused Sarah to shrink against the door. "But I better not hear of your lying about my brother again." He had spoken as softly as his mother had, yet his words flew as a sword into the heart of the vengeful Sarah.

Clasping her breast and crying out in the face of such courage, she fled the house of the carpenter. Never again would she dare enter.

Still burning from the memory of that day, Sarah joined the cries, "Do away with him. Who does he think he is? What right does he have to pass judgment and try to teach us." Adding to the fury of the crowd, Sarah grabbed something to throw at him.

"Please, please, not here. Not in the synagogue." Rabbi begged them to stop and think, but Sarah's voice was shrill and loud. She followed them to the top of the hill just above Mary's home.

Mary heard the commotion and ran to see what was happening. Her heart lurched when she saw Jesus being pushed toward the cliff. Why didn't he resist? Where was the protection promised him? "Stop! Stop! Please listen to him! He has an important message!" screamed Mary at the raging crowd.

Pushing and clawing her way to him, Mary fell at his feet. Seeing the weeping woman pleading for her son, the crowd fell back, ashamed. Sarah tried in vain to whip them into action. Seeing no help forthcoming, she rushed forward to shove him over by herself. Jesus caught the feeble old woman and saved her from toppling over the steep cliff herself. Simon was allowed to pass forward through the crowd. He helped Jesus lift the trembling Mary to her feet and turn her toward home.

Jesus stood and looked at his beloved friends, neighbors, relatives, and customers. Tears of sorrow running down his face, he left without another word. To these people he would always be just "Jesus, the carpenter's son. " But he knew and understood his true identity: he had accepted his mission.

The crowd melted to let him pass unhindered. Some felt a loss at his going, others felt shame for their actions, but most felt joy at ridding the town of a lunatic.

The lonely days stretched into lonely months. Mary realized Jesus was wise to stay away from Nazareth, but she longed to see him . . . to talk to him . . . to ask if the stories were true.

Rachel and Dan had moved into the old home. It was bigger and the garden spot much more fertile. Things had been going badly for the family since Jesus began teaching. Dan had not been able to keep working as steadily. The sale of their house helped considerably to relieve the debts that had piled up. Rachel's son, Joshua, and Simon were both away from home, learning the trade of tanning leather. Capernaum had a lovely shop and Peter's father-in-law knew the proprietor. Arrangements made, Mary kissed her youngest son goodbye, then welcomed her daughter and family into her too silent home. Once again the laughter and sounds of little feet filled the home.

"Simon's letter said Jesus is at Salome and Zebedee's again. He spent some time with the boys. Their overseer let them have a day to go fishing with James and John on their big boats. Now Simon is wishing he had become a fisherman." Mary was grateful Simon wrote often. His letters told of Jesus and his work.

"It is a good thing Simon writes or we would never know what Joshua is doing." Rachel smiled at the baby nursing at her breast. "They grow up so fast and are gone so soon."

"I know. Too fast and gone too soon." Mary began weaving.

The loom had worked beautifully since that short visit of Jesus. No warning, just a shadow in the doorway and a voice saying, "That loom squeaks so loudly I heard it from the bottom of the hill." Startled from her daydreaming, Mary had been unable to believe her ears. But her eyes confirmed the good news. Trying to untangle her feet from the yarn, she had become tangled worse and worse. Jesus had to untangle her skirts, feet, and the yarn. Then they were both able to say, "Hello, I love and miss you."

The day had passed too quickly, yet between eating, talking, sharing news, and just enjoying being together, Jesus had worked on the loom so that it did not squeak. "I just needed to take some of the swelling out of one joint. Did it get wet or something?"

"No, I don't recall it getting wet." Hearing a muffled giggle from Rachel, Mary had started to laugh. "Oh, yes. It did get wet. Your little nephew decided to wash my feet for me. I had been thinking of your father and was off in another world. Next thing I knew, my feet were wet and cold. Of course I jumped. Poor dear. I frightened him so badly he fell backwards on the floor, upsetting the water. Never have I seen such a little bit of water go so far. We both had to change."

"Poor Benjy was so afraid he would be scolded. But he and Mother have a signal worked out now. He is to whistle before he touches her when she is thinking like that. I can still see Mother's face." Rachel had melted into laughter.

"No wonder it squeaked. You probably forgot all about the loom in your concern for Benjy. No harm done. It is fine now." Jesus had smiled, but he seldom laughed anymore. He seemed to carry the weight of the world on his shoulders. Mary had noticed a slight stoop or slump when he sat down.

Rachel's words broke into Mary's thoughts, "And they claim she is an adulteress. Can you believe that?"

"Believe what? About whom?" The weaving seemed smooth and tight, in spite of her daydreaming.

"Mary Magdalene. Mother! Weren't you listening? Where were you this time?" Rachel's exasperation caused her to speak rather sharply.

"I am so sorry. I was thinking of Jesus' last visit. Please start again. This time I will pay attention." The loom began its rhythmic hum once again.

"Reports are that Jesus has 'taken up with' Mary Magdalene. She is reported to have been possessed with devils—one of which is adultery. He cured her of it and has had her in his company ever since."

. . . Behold Thy Son

"That is not uncommon. Many men and women travel with him. The twelve seldom leave his side." Mary saw no reason for her alarm. This was not unusual behavior for a teacher and his followers.

"Isachar and his wife went to hear him over at Capernaum last week. They saw with their own eyes how he looks at her. She served him as a wife would do. And she looked at him in the same way." Rachel jabbed her needle into the cloth as if to emphasize the point. "Ouch!" She sucked her finger, looking sheepish.

"Serves you right for believing such nonsense." The two laughed lightly together. The sleeping baby stirred in its basket at Rachel's feet.

Benjy came bursting through the open door. "He's here! He's here! And he brought a lady."

"Who is here? Catch your breath so you can talk plainly." Rachel steadied the excited boy.

"Who is here with a lady?" Mary was at his side feeling his head to see if he was ill.

Brushing his grandmother's hand aside, Benjy sputtered. "Jesus. I saw him down the hill. He had a group of people but sent them on to Cana and is leading the lady by the hand up the road to here. I saw it! I really did!"

"He has found her. Jesus is bringing his chosen companion home." Mary frantically began straightening and cleaning the already spotless home. "Rachel! We must not disgrace your brother with our untidiness. Quickly! Clean up these messes. Wash your face and comb your hair! Oh dear! Where is my scarf?"

"Mother, Mother, you are jumping to conclusions. Slow down. You will make yourself sick." Rachel tried in vain to pull Mary back to the loom.

"You said yourself, not five minutes ago that Jesus had chosen a wife." Mary refused to sit.

"He's here! He's here!" Benjy bounded from the gate to the door and back again. "I knew it was you. I just knew it!"

"Hello there, young fellow." Swinging the squealing boy up into the air, Jesus' laughter floated through the open door. Mother and sister rushed to the door, remembered their manners, stepped aside to let the other through first, then started—together—once more. "Dancing in the doorway? What is the occasion, dear Mother and sister?" Jesus stooped, set the boy down, and gathered them into his arms.

Turning back to the doorway, he held his hand out to the woman waiting—a bit frightened—just outside. "Come in, my love. I believe things are quiet enough now. It is safe for you to enter." A blushing, trembling, beautiful woman stepped into the cool room. "Mother, Rachel," bowing to the small boy, "Benjy, please meet Mary of Magdala. She is my choice—if and when there is time."

Stunned at the announcement, so long awaited, neither Mary nor Rachel could find words to speak. Mary embraced the beautiful woman and led her to a seat. "See, I told you they had given up on me." Jesus slipped an arm around Rachel who poked him in the ribs with her elbow.

"We did not. It is just that we have heard . . . " Embarrassed, Rachel went no further.

"Heard the stories?" Mary Magdalene spoke for the first time. Her voice was soft and trembling. "I told you they would." She looked to Jesus for support.

"Oh," broke in Mary, "we heard them but considered their source." She began preparations for washing their feet. "We know our Jesus well enough to know he would not choose someone with a sordid past. Besides," Mary blushed at the memory, "there were those who were cruel in their accusations of me at the time Father and I were wed."

Relieved, Jesus took the basin from his mother. "I knew I could count on you, Mother. Part of the stories are true. I did cast the devils from her, but she is pure—pure as the driven snow. And she understands my work." Mary watched as her son bathed the feet of his beloved. "Because of the devils, men have feared her and left her alone. You see, she is beautiful beyond belief."

"It is such a relief to be free of the evil spirits. I was powerless. I didn't know what was wrong or what to do. My family nearly deserted me. Then I heard of your son. I would creep down to hear him speak, but would become so torn inside that I would run screaming into the closet. My father dragged me to him in despair, begging for help. When Jesus' eyes looked into mine, two forces began a final war inside my body. Screaming in pain, I lashed at him to destroy what I felt had caused the awful pain. He caught my arms in his strong hands and held me powerless. It took my father, Simon Peter, James, and John to hold me quiet enough for Jesus to anoint my head and cast out the evil spirits. So great was the relief, I fell unconscious to the ground. It took several days to

. . . Behold Thy Son

recover because I was so drained." Mary Magdalene looked from one face to another wondering what the women were thinking.

"I, too, felt the power of those devils. Looking into her tormented eyes, I found the reason for such torment. Satan knew of her special mission on the earth and had done all in his power to destroy her. But her strong will prevented him from harming her. He fought hard, but the power from my Father and my love were stronger."

Mary Magdalene slipped her feet into the fresh, cool slippers. "Oh, how lovely and soft." Mary's blush betrayed her hand in making them.

"Yes, Mother is an excellent weaver." Jesus stepped out to throw the water onto the garden. "Your garden is doing well. James must still help."

"Yes, he is very strict on what is done and not done to 'his' garden. We had fresh greens for supper last night."

"I love fresh greens," cried Mary Magdalene. Then she saw Rachel's face. Trying to sort out her feelings, Rachel was torn inside. She knew she should trust her brother's judgment, but . . .

Jesus, following Mary Magdalene's eyes, realized Rachel needed more time. "Rachel, Rachel, why are you so cloudy?"

"You are so . . . so old . . . and still so . . . unmarried."

"My family is wealthy and were able to provide for me. Because of my 'illness' as they called it, no man would have me to wife." Mary Magdalene wondered if Rachel believed her.

"You should see her mother. Almost as pretty as mine." Jesus kissed his mother's blushing cheek.

"Now, could we ask for some food?" he asked. "We are very hungry."

Remembering her duties as hostess, Rachel began preparations for a quick meal. "When will you be married?"

"Not at the present. His work won't allow time for it," responded Mary Magdalene.

"It would be too dangerous." Seeing his mother's horror, Jesus went on quickly. "Then the priests would be able to use her to hurt me. I am in no danger, Mother. Not yet."

Mary's thoughts matched the hard rhythm of bread kneading. Always grateful for a chance to release some of her tension, she had decided to begin this task earlier than usual today. Rumors had become more cruel and threatening. Each day dawned darker and more ominous than the day before. Even James and Joses had begun to wonder if they were wrong to defend their elder brother.

Mary thought of a family dinner when James voiced the problem. "But, Mother, he is bringing shame and disgrace to our family. He is encouraging people to revolt."

"Yes, and I heard he actually refused to pay taxes."

"Now, James, I know that is a lie. Simon Peter himself told me what happened. It was not at all like what Rabbi said." Mary had served them fig cakes, hoping to soften them a bit. "What Jesus said was, 'Of whom do the kings of the earth take custom or tribute? Of their own children or of strangers?' I believe it was Simon Peter who followed his instructions and found the gold piece in the fish to pay the temple taxes."

"That's another thing." Joses loved those fig cakes. "How did Jesus know about that gold in the fish? Where did he get that kind of power?"

"*We* don't have that kind of power. You don't and certainly Father didn't. So it must be from the devil. There is no other answer . . . is there?"

How could Mary answer and make them understand. Joseph certainly did not have that power. But Jesus was not Joseph's son. And his Father certainly *did* have that power and could give it to His son. Yet, try as she might, Mary had been unable to tell her sons that Jesus was different and why. Something always stopped her. Somehow the words would never come. Why?

This was so hard for Mary to accept and understand. Surely, now it should be known. Perhaps the knowledge would help stem the tide of lies and bitterness that was growing. James, Joses, Jude, and Simon, but especially the girls were beginning to believe the rumors. She could no longer convince them that Jesus was a good, fine man.

"Well, he is certainly holding himself above the rest of us. Always putting on airs." James had stalked to the garden.

"Where did he get the right to cleanse the temple? That is what I can't see!" Joses had noticed the fuel box empty and started for more.

"I have wondered and wondered about that, too. It must have started the day we presented him at the temple. He became so frightened with all the noise and confusion. We have never taken a baby back there—unless it was required."

"Oh, Mother! You are forgetting the time he ran away and spent

. . . Behold Thy Son

three days in the temple alone." James had laid the greens on the table.

"He was in a different part of the temple. It was the money-changers he drove out. The sight of all that captivity and blood always made him sick, to say nothing of the craftiness and lying of the moneychangers."

"Caiaphas permits it. They are one and the same group. Another thing, eating and drinking with Samaritans, publicans, and sinners."

"Don't forget, brother, Matthew is a tax-collector."

"But an honest one, boys." Helplessly, Mary had grasped at any help she could see.

"Says who? Our brother? Our brother who keeps that . . . that . . . woman with him?" James had shuddered.

"That woman is pure and honest. I know that. If you had come when I sent for you, you would have met her and known for yourself. But you were 'too busy,' so you said." Mary's tone let them know her displeasure at their conduct.

"It is time he married and settled down. His constant wandering and relying on the kindness of people could make married life a bit haphazardous, though." Joses had smiled, then begun in mocking tones. "Please, may my wife, six children, and I eat at your table and sleep at your hearth? We have nothing with which to pay you but a message of hope, love, and faith."

"Stop it! Joses, You should be ashamed of yourself. You know your brother is not a loafer. When not teaching or healing the sick, he is busy mending, fixing, and building for those kind enough to let him stay." A lioness had no more courage than Mary at that moment.

James had put an arm around his angry mother and led her to a seat trying to soothe her ruffled feathers. "What upsets me is his apparent lack of reverence for the Law. Most of his work seems to be on the Sabbath. That is what I can't understand."

"Nor do I," Mary had sobbed, "nor do I."

Long after the boys had gone, Mary had pondered the issue, trying to understand why her son had forsaken the Law. "Not really forsaken it, just sort of set parts of it aside." Talking to Rabbi had confused her even more.

Finally she had gathered together some special treats she knew he would like and inquired as to where Jesus could be found. Reports confirmed his stay in Capernaum for the winter. Mary had suggested Jesus look up her cousins and seek lodging with them. Since that first visit, her son had been as welcome as could be in the home of Zebedee and Salome. James and John were just older than Jesus, but they immediately became fast friends. Reports were that they were among the first to believe and accept his teachings.

"I shall go to him. I can see Simon and Joshua, too. Joses and Naomi are in Jericho, but perhaps James would take time to go hear his brother."

"What is that you are saying, Mother?" Dan had been delighted to catch her talking to herself again.

"I said . . . You know perfectly well what I said, Dan. You just want to tease me for talking out loud again." Mary had set aside her mending to get herself a drink.

"If I heard you right, you are planning to ask James to take you to see Jesus at Capernaum. You have heard of his plans? He thought he was being so careful that no one could suspect him."

"Suspect him of what?"

"Of wanting to go hear his brother." Dan had taken the empty water jug, and replaced it with the fresh, full one.

"Why should he be ashamed of that? When does he plan to go?" The fresh water had been so cool and tasty that Mary drank two dippers full.

"Two days hence. Rachel would like to go, too, if she would only be honest enough to admit it."

"Then I shall provide the reason for them both. They can take a poor, distraught mother to see her son."

"You are so special, Mother. Please don't ever change." Dan had hugged his mother-in-law. "No wonder Jesus is so wise and good."

Mary had grasped his hands. "Then you believe? You believe Jesus' teachings?"

"You forget we are best friends from way back. Rachel's unbelief and fears have kept me from being open in my support. Perhaps this visit will help swing her in the right direction."

Mary gave the bread one last punch. But it hadn't. It only served to draw her farther away.

Jesus was not at Salome's. Nor had he come when they sent word they were there. After the second day, Mary and the family had gone to where Jesus was teaching. Not able to get to him, word was sent on. The message he returned had infuriated Rachel, upset

James, and puzzled Simon and Joshua. "Who is my mother? and who are my brethren?" Mary understood, "Whosoever shall do the will of my Father which is in Heaven, the same is my brother and sister, and mother." He was reminding her once again that his Father's work came first, and they were no longer first priority. Even when he came for supper, Rachel had not softened her heart. The family could not realize the importance of believing and following their brother if they wanted to be a part of him.

Rachel returned from the market prepared to make bread. "Oh, you beat me to it. Thank goodness. I am so tired that I would appreciate a chance to rest." She sank to the bench.

Drying her hands, Mary pulled her daughter out into the warm afternoon sun. "Come, let us enjoy the sun a few moments. We've hardly used the new bench Dan fixed for us."

Allowing herself to be ushered outside, Rachel sank to the bench. "I do not see how you do it, Mother. You are always so cheerful. I know you are worried about Jesus and since Grandmother Rachel's death, I know you are lonely."

"Yes, many times a day I find myself on the way out the door to share something with her. Then I think of her visiting with my dear mother and father and your father, catching them up on all the news."

"Have you forgotten Jason?" Rachel's eyes softened as she remembered his tragic death.

"No, I would never forget dear Jason." Laying her head back, Mary closed her eyes. Memories flooded her mind. "I wonder who greeted Grandmother Rachel first."

"I know who will greet Reuben first," laughed Rachel.

"No doubt there." Happy sounds of the village filled the sunlit courtyard. "Did you hear of Lazareth's death? He and his sisters have been so kind to your brother. How marvelous that Jesus was able to call him back. They need him so very much."

"Why didn't he come raise Rachel? He was close enough to come." Bitterness made her words snap in the hot air.

"Because Rachel was tired. Her life was ended. No need to bring her back to the hardships she would face."

"Reuben needs her. He is lost without her."

"Yes, but Rachel could not have been left. Reuben has more strength than Rachel. Since Jason's death, Rachel has clung to Reuben, frantically." Mary leaned into the warm sun.

"That is true." Rachel sank back and relaxed again.

"Mother! Rachel!" Simon rushed up the hill, through the gate and into the house before the startled women realized what was happening.

"Out here, in the garden. Simon, why are you home? Where is Joshua?" Rachel hurried to the door.

"Mother, are you here, too? Jesus is in danger! I heard the priests plotting how to trap and kill him. Telling Jereboam I was ill, I left to come and seek your help. Jesus will listen to you. You must go to him!" Simon was breathless, frightened and half sick with worry.

Knives tearing at her heart, Mary sought to quiet her son's fears. "Jesus will be safe. His work is important. He has the promise that his life will not be taken until his work is finished."

"Mother! Do you believe that?" Rachel stood open-mouthed, unbelieving.

"Better close your mouth or a fly will drop in, and you will have no need for supper." Somehow, Mary needed to find a way to help Rachel believe in her brother. Turning back to her son, Mary wiped the dust from his face. "Why do they want to kill him?"

"Because he is setting himself up as a god. He says he is the Son of God—the Only Begotten in the Flesh." Simon shook his head.

"You know that is a lie!" exploded Rachel as she sank to the bench.

"Go on, son." Better not answer just yet.

"He keeps himself as someone different and above the points of the Law. No need for him to pay the temple tax."

"But he paid it, after explaining it was his Father's so he should be exempt. He did not wish to give offense." Mary sank to the bench.

"With money from a fish." Rachel shook her head. "How did he know that money would be there?"

"The priests were furious when he paid. They were going to use it to accuse him. No matter how they try, he destroys their plans. Now they are looking for people to testify for money." Simon sank to the ground at his mother's feet.

"Satan is getting worried. Jesus must be doing good work."

"Mother! How can you joke about this?" Rachel was very, very angry.

"Who's joking, my daughter? Not I."

When Luke came seeking audience with the Teacher's mother, Mary felt drawn to him. He was not the usual visitor, seeking ways to trap her son. Instead, he seemed to be searching for reasons to believe in him. After visiting in their home three days, Luke asked if she would walk with him. "I want to visit some of the places your son loved." A basket lunch swung on his free arm as they climbed to the pastures.

"You believe him, don't you?" Mary was resting from the steep climb.

"Yes, I do. Many times in my work as physician, I have felt a power greater than my own, guiding me, giving strength where none had been before. Gentle mother, I know he heals the people. I see and examine them before and after."

"Why are you questioning, then?"

"Because I cannot understand how and why he does it. He is in grave danger. It is getting worse, yet his only concern is for others."

Thinking on it afterwards, Mary could not remember how or when she began. Yet, before they left the hill, the gentle Luke had been told the whole story from the visit of Gabriel to the last visit with Jesus. She also shared Elisabeth's and Zacharias' experiences. Why had she been allowed to tell him and not the family? Would it help protect her son?

Perhaps he can use his power and influence to turn the tide. When the truth is known, the people will have to believe.

However, Luke did not share her story with anyone. Understanding more clearly than Mary the danger her son was in, he knew what lies and stories would be used against mother and son if the truth of Jesus' birth was told abroad. He felt the people were not ready for it. It would be casting pearls before swine. He did write it down before he left the humble home. Perhaps he could share the story with Peter, James, and John.

Chapter Fourteen

THE TREE

The tiny garments, stitched so lovingly, led Mary's thoughts to the first baby clothes she had made. "How I wish we had some of that white silk Elisabeth and Zacharias gave me for Jesus."

"Why did you go to them, Mother? Were you that lonesome for your parents?" Rachel held the finished gown up for inspection.

"You have done an excellent piece of work. Such tiny stitches and so even, too." Mary's hand caressed the soft cloth.

"Grandma, why do you always hum or sing?" Little Rachel tugged at Mary's sleeve. "I love it when you sing."

"Because my heart is so full of love and gratitude, my dear. Would you like to learn this song?" Mary helped the child into her lap.

"Oh, yes. Please help me learn it." The room soon became filled with merry voices.

Rachel seemed out of sorts. The music was her mother's excuse for not answering her questions. Impatiently she sent her daughter to the garden for onions. Once again she asked why Mary had gone to Elisabeth's in such a hurry. She had heard the old stories again that very morning as she approached the well for the day's water.

Trying to frame an answer, Mary leaned back and looked at her daughter. Anciently, Rachel was the younger sister and by far more fair and desirable than her sister Leah. My daughters are not like that, she thought. Rachel is oldest and not as attractive as Leah. Maybe it is because Leah is tiny with a fair complexion. Rachel is built like Reuben's Rachel and Leah is more like me—never an extra bit of fat.

"Mother! Aren't you going to give me an answer?"

"Rachel, Rachel, I have told you a dozen times why I went to Juttah. You are never happy with my answer. That is the only answer I can give you. I *had* to go to find strength and purpose."

A neighbor's call pulled Rachel outside. Grateful for the respite from her daughter's doubting questions, Mary gathered up her sewing and slipped away for a quick nap.

Sleep, however, refused to come. Thoughts kept racing through her mind. Not of Jesus, but of John. John. Poor John. He had lost his father while still a baby. Elisabeth had to stay in hiding to protect her son. Certainly John's had not been a normal childhood. Thank goodness he would no longer be hurt. What a terrible way to die and for such a foolish reason, to satisfy the selfish whims of a wicked woman. No wonder Jesus had grieved so deeply. They had been so close, closer than brothers. Each had sensed the importance of the other's work and had been drawn closely together.

Jesus had mourned John's imprisonment almost as if he knew it would be the end for John. Then the disciples of his beloved cousin brought the tragic news of John's death. "How like my firstborn. He sought solitude to pray and find comfort from his Father. Still, when the crowd followed, *their* comfort became his main concern. Seeing so many sick and infirm, he stretched forth his hands and healed them."

"What are you talking about, Mother?" Rachel had returned and found her mother by following the sound of her voice.

"Was I talking out loud again? My, I must be getting old."

"Not old, Mother, just worried and concerned."

"I was just thinking about Jesus and how he found comfort in healing at the time of John's death."

"Yes, that is what one would expect from Jesus. Others and their sorrows have always come first with him." Gathering her little daughter into her arms, Rachel sat on her mother's bed. Perhaps now she would get some answers.

"Can you believe the reports, Mother? Five thousand men, their wives and children fed out of thin air."

"Why not? He changed water into wine. Or have you forgotten?"

164

"No, I have not forgotten. I can't, for the life of me, figure out how he did that. But I have figured out how he fed the five thousand." The sleeping child was laid gently in her grandmother's welcoming arms.

"How?"

"Well, it is really quite simple. They all had lunches and things tucked away, so as the blessing was said, they pulled them out and shared." The smug look on Rachel's face alarmed her mother.

"Rachel, Rachel, where is your faith? Why won't you believe? No, daughter, that is not how it was done. He has power we do not understand." Mary's troubled eyes searched Rachel's face in vain. Rachel would not let herself believe.

"What happened next is very acceptable. True to your brother's nature, he sent the disciples on the ship so they would not be harmed by the angry crowd. Next he told them he was not the king they were looking for and sent the people home to think on his words."

"James said he slipped away again for a period of prayer and meditation. James could not understand why Jesus would not let them crown him king. The people were so willing and anxious, but Jesus would not." Rachel pulled the robe over her daughter and mother.

"Because they wanted him to be king and keep them fed in that easy, miraculous way. They would then have no need to work or do anything for themselves. Can you see Jesus agreeing to such plans?"

"No, Mother, I can't. Work is too good for us for Jesus to ever be a party to such foolishness." Silence seeped into the room. Mary almost dozed off when Rachel's question jarred her awake.

"How did he do it? James said it was real. But I can't see how he could." Gone was the antagonism from Rachel's face. Now puzzlement and bewilderment were easy to read on her whole being.

"Could what?" asked the sleepy mother.

"Still the storm. How can Jesus command even the waves and wind to be still? If James had not been there and seen it with his own eyes, I would never believe it."

"If Jesus can command the loaves and fishes to multiply and feed five thousand, their wives and children, why not command the waves and the wind?"

A long, thoughtful pause, then a very small, trembling voice began, "I guess it boils down to that, doesn't it? I have to decide if

. . . Behold Thy Son

he really does have powers or not."

"Yes, my daughter, it boils down to that. You must decide for yourself. James and Jude are beginning to see and accept. But you must decide for yourself."

"Mary, isn't that son of yours going to come and show us the signs and wonders he does everywhere else?" The women looked up from their washing, waiting for her reply. Even Rachel had paused.

Only Mary continued her work.

"Mother, didn't you hear Dorcas' question?"

"Yes, I heard. But I have no answer. He did come again. He tried again. Yet once again our people rejected him and threw him out." Mary's arms scrubbed even harder.

"Small wonder! He did not heal or do any great thing. He just looked into our lives and stood as judge."

"What right does he have to judge and teach us? He is not Rabbi!"

"But you have to admit, Dorcas, Jesus is different."

"Oh, different is right, sister. He is aloof and superior."

"You are mistaken," cried Miriam. "He is not aloof, just quiet and kind. He is more like his father every day."

"Humph!" snorted Dorcas. "I guess I didn't know Joseph as you did."

"No," murmured Mary, "you don't know his Father."

"Rachel, I guess your theory of the way your brother fed the people got blown to the winds."

"How is that, Esther?" Rachel began to lay the clean clothes out to dry.

"Well, this time when he fed the crowds, they had been with him for three days—four thousand men, their wives and children. Not so many, but after three days their lunches would all be gone."

"You don't mean you believe all that . . . that stuff?" exploded Dorcas.

"Yes, I do. There is too much to ignore. I knew and trusted Jesus before and I know James and Jude. They are beginning to swing back again. Dan has never doubted Jesus. Or am I mistaken, Rachel?"

Red-faced, Rachel choked on the words. "No, Dan has always taken Jesus' side. We never discuss him any more."

A knife turning in her heart would cause Mary no more pain

than the strugglings she read on her daughter's face. At first the family had been flattered and thrilled at the success of their oldest brother. But as the tide of public opinion turned and Jesus declared his Sonship, Joseph's children had pulled away in shame. They knew their father was rightful king of the people. But to intimate he was God and Father in Heaven? Oh, no! Anyone would know better than that. Joses seemed most affected and had left the family who loved him so very much. James and Jude had found him and persuaded Joses that Mary still loved and needed him as her special son.

It was true—Jesus and his work was tearing the family apart. Mary read disbelief and fear in their faces. James and Jude were beginning to find a semblance of peace. Dan had been so patient with them. But his efforts had been in vain where his wife was concerned. Tension in their once happy home became thicker every day. Mary feared for her daughter. Prayers had not seemed to help. Even gentle Leah's pleas had been turned aside.

If only I could tell her that Eloheim is his father. Joseph is her father, but not Jesus'. Why? Why can't I tell her?

"Mary, I can't believe they will kill him." Esther's arms tried to convey comfort and solace to the troubled woman.

"Jesus will be protected. I have his promise for that. It is Rachel for whom I mourn now. I cannot help her find peace. No matter where I turn, she becomes more upset and confused." Together, the women watched Rachel's hurried and clumsy efforts to finish and leave so she could cry in private.

Shamed by the feelings that her thoughtless questions had stirred, Dorcus struggled to help the trembling Rachel. Grabbing an armload of damp clothes from the rocks, she threw them toward the basket just as Rachel moved it closer to herself. Horrified, Dorcus watched the clean clothes land in the sand. "Oh, Rachel! I'm so sorry. I didn't know you were going to move the basket. Here, let me wash them again for you."

"Oh, just leave me alone, you . . . you. . ." Rachel's anger caused her to be careless and she landed in the water with a splash. As the horrified women watched helplessly, Rachel floundered and lost her footing once again. This time, splashing water on them all.

"Rachel, Rachel," laughed Mary. "Thank you for cooling us all off. However, if you refuse to let me help you out, we will all have to start our washing again."

Rachel accepted the outstretched hand. Glaring from one face to

. . . Behold Thy Son

the other, she defied them to laugh. Then she looked closely at her tiny mother who was helping her up. Mary's eyes were dancing and her mouth was screwed up tight to keep from laughing. "Oh, Mother, you are all wet and you didn't even fall in."

"I know," burst out as Mary lost the battle and doubled over with laughter. The air rang with laughter as Rachel flopped by her mother on the bank, laughing so hard she hurt. Tension gone, all joined in a good laugh. Only the doves seemed upset—flying away in a startled sweep.

Washing done, visiting at a standstill, Mary and Rachel climbed the steep path to their home. "Here, Mother, let me carry it. You are too tired." Rachel pulled at the basket in an effort to free it from her mother's grasp. "No, dear. I am fine. That laugh did me a world of good. Thank you, Rachel, for being a good sport. My, you did look silly." Laughter poured out again, causing Mary to stumble.

"Careful there, Mother. Let's sit right here and rest. We have a few moments before we have to get home. I have one more question for you." Rachel pulled her mother down on the wall beside her.

Oh, dear, what now? thought Mary.

"You did it again today. And I want to know why." Rachel turned so she was looking directly into Mary's face.

"Did what?" Mary looked into her daughter's troubled eyes.

"You do it all the time. When you talk to Jesus about Father you call him Joseph. But you call him 'your father' when talking to the rest of us. And today, when Dorcas said she guessed she didn't know Joseph very well, you said, 'No, you don't know his father very well.' Why do you do that? Are Sarah's stories true? Isn't Father Jesus' father, too?"

"Surely, now the time is right" thought Mary. "Surely now I can tell her the whole story." But such was not to be. Anxious voices burst upon them as Benjy and Simon flew around the corner.

"Mother! Where are you?"

The startled Mary shrank back to avoid being run over. But solid and firm as a rock, Rachel stood her ground and caught her son's arm as the boys ran by. "Right here, Benjy. Whoa, Simon. What on earth has you boys in such a whirl?"

"They've done it! Mother! They've done it!"

"What? Simon, who has done what?" Reaching up to her growing son's head, Mary brushed the reddish curls from his eyes.

"The rulers, the Pharisees, and others. They've found witnesses to testify against Jesus. They are willing to lie and help put him to *death*!

*   *   *   *   *

Hordes of pushing, rushing, restless people shoved Mary and her party toward Jerusalem. "I don't know when I have ever seen so many people here."

"Nor such a boisterous and rude crowd, Mother." Dan reached to steady the stumbling Mary. "You must watch your step, or they will push you down and tromp you into the ground. Here, let me trade you places and you walk by the donkey."

"I am all right. Really. It gets too hot in there. I prefer to walk out here. Sometimes I can catch bits of conversation, so we can understand why the crowd is so upset."

Upset they were. Some supported the "New King" but most judged him an imposter. The arguing and bickering bounced from group to group as the pilgrims strained forward to attend the Passover ceremonies. Instinctively, Mary knew they were speaking of her son, but fear kept her from asking questions. Perhaps she was mistaken and someone else was the cause of the agitation.

James and Dan watched their tiny mother anxiously, hoping she would not realize their brother and friend was the cause of the unrest. How could they shield her from further pain and sorrow? How much could this tiny giant stand? How much would she be called to endure?

The animals had to have water. Reflecting the feelings of the crowd, they had hurried without any urging. Their wheezing and heaving sides spoke plainly of their need for water and a rest. The little donkey seemed to be limping a bit. "Perhaps a stone in his hoof," murmured Dan under his breath.

"What did you say, Dan?" Mary's eyes twinkled for the first time in several days. "Getting old aren't you? Maybe I'd better hold *you* up."

"Mother, you finally caught me. Yes, I am getting old." Dan staggered and swayed, allowing the laughing Mary to ease him to the well's edge. "Oh, thank you. Thank you. I am getting so old and feeble."

"You can say that again," snapped his short-tempered wife.

"I am getting so. . ."

"Stop that! There is no time for such foolishness." Rachel's face had not felt a smile for many days.

Mary's arm slipped around her daughter's ample waist as she tried to smooth the ruffled feelings. "Now, Rachel, there is always

. . . Behold Thy Son

time for foolishness. Especially if it helps ease the tension. And there has been too much tension these last few days."

"Last three years, you mean. It is all his fault. If Jesus didn't make such fantastic claims and do such strange things, we would all be better off." Grabbing the bucket from Dan, Rachel did not see the hurt look in Dan's eyes, as she poured the water for the donkeys.

James paused as he spread the blanket for his mother. "What about those he has healed—those to whom he has given new hope? Should he not have done that?"

This was too much. Rachel melted into a sobbing heap. Mary knelt beside her and comforted her as she had when Rachel was a child with a scraped knee or smashed finger. Rachel's heart was hurting far worse than her knee or finger ever had. Dan and James stood bewildered. What should They do now?

"Feed the donkeys, son. They are so tired and hungry. We can wait." Turning back to her daughter, Mary drew the scarf forward to shield the swollen eyes from the glaring sun. "Go ahead. You will feel better when you let it all out. You have been working so very hard."

"Mother, why can't I understand and believe? Why is it so hard?"

Searching Rachel's face, Mary prayed earnestly for the right words. "Because he is your big brother. Yes, he was special and did special, kind things at home. But he is still your big brother. Somehow, we forget that big brothers, neighbors, or good friends can really do great things. We know them in their weak, struggling moments, as ordinary people. Perhaps we wish those we know and love to rise no farther or faster than we are able, for fear we will be left behind, or hurt. Maybe it is just plain jealousy. But I have seen no jealousy on your part. I feel sure that is not your problem."

"It is not, and Jesus has no weaknesses. Or at least he didn't before he went off that first time. The only weakness I knew of was his love for fresh honeycomb—the first from the hive—or fresh, ripe dates. But now, he seems to have gone soft in the head. Imagine, Jesus—my brother—allowing himself to be led into the city astride a donkey and proclaimed King of the Jews."

"Are you sure it was Jesus?" Mary's voice was low and shaky.

Nodding, Rachel turned to point out a fellow traveler. "He told me very plainly. That man in the rich turban. He was there and saw it himself. The priests are paying him great sums to find someone to testify in the courts against 'Jesus the Nazarene Carpenter.' That man with him is willing to swear Jesus is teaching treason." Rachel turned in time to see James catch her mother. Mary had struggled to her feet to see who Rachel was pointing out. Her strength failed when she heard why the man was so important. Horrified at what she had caused, Rachel's tears gushed harder than ever. Dan tried his best, but Rachel would not be comforted.

James laid his mother out straight. Then he knelt so he shaded her face. "Please get this wet, Dan. I must get her cooled off. Rachel, please! Be careful what you say. You certainly need not tell *all* you know—every time."

Rachel howled harder and louder. The two men looked at each other over the women, shrugged their shoulders, sighed, and thought, Women! What to do with them?

Finding no one at John's, Mary and her group debated what to do. Usually someone was there to welcome the weary travelers. "Perhaps they are all at the temple," Dan said as he drew water for the animals. The cool water from the cistern felt very soothing to the hot, weary beasts.

"Not at this hour, Dan. It is much too early. I fear things really *are* coming to a conclusion. Simon and Benjy's story has been verified as I listened to the crowd." James removed the packs from the donkeys and carried them into the shade. "But let's not say anything to further upset Mother or Rachel."

"Amen to that! We don't need a repeat of last time. I didn't think Rachel would ever quiet down. That was a flood to end all floods. How can I help her find peace of mind, James? Rachel is so upset. I must find a way to help her see and understand Jesus' work." Dan looked old and tired. Helplessness and despair clouded his handsome face.

"If only she could believe. She has had witness after witness. But Rachel seems to be looking for a burning bush. I told her she is not Moses and to quit searching for that burning bush. She only got angry. I could joke with her—before—but now, it only makes her angry."

"I know, I know," murmured Dan shaking his head in despair. "How well I know." A commotion in the streets caught their attention as it grew louder and stronger. Listening, the men realized the noise was coming up the street toward the yard. Dan went to the gate and looked out. At his startled cry, James rushed to his side. Both men were horrified at the scene. Roman soldiers were pushing the unruly crowd aside for a man. No, there were two—one had been stripped and beaten, the other was a foreigner of some sort. At least he looked like a foreigner in those clothes. He had not been beaten, but seemed eager to help with the heavy log. It was hard going over the uneven and crooked streets, especially with the mob taunting and trying to impede their progress.

"Crucify him! Crucify him!" rang from the mob.

"Poor devil. I wonder what he has done," murmured Dan.

"Say, look!" James pointed to one of the women following, begging for the man's life. "Look, that is Salome, John's mother. Oh, no!"

"James," gasped Dan as he clutched the gate. "That's Jesus. That is Jesus they've whipped and beaten."

"They are going to crucify him!" James flew out the gate, rushing and pushing, trying to come to his brother's aid. "Jesus!" he yelled. "*JESUS!*" Jesus stopped, turning toward him. Never before had James seen such a look on a man's face. No fear, not even hate. Pain? Yes, there was terrible pain, but not from his physical wounds. And calm. Jesus was calm and unafraid. Strength seemed to fill his whole being, radiating from his countenance.

"Why doesn't he *do* something?" Dan's question caused James to jump. When he looked back, Jesus was being pushed on. "I don't understand it, James. He seems so calm and full of strength, yet he does nothing. Surely he could escape if he can calm the sea and the winds."

James drooped. "Just when I was beginning to see and believe." He suddenly straightened. "Dan, what can we do? We must do *something!*"

"Let's follow. Perhaps we can find an answer." Forgetting the women, they hurried off. But they didn't get far. A flying fist found its mark when James told a man to watch what he said about his brother. Heartsick, Dan carried his friend back to John's home. He could do nothing for Jesus now. There were too many guards. But he could help James and the women.

Rachel was alone and terribly upset again. Mary had simply disappeared. "I don't know where she went. We heard that terrible noise and I came in to shut it out. I thought Mother was right behind me, but I can't find her anywhere!"

Dan sank to the table, buried his head in his arms and sobbed. He felt deserted and drained of all his strength. Frantic, Rachel looked at her husband, then her unconscious brother, and back again. *"Dan!"* she shrieked. "What's wrong? What's happening? *Tell me!"* But Dan could not speak. First Jesus, then James, and now Mary was gone, and he had no strength to go search for her. How could he tell Rachel? She would never understand. Not ever.

Mary heard the noise and stepped into the courtyard. She saw James and Dan watching at the gate. She cringed and turned back to the house as she heard, "Crucify him! Crucify him!"

But James' cry of "Jesus! Jesus!" cut into her innermost soul. Running to the open gate she searched the crowd. The first face she recognized was that of the beautiful Mary Magdalene. But distorted by grief, fear, and pain, it was not a lovely face now. Then Salome's face came into focus. She, too, was very upset.

Pulled by some unseen force, Mary found herself drawn into the crowd.

"King of the Jews? Oh, no. We don't want him as our king!"

"Crucify him! Crucify him!"

"Yes, crucify him! He's a blasphemer!"

"Son of God indeed! He is only a carpenter's son!"

Jesus? Where *was* Jesus? James had called his name. Pushing and pleading, Mary fought her way to the side of the two women. Then she recognized John. He was trying to clear the path for the women. "John! John! Where is Jesus? Where is my son?" John turned, looked down at the frightened woman, then turned sadly back to look on the man struggling with his heavy load. Mary looked, too. She winced as she recognized the terrible instrument of death. She had been forced to witness such executions before. Loving arms went around her, giving support and comfort. Mary turned to look at Mary Magdalene, then at Salome. Neither could utter a word. Mary had not seen such grief since Rachel's Jason had been killed. She looked up at John. But he was still looking at the back of the man struggling under the weight of the crosspiece. Tears ran freely down his face. "Where is Jesus? Where IS my son?" she whispered.

The guards had stopped at the base of Golgotha. The two men already hanging on the crosses cried out in great anguish. Mary saw the hole and pole waiting for the next unfortunate person. The beaten man stumbled and fell. No, he was pushed down by the guard. Mary watched in horrified fascination as the crosspiece was lashed to the pole. The man was brutally stretched out on the crosspiece so the guards could drive the nails into his palms.

. . . Behold Thy Son

"Two nails!" shouted the captain. "Remember the second nail. One through the palm and another through the wrist. He's so large and strong, he will rip his hands free and escape if you don't."

Lightning flashed and thunder cracked as the second nail was driven in. The clouds had come up very quickly. It was still forenoon but getting very dark. Thunder came more and more often. Lightning began to strike repeatedly. But this only served to stir the mob to greater fury. "Crucify him! *Crucify him!*"

Mary had been pushing her anguished thoughts away. She would *not* believe it! It couldn't be Jesus on that cross. He had promised her he would be protected. His work had just begun. No! It was not he. It couldn't be!

The guards were jerking the heavy cross up. The man writhed in pain. He had not cried out—not even once. The crowd grew silent as the guards struggled with their burden. Only the straining of the guards and the moans of the tortured men were heard as they struggled to place the pole in its hole. It slipped and fell back to the ground with a heavy thud. The man groaned. The crowd cheered. Mary Magdalene cried out. John covered his mother's face with his robe. Once again the pole was jerked into place. This time they were successful. With a sickening thud, it fell into the ground, tearing the man's hands as he bounced with the cross. He groaned but did not cry out. Nor did he pass out with the pain as most men would have done.

Mary screamed! "JESUS! JESUS!" Mary Magdalene caught the frantic woman as she rushed to her son. John and Salome grabbed her other arm and her robe. They pulled the sobbing woman away from the reach of the Roman soldiers and their whips. She did not faint; she would not allow herself to do so. She must do something for her son. But what? Why didn't he help himself? Why didn't he call for heavenly help? Why?

"John, John." Mary pulled frantically at his sleeve. When he turned his eyes to her, she asked, "Why are they putting up that sign? What does it say?"

"I can't read it yet. There, now I can." The guard crawled back down his ladder. "It says, 'Jesus of Nazareth the King of the Jews.' Humph! A fine way to treat the king." John spat in disgust.

"He's not *our* king!" rang from the mob. "We don't want him!"

"Father, forgive them; for they know not what they do." Jesus spoke in a voice that filled their souls. It was not a bitter voice, but rather a soft, quiet voice filled with pity and forgiveness. Yet it reached the ears of all who were around the cross.

"Did you hear that! Forgive us! Forgive *us!*"

"Imagine, *he* is forgiving *us!*"

"I can't believe it!"

"Nor do I!" The crowd became more and more unruly and shouted louder and harder.

Mary Magdalene stood transfixed, watching the guards. "What on earth are they doing now?"

Salome answered, "They are casting lots for the clothing of Jesus and the two thieves. I have seen them do it at other crucifixions. They are heathens! That is all they are—heathens!"

"If thou be the king of the Jews, save thyself."

"Yes, where is your power to calm the winds and storm now? We could do without the storm right now!" Clap upon clap of thunder rolled across the heavens. The sun was hidden from view. But it didn't stop the people for long.

"Jesus, you said you'd destroy the temple and then rebuild it in three days. Why can't you get down off there and save yourself?"

"Don't you know?" railed a priest. "He can only save *others!*"

"Jesus, you come down from that cross. That'll prove you are King of the Jews. Then we'll believe you." Raucous laughter rolled through the mob.

"Jesus," whispered Mary, "why have you let them take you? Why have you *let* them do this to you? Use your power. You can save yourself." Burying her face in her hands, she sobbed, "God, where *are* you? Why haven't you protected our son?"

As if in echo of Mary's words and thoughts, one of the Sanhedrin stepped forward, faced the crowd, and signaled for silence. He had to shout to be heard above the rain, thunder, and wind. "He believed in God. Yea, he trusted in God. Let God deliver him now—*if* He will have him. For he said, 'I am the Son of God.' What, I ask, is the 'Son of God' doing on that cross?"

Mary sobbed harder. She ached to do something, but what? What could she do?

Jesus doesn't even know I am here. I must go to him and beg him to use his power. He must use it!

She struggled to her feet and toward the cross. She felt the crack of the whip in the air as it snapped a warning, just inches from her face.

"Stay back, lady, stay back!" barked the guard.

"But I must go to him! I *must!* I am his mother," cried Mary.

. . . Behold Thy Son

From the cross came a groan, a groan deeper than had issued forth before. Mary looked up at her son. Her arms outstretched, she called his name. "Jesus! Jesus!"

Jesus looked down at his mother, then at John who had rushed forward to protect her from the whip. A soft, sad look came over him. Tears of compassion for the suffering he was causing her ran freely down his face. He strained as if to reach out and touch her. The nails tore the flesh of his hands, but he seemed not to notice. Jesus' whole feeling was for his dear, suffering, bewildered mother for whom he could do nothing.

The crowd sensed the meaning of the scene before them and momentarily became silent. They all had mothers, and most of them had children. For one brief instant they sympathized with the tortured man and his mother.

"Woman"—that greatest title of love and respect—"Woman, behold thy son! John, behold thy mother!" Jesus strained forward again as if to touch and reassure his beloved mother. The blood gushed from his wounded hands and splashed on a guard below.

"What the ——?" he shouted. The mob shook off its momentary feeling of sympathy and began to rail and revile with renewed vigor, as if it would erase from their minds the picture of mother and son.

"Come, Mother, you heard Jesus. We must go." John tried to pull the grieving woman away, but she stood as if anchored to the spot.

"No! I will *not* go! I must stay here. My son is on that cross. Why is he on that cross? Won't someone explain it to me? Has he done such terrible things?"

"No, Mother, he has not." Gentle arms succeeded in drawing her a little way away. Mary Magdalene—torn by her love for the mother and the son—turned to look back.

Suddenly realizing she was being taken away, Mary twisted away from both of them and ran back up to the cross. The guards, pitying the weeping woman, did not strike her as they had others who had approached too closely.

The gruff captain took her gently by the arm and led her away. Looking into her face he realized with a start that he had seen this face before. But where? "What is your name?" he asked.

"Mary," so softly he had to bend close to hear. "Mary, wife of Joseph the Carpenter of Nazareth and mother of Jesus. *Jesus!*" Again she tried to return to her son. But the firm hand held her tightly.

"No, gentle mother. It only makes it worse for you and him. Please, go with your friends." The sobbing Mary was returned to John and Mary Magdalene who marvelled at the gentleness of the captain. Roman executors were known and chosen for their callousness and harsh treatment of those they executed. Muttering to himself, he returned to his men and their game of chance. He surely did want that robe. It was of extra fine quality, especially for these hill people.

The ground shook violently. Thunder rolled and lightning flashed. Although it was just past noon, the sun was darkened as if it were night. Mary Magdalene could stand it no more. She turned to John's mother, shouting above the noise. "Please, support her and help her home. I must return to my Lord."

As Mary Magdalene returned to the cross, she saw the captain standing white-faced, staring at the cross. His lips were moving but she could not hear. She drew closer and was astonished to see him fall to the ground in deep anguish, crying aloud. Aghast, she listened to his tortured words. "Mary the beautiful, young wife of Joseph. They were traveling from Nazareth to Egypt. The two boys. The beautiful child, Jesus. I have crucified him. Why? Not that he deserved it, but because Pontius Pilate could not pacify the Jews any other way. To think he escaped Herod's blood bath and then I . . . I . . . I have to . . . crucify . . . him. Oh!" He could go no further. His whole soul was in deep, deep, bitter torment. Mary marvelled at his grief. How did he know about Jesus? She must remember to ask Mother Mary about it.

Thunder rolled continually. It seemed as if the earth itself were mourning the death of Mary's son. People jostled, pushed, and shoved as they hurried home to get out of the storm. But as the earthquakes rumbled, panic made their progress almost impossible. John pulled his mother and Mary into a doorway for a rest and to allow the crowd to thin out.

Two men joined them without pausing in their conversation. "That was some sight. Best thing I've seen for years!"

"Me, too. It did my heart good to see him nailed there. About time, too. Imagine! He wasn't satisfied with being King of the Jews, he had to claim he was the Son of God."

"Yea! Son of God!" He spat into the mud, narrowly missing Mary's feet.

"I tell you he *is* the Son of God. I know it! I am his mother and

. . . Behold Thy Son

who would know better than I?" Mary shook the man's robe. For a little woman, she was surprisingly strong.

John pulled her away and started home again. He didn't listen to her muttering and sobs. After all, what mother can watch her son be crucified and not lose her mind? He sickened at the memory of those huge nails being driven into the flesh. The rain was falling in torrents making their journey even more treacherous. At last John pulled them into their courtyard. But a crowd was waiting to taunt the followers of Jesus.

"We said we'd get him and we did!"

"Yea, he'll not be bothering us anymore!"

"Not unless he gets down from that cross, he won't!"

Grateful to be out of their way, Mary hurried into the house. She fled into the bedchamber and sank to the floor. Sobbing harder yet, she talked to her God, demanding to know why He had allowed their son to be treated so cruelly. Those listening grew more and more concerned as they caught a phrase here and a word there. "Our Son . . . alone . . . Joseph gone . . . I tried . . . A good son . . . respected his elders . . . teacher . . . wise beyond his years . . . so loving and tender . . . obedient . . . you promised . . . your son . . . why? *Why?*"

A flash of lightning lighted the room. Thunder shook the whole house. John looked around in terror. Would the house stand? Or would the earth open and swallow them? But the storm passed. That was the last of the thunder. Blessed, gentle rain came to cool and calm the earth and all who dwelt there. Could it just now be nightfall? It had been so dark since before noon. But John could see the sunset. The whole earth appeared to be on fire. A movement caused him to turn back to the bed chamber door.

Mary was standing in the doorway. Gone was the torture, fear, and pain. Peace and calm was shining from her whole being. Speaking softly, yet with great authority, Mary surprised them even more. "Yes, it was necessary. Jesus *had* to die. And he did."

John rushed to her side. "But, Mary, he is not dead. It takes days to die on the cross. Those thieves have been there two days already. Jesus is healthy and strong. It may take a week."

"No, John. He is dead. I know it." Going to the doorway, Mary looked at the sunset. "How fitting. I have never seen a lovelier sunset. Look! There is a double rainbow!"

What had happened? Where had Mary received such peace? Why was she suddenly so . . . so . . . changed? Before such questions could be voiced, Mary Magdalene burst into the house and collapsed onto the bench, sobbing violently. Mary went and took her into her arms as she would a troubled child.

"There, there, daughter. Cry it all out. It helps. That's it. Let it all out. But fear not, it is right."

"Right that he should suffer so? And die so young?"

John started—unbelieving. "Die? Is he dead already?"

"Yes. He is . . . he is gone. God be praised. His suffering was cut short." Mary Magdalene straightened and wiped her face.

"You saw him? You know for certain?" John still could not believe it. Men, especially such strong men, did not die that fast on the cross. Not in six hours or less.

"Yes. He cried with a loud voice, then gave up the ghost. The soldiers went to see if the men could be taken down before the Sabbath. The thieves were still alive, so they broke their legs to hasten death." Mary Magdalene shuddered, unable to go on.

"Did they break my son's legs?"

Shaking her head, Mary Magdalene sighed, stood up and began again. "No, he made no more sound and hung as if dead so they thrust a sword into his side. Water and blood burst forth." Remembering the fright on the guards' faces brought a brief smile to her face. "The soldiers were frightened and nearly ran away but the captain's whip made them remember their duty."

"Then we must go get his body and bury him." John rushed to the door. An outstretched hand caught his robe.

"No, John. He is being cared for. Joseph of Arimathea requested Jesus' body from Pilate and was hurrying to reach his tomb before the Sabbath. I followed to find out where and had to hurry to get home in time for prayers. Jesus is in a garden close to the cross."

"Then he is among friends?" John was still not satisfied. "Joseph is of the Sanhedrin."

"Yes. Joseph is a believer, although he lacked the courage to follow openly. He would come in the night to talk privately with Jesus." Mary Magdalene went for a drink and brought one for Mary.

"Thank you, daughter. You are so thoughtful. I see why Jesus loves you so very much. Come. It is time for Sabbath prayers. John, will you be leading us?"

Everyone marveled at the calm, confident manner of Mary.

What has happened, and where has she received her strength?

. . . Behold Thy Son

Chapter Fifteen

OUR SON—THY SON

The smell of fig cakes filled the humble home. So many at once suggested a celebration or party. Mary and her daughter Rachel were bustling around cleaning and preparing. Fish were laid aside in readiness for the arrival of the guests. "I like to put them on just before supper. I do hate overcooked fish," Mary said.

"Mother, your fish are always perfect. I have not gained that skill. No matter how hard I try, Dan always says, 'Good, but not as good as your mother's.'" Rachel patted the flat bread into shape.

"I do wish Joses and Naomi were not in Jericho. They belong here, too. I do miss them and their little one."

"Mother, there is no call for an artist around here. He had to go there to find work. He does love his work and is so good at it."

Finally, all was in readiness. Mary gave one last look around before taking up the scriptures for her spiritual feast. "Oh, but I love this time of day. Family will soon be here. We are all prepared. Our home smells so inviting. And now I have a few moments to study. Would you like me to read to you, Rachel?"

"Please do. You make the scriptures come alive and so much easier to understand."

"Any particular place or passage?" Mary hoped not. She had a particular one in mind.

"No. You choose, Mother. You will know what to read. But give me a minute; the baby is stirring. I need to change her." Rachel slipped into the other room as Mary began to search for the passage to share with her daughter.

Not surprisingly, Isaiah was her choice. Mary's love for this book had begun as a tiny child on her father's knee. A passage caught her eye. She began to read aloud unaware of anything or anyone around. This passage had never made sense before, but now as Mary read she felt as if a light had been turned on in her mind. It was as if the pieces of a puzzle were falling into place. Everything suddenly made sense.

"'He was oppressed, and he was afflicted, yet he opened not his mouth: he is brought as a lamb to the slaughter, and as a sheep before his shearer is dumb, so he openeth not his mouth.'" The scriptures fell into her lap as Mary looked into the distance. "Rachel, Simon Peter said Jesus would not answer the questions or defend himself from the beatings and reviling. Simon Peter and John said he was as humble as a lamb waiting for the sacrifice."

Returning again to the scriptures Mary read on. Then she called out, excitedly. "Rachel, he won't know children of his own for he died before that was possible, yet listen, 'and who shall declare his generation? for he was cut off out of the land of the living: for the transgressions of my people was he stricken. And he made his grave with the wicked, and with the rich in his death.' Mary Magdalene watched as Joseph of Arimethea, a rich man of the Sanhedrin, took my son's body from the midst of thieves who died with him and laid it to rest. I went there myself when Sabbath was over. Rachel, that is what this verse said. Listen!"

Rachel listened as her mother reread the scripture telling of her brother. Was it really about her brother, she wondered? Mother was certain. What made her so sure? Why was she so changed?

"'Yet it pleased the Lord to bruise him; he had put him to grief.'" Again the scriptures lay in her lap. "Yes, it *was* necessary. Jesus had to die. I am not yet able to fully understand it, but if I keep studying and praying I will. 'Because he had poured out his soul unto death: and he was numbered with the transgressors; and he bare the sins of many, and made intercession for the transgressor.' Yes, Jesus hath poured out his soul."

"Mother, please tell me again of his visits after his death. It still troubles me." Now Rachel earnestly wanted to believe, yet too many questions had not been answered. "If only we had stayed with you and James and not hurried home to comfort the little ones."

"Oh! Here comes the family. Rachel, time to put the fish on. They should be on the back for a bit." Mary knew Rachel would get her answers soon enough.

The lamp was burning brighter than usual, especially for such a humble home in Nazareth. Thrift and economy usually demanded it be left as low as possible. Smiling as brightly as the lamp, Mary passed fig cakes and fresh milk.

"Mother," Simon took two cakes each time around (as the youngest he took special privileges), "Why haven't you told us these things before? It would have been so much easier to understand and accept."

"Yes, when I think of the many times Jesus tried to talk to me and the excuses I used to avoid it, I am ashamed. No wonder he spent so much time with Simon Peter, James, and John in Capernaum." James looked at his young son sleeping peacefully in his arms.

I wish Jesus could have known the joy of a child of his own. He loved them so. He made a wise choice in Mary Magdalene. Maybe at another time.

Startled at his own thoughts, James looked puzzled.

What do I mean, another time? But that is what he said, I think. Oh! I wish I had listened and understood more of what he tried to teach us . . . At least we were not cruel and vicious to him.

Leah's voice broke into James' thoughts as she begged her mother to tell once again the wondrous things she had shared with them at supper.

All had seen and marveled at the changes in Mary when she returned with James, bearing the news of Jesus' resurrection. No longer fearful and worried, Mary radiated calm, peace, and utmost joy. These past three years had been increasingly harder on her. Deep lines had marred the beautiful face. It seemed as if each ill report about her eldest son cut as a sword into her very soul, leaving an ever-widening wound. Rachel had found Mary crying and praying the day before she had announced her intentions of going to the Passover. Rachel had caught a phrase or two which sounded like "Simeon, how did you know? . . . A sword through my very being! How can I stand it? Why must it be so?" When Rachel questioned her mother, she had answered by telling of the day Jesus was presented at the temple and how the priest had told her that her son's life would be as a sword in her soul, twisted to and fro. "And it is! It is! I cannot stand it any longer. He is in grave danger. I *know* it! I can feel it! I must go to him—now!"

Thinking they had talked Mary out of her plans, Rachel and Dan were dismayed when Mary came to breakfast packed and ready to go with them. Nothing short of force could change her mind. Mary had to go to her son. She had refrained long enough.

. . . Behold Thy Son

But now, gone were the tense lines. Softened by peace and joy, Mary's face looked almost as young as her daughters'. Her beautiful hair was streaked with white. No longer hunched and fearful, Mary stood straight and tall—as tall, that is, as she could. All her sons towered over their tiny mother. Even her daughters had received their height from their handsome father.

Jude's little toddler looked up at her grandmother. She was so like Mary in every detail that Mary had been the only name for her. She would be tiny, as well as fair and beautiful. May she be as sweet and loving as her namesake, thought Esther, as she watched her tiny daughter climb into her grandmother's lap.

"Please, Mother, I want to hear it again. It is so beautiful." Leah handed a wet towel to her mother to wipe the child's sticky hands.

"Where should I begin?"

My, Joseph would be proud of his family. They are all fine, honest, sincere men and women. They have chosen their companions wisely and are rearing beautiful, obedient families.

"All right, I will begin at the first again."

Mary retold her beautiful story, adding details she had forgotten the first time. As questions arose, she answered them before going on. Young Ephraim wanted a complete and detailed description of the wisemen.

"What happened to the gifts, Grandmother?"

"Your grandfather said we must be careful and not arouse any suspicion in Egypt, so we simply kept them hidden. The gold helped us come back to Nazareth. Then we used the frankincense to pay for the fixing of the shop and settling our debts when we returned. The myrrh was given as a gift at the temple when we were finally able to return again from Egypt."

"Wow!" Wide eyes testified sleep was a long way off. "Were you scared when the wisemen came?"

"Yes, my child. I was scared. But they were so kind and courteous I soon lost my fear. You know, Jesus was never afraid of anyone—even as a tiny babe. He had just learned to walk and was delighted to walk from one wiseman to the other and back again. He showed no fear. He took the tall one by the hand and led him to the door then lifted his arms and begged to be carried. The wiseman laughed, picked him up and they explored the garden together. They brought a green lizard in to me."

"Mother, do you remember who they were? Their names, I mean?" James always wanted things proven and straight. Every last detail must be explored and pinned down.

"I was so frightened at first I did not remember their names. Later I found a passage in Psalms which talked of kings coming to the child."

"Where is it, Mother. I'd like to read it." James handed his sleeping son to his wife and took up the scriptures.

"The 72nd Psalm."

James found the passage and read it aloud to the quiet family group. "'The king of Tarshish and of the isles shall bring presents: the kings of Sheba and Seba shall offer gifts.' Mother, were these the ones who came?"

"As I said, I don't remember their names. Your father did, but I have forgotten them. The fact they came was what I marvelled at." Mary's audience remained spellbound as she retold her story, verifying it with scriptures to help them see why it had been that way.

"Why didn't you tell us before? Didn't you trust us?" Rachel's face glistened with tears. "Did you ever tell Reuben and Rachel?"

"No. I tried but was prevented. I really did try to tell you. But I could not even discuss it with Jesus. Something always held me back. My tongue was stopped. It semed to be God's will that I not speak about it."

"At least you had the scriptures to guide and give comfort, especially after Father passed away." Jude reached for more cakes but his wife's stern look stopped him.

"No, not really. No matter how often I reread them, they did not apply or make sense until afterwards. I just had to . . . store things in my heart and wonder about them. But now," Mary glowed even more brightly. "Now, I am beginning to understand. Now I see what they mean. Jesus *is* resurrected. He *is* our Savior and King. He has taken his rightful place at his Father's side."

"But what of Mary Magdalene? Is she coming here?" Rachel was still a bit uncertain.

"No. She feels she can best help by staying close to the Twelve helping them as she did before. Those men would forget to eat if the women did not watch over them." Mary stood to begin preparations for night.

James had a faraway look in his eye. His wife and Jude's knew only too well their men would soon be back in Jerusalem with Simon Peter. "Mother, thank you for sharing your thoughts with us. You have answered so many questions. It fits into what Simon Peter, James, John, and the others told us after the crucifixion. Jude,

. . . Behold Thy Son

when can you be ready?"

"In two days. Can you wait that long?"

"Yes, I can. It will take me that long, also."

The moon shone down on a radiant Mary. Her family was united once again. Even Rachel was believing the truth. At last she had peace—if only for a minute. Her troubles were not over but she could now face them squarely.

Looking into the star-filled sky, Mary's thoughts turned once again to Joseph.

Thank you, my darling. Now I see why you were taken. You had laid such a good foundation. He learned well. But Jesus also needed to learn of widows, orphans, and those alone. He found how much they need our added love and support. Our family pulled together even more and now they are pulling together again. You gave me fine sons and beautiful daughters. Thank you.

Silence prevailed but the night creatures could not be silent on such a night as this. They filled in the space left by the humans and day creatures as Mary began to pray.

"I thank thee, Father, for allowing me to tell my family. For the understanding and peace. Please let me be with him again. Forgive, I beg, my doubts and fears. Thou, too, must have hidden Thy face from that terrible sight. How couldst Thou stand it? How great Thy pain must have been. Thou art so gentle and tender. Thy heart must have broken nearly in two. No wonder the earth groaned so . . . But I . . . " Mary buried her head in her hands, sobbing. "But I thought only of *my* anguish and wanted to curse, yea, almost did curse Thee for allowing it to be. Please . . . Please forgive me." Mary's sobbing figure was bathed in soft moonlight.

When she straightened once more, peace had been restored. Mary's life and mission were acceptable. She knew that, and was at peace.

Mary—mother of the Son of God, handmaiden of God—returned to the house. There was much to be done. Grandchildren are to love and teach. But she knew she would manage. Besides, now she could write that letter to Joses and Naomi. They must learn of their brother's work.

Mary turned for another look at the beautiful full moon, then softly shut the door.

THE END